THE THRILLING LIBRARY:

BY

G.T. FLEMING-ROBERTS

THRILLING PUBLICATIONS

2017

TABLE OF

CONTENTS

WILL MURRAY

FOR SOME unexplained reason, magic fascinated the pulp writers of the 1930s and '40s.

The king of them all was Walter B. Gibson, who created The Shadow out of a mesmerizing radio voice and his close association with Blackstone, Thurston, Houdini, Dunninger and other notable magicians. Gibson was as famous for his books on stage magic as he was for his prolific pulp output. He knew all the tricks, from Hypnotism to escape stunts, and employed them freely in spinning his Shadow stories.

Lester Dent had the Marvelous Merton. Norvell W. Page concocted Aubrei Dunne. Paul Ernst had Karlu. Walter Gibson mixed together a number of actual illusionists and produced Norgil the Magician. Many were one-shot characters.

Jimmy Christopher demonstrated a magic trick in every one of Frederick. C. Davis' *Operator #5* novels for the edification of his young assistant, Tim Donovan—and his readers.

No doubt conjurors in other media helped to popularize the trend. Beginning in 1932, Chandu the Magician enjoyed a successful radio run. Lee Falk and Phil Davis' Mandrake the Magician comic strip kicked off in 1934. It's still running today. Magic still fascinates America.

The tuxedo and top hat became the trademark of a new type of suave criminologist. Probably any pulpster who was anybody dreamed up a polished prestidigitator who solved crimes. Clayton Rawson's Don Diavolo, the Scarlet Wizard, was one of the most prominent. Rawson also wrote about the Great Merlini. Ken Crossen's Green Lama, a wizard of a sort, was sometimes assisted by a stage magician, Theodor Harrin.

If being a denizen of the Pulp Jungle made a writer part of a special subculture, then there was a subset of that subculture where pulpsmithing and slight of hand intersected. An amazing number of them were amateur or performing magicians.

"Walter Gibson and I were very good friends until we were separated by the entire country," Ken Crossen once reminisced. "It's difficult to do magic at that distance. But we used to meet fairly often. I don't think we ever talked about The Shadow or the Green Lama. Walter (writer and magician), Bruce Elliott (writer, editor and magician), Clayton Rawson (writer and magician), sometimes Ted Annemann (magician) and I spent many an evening together. If any of the leading magicians were playing within fifty miles of New York City, we would go at least once during the engagement. And after the show we'd all go out and find an all night cafeteria and stay there, drinking coffee and doing magic until daylight."

G.T. Fleming-Roberts was not a member of that inner circle. An Indiana native, he rarely visited New York and conducted all of his business by mail or through his agent, August Lenniger. But the same bug that compelled Lester Dent to schedule many of his trips from Missouri to Manhattan to conference with his Street & Smith editors the same week that magic conventions were being held in that city, evidently infected Fleming-Roberts.

In 1937, Fleming-Roberts came up with a crime-solving conjurer of his own, the Great Diamondstone. Fleming-Roberts had been writing for only about four years and was then ghosting *Secret Agent "X"* for Magazine Publishers. Later, he would create the Ghost—ultimately renamed the Green Ghost—a magician-sleuth for the Thrilling chain. But Diamondstone came first.

Diamondstone's first outing, "The Crime Conductor," appeared in *Popular Detective*, March 1937. Over the next two years, five sequels followed. Modeled—or at least named—after the famous stage illusionist Harry Blackstone, Diamondstone predated Walter Gibson's *Crime Busters* headliner, Norgil the Magician, by six months.

As befitting a stage performer, Diamondstone the Great Magician is a striking figure of a man crowned by blond hair, with red-gold eyebrows over blazing blue eyes. He employs no aides or assistants. His only confidante is his black manservant, Absalom. Diamondstone's specialized skills adapt perfectly to unraveling mysteries and unmasking schemers. Magicians are after all professional deceivers, so this may be a variation of the old adage, "Set a thief to catch a thief."

The Diamondstone stories hop around the country, sometimes delving into theatrical crimes, as in "The Murder of the Marionette," and are marked by Fleming-Roberts' clever plotting and smart stylistic touches. He was a top pulpsmith.

Misdirection is the stock-in-trade of the performing professional illusionist and escape artist. Mystery writers also employed it to keep their culprits before the eye of the reader, yet unsuspected until the climax.

Fleming-Roberts employed a version of this devious thinking he called "reverse reasoning" to concoct his tricky plots and keep his readers guessing. He explained his method in his 1942 *Writer's Digest* article, "The Turn from the Trite" this way:

> Now, as probably everybody knows, there's no device which has been used any more frequently in detective stories than the murder committed inside the locked, practically hermetically sealed room. It is still a good gag, and there must be a number of as yet unexplored ways in and out of that sealed room. But in a yarn I was working on not so long ago, I found myself with a locked room, a dead man inside it, and no new way up my sleeve for getting in and out. In fact, I had used the very old gag of working the lock from the outside by means of a piece of thread manipulated to turn the key on the inside. Unfortunately, the gag had to come quite near the beginning of the story. I felt certain that if that old hackneyed situation could be saved, the rest of the yarn was sure money. There was my detective and a number of other people standing outside this room in an office building, and everybody, including the reader, was perfectly aware there was a corpse in that room. There had to be a corpse in there, or my story was a dead duck.
>
> Detectives, as you've probably noticed, have a couple of tried and true—and trite—methods of getting into locked rooms. They smash the panel with burly shoulders—or maybe it's the more logical fire ax—or they pick the lock. My shady detective was more the lock-picking, skeleton-key type. But instead of doing the expected, my detective simply looked at the door and said, "To hell with it. If I open that room now, every time some rat nest of an office in this building is burglared, I'll get the blame." And he walked away.
>
> Disappointing to the reader? I don't think so. I think that turn from the trite saved a situation that might otherwise have ruined an acceptable story.

The origin of the author's inside knowledge of magic is unknown, but it must be remembered that the period before World War II was a Golden Age for professional magicians, many of whom toured the country with huge caravans of equipment and support staff, often playing to sold-out theaters. They were celebrities on a par with modern musicians or actors. Any American who lived near a fair-sized city is likely to have caught any number of special performances.

In many respects, Diamondstone was a trial run for George Chance, the future Ghost. Both were retired from the stage when they took up crime solving. Both were men of independent means, the better to support their amateur sleuthing. Neither charge fees for their investigations.

G.T. Fleming-Roberts' steadfastly refused to reveal Diamondstone's first name. He also left behind another unsolved mystery involving Diamondstone. In 1942, after *The Green Ghost* was cancelled, a story of his entitled "Dance with a Dead Man" ran in the March issue of *Exciting Detective*. Listed under the familiar hyphenated byline were two previously-published stories. One was "Diamondstone Returns."

Exhaustive research has failed to bring this tale to light—or any further Diamondstone tales. But later in the year, Fleming-Roberts revived the Green Ghost in *Thrilling Mystery*. One wonders if one of those episodes was "Diamondstone Returns" revised into a Green Ghost exploit. And if not, then where did that mysteriously missing tale end up?

One possibility: The final Diamondstone tale appeared nearly a year after the one before. Could "Three Wise Apes" have been originally titled "Diamondstone Returns?"

The dwindling of both magic-inspired series did not mean that G.T. Fleming-Roberts was done with magically-oriented detectives. During his active military service in World War II, he launched another series in the Diamondstone mold. Jeffery Wren was a former vaudeville magician who ran an Indianapolis magic shop, and was drawn into seven cases in the pages of *Dime Detective* between 1944–46. Wren specialized in exposing fraudulent spirit mediums, as these stories were not as pulpy or violent as Fleming-Roberts' prewar output. Times had changed. As the author himself explained to the *Indianapolis Star Magazine:*

> "The menace nowadays has to be something commonplace and familiar.... Adults are now reading the magazines—kids dropped them in favor of comic books—and you can't scare grownup mystery readers with a slinking figure in a black cape or a nasty old clutching hand."

The tradition of mixing magic and murder continued far beyond the pulp era in which Fleming-Roberts operated. Decades later, a group similar to the one Ken Crossen described coalesced in Manhattan. In its heyday, the Witch Doctor's Club of writers and performing magicians consisted of Walter Gibson, Bruce Elliott, Clayton Rawson, John Dickson Carr, Jim Steranko, Martin Gardner, Isaac Asimov and Orson Welles. The group met monthly in various restaurants, and new members were required to perform magic for the benefit of the others.

Why did so many pulp mystery writers migrate to magic?

"Magic and Mystery," Walter Gibson once observed, "are so closely interwoven that it is hard to tell where one leaves off and the other begins."

To which Ken Crossen added, "It's just like writing whodunits. You have to love to fool people."

THE CRIME
CONDUCTOR

CHAPTER I

THE COCK-EYED KING

IT WAS an afternoon in June when he first learned of the lightning-rod propensities of the Cock-Eyed King to attract sudden death.

He was sitting at his desk in the study, a big, golden-haired man, fiddling with an orange, some thread, and some wax. Not fat, there was still something elephantine about him: his breadth of shoulder, perhaps, or the way his yellow oxfords crushed the peanut shucks beneath the desk. Clumsy, too, you might think him, if you had never seen him handling eight multiplying billiard balls, a pack of bewilderingly rising cards, or vanishing a jangling alarm clock.

His name was Diamondstone—"The Great Diamondstone" back in the magician's heyday before some traitor had explained the workings of all illusions. Retired, wealthy, almost mad with inactivity, Diamondstone had mounted his hobby of crime detection. He had found it hard riding. Too many people thought "magician" and "charlatan" were synonymous.

A few people did not know that Diamondstone was a magician. Kitty Marris did not know it. The Menace did not know it, else he might have thought twice before crossing blades with Diamondstone.

Absalom put his head in the door—Absalom who was like a bit of worn brown velvet stage property; Absalom who had done everything to assist Diamondstone in his old stage act, from playing Hindu yogi to being the legs-end of a sawing-a-woman-in-half stunt. His liver-colored lips were sloven; his Southern accent negligible.

"You care about seein' a young woming named Kitty Marris?" he lazily inquired. "She say it most important."

Diamondstone kept on with his orange and string. He was laughing inwardly with a little of the laugh leaking out of his innocent-looking blue eyes.

"I say"—Absalom cleared his throat—"you want to see a young woming—"

"Uh-hum. Very much." Diamondstone thrust a length of the thread into his mouth while he pressed a bit of wax to the orange.

Kitty Marris was shown in. Diamondstone noticed that she was young and small. He got the threads out of his mouth lest she think him a new diet faddist or a sort of male seamstress. He smiled beneficently and told her that she was about to witness the mysterious and marvelous levitation of an orange.

Kitty Marris began jerking off her gloves. "Please, no. I don't know what that is, but I'm sure it wouldn't help."

Diamondstone took her by the shoulders and perched her in a chair. He stood back, thoughtfully shucked a peanut, and came to the conclusion that Kitty Marris was unusually pretty. There was a coy wisp of brown hair that didn't belong over her right eye, but it looked nice there, anyway. At the moment she looked as though she had inadvertently sat down on a box of eggs, she was that ill at ease.

"It's about my friend, Dr. Meanwell," she blurted. "He's here in the hotel because of the convention of the Midwest Society of Philatelists. Philatelists, you know—" She paused, looked nervously behind her.

A thin, crystal line of pungent liquid described the shortest distance between the black gun and the bell-hop's eyes.

Diamondstone wished she would calm down a little. He nodded pleasantly.

"I know. They're postage stamp collectors." He flicked a blue silk handkerchief from the breast pocket of his coat and started poking it into his left fist. He smiled broadly. "If you're going to have hysterics, which would you rather have them in—a blue handkerchief or a red one?" He pulled a handkerchief out the bottom of his fist and it had become a brilliant red.

Kitty Marris' laughed a little. "Have you ever heard of the Cock-Eyed King?" she asked.

Diamondstone's teeth crushed a peanut audibly. "Wait. A race—Ah, I see it isn't a race horse. Nope. Never heard of it."

Again Kitty Marris looked nervously behind her. "I—I— Oh, I can't go through with this!" she sobbed. "Look. In my purse—" She fumbled with the clasp of her purse. "Dr. Meanwell owns the real Cock-Eyed King. He's horribly afraid he'll be murd—"

Her pocketbook opened suddenly. She seemed to listen, heard something. She uttered a small cry, sagged in her chair, and slipped sideward to the floor.

Diamondstone's mouth opened and remained so for a fraction of a minute. Then he stooped, slid arms beneath the girl's back and knees, and carried her to the open window. His red-gold brows were drawn tightly together.

"Absalom! Water!" shouted Diamondstone.

HE PROPPED the girl against the window and breathed deeply as though he hoped to force her to do likewise.

Footsteps. Diamondstone looked steadily into the girl's quiet face. Her warm, dark complexion had blanched not at all. She had arched an artistic eyebrow. Footsteps neared.

"The kid fainted," Diamondstone said, without looking around. He reached back with his left hand and groped. "The water, Absalom." His fingers encountered something hard and chill. "Oh," he said, quietly.

His left hand returned to the girl. Gently, and still without turning around, he lowered her to the floor. Then he pivoted in a slightly stooped position.

His eyes traveled up a pair of trouser legs of the blue-grey stuff worn by the hotel bell-hops. He saw a braided sleeve and the blue steel automatic that sprouted from the sleeve. He raised his eyes to the bell-hop's face and saw only a triangle of white handkerchief with two shrewd, black eyes glinting above it.

Diamondstone smiled unpleasantly. He slowly raised his hands.

"You got it." The bell-hop had a too-old, rusty voice.

"Uh-hum," agreed Diamondstone. Why argue with a man who has his mind made up and holds the business end of an automatic?

"Well, give it to me."

"Just what?" asked Diamondstone.

"The Cock-Eyed King, you dope!"

The masked man had left the door of the room open. Absalom's withered face, faded with fright to the color of a cross section of liver sausage, appeared. The tips of Diamondstone's fingers waved almost imperceptibly.

DIAMONDSTONE AND his servant seemed synchronous beings, for they moved at once and swiftly. Diamondstone's right arm came down like a semaphore. There was suddenly in his right hand a small, black gun that spoke in a sharp whisper without so much as an introduction. A thin, crystal line of pungent liquid described the shortest distance between the black gun and the bell-hop's eyes.

The bell-hop went blind and crazy all at the same time. He shot, yes, but no one ever found out what became of the bullet. Kitty Marris, suddenly out of her trance, screamed. Diamondstone, the black gun palmed, slapped the masked man across the jaw. The man reeled, dropped the gun, and clawed at his eyes. Diamondstone's extended left leg helped him unceremoniously to the floor. Absalom came into the room, dragging a length of rope.

Diamondstone landed with both knees on the bell-hop's back. Blind, winded, still the masked man put up a fight until Diamondstone managed to get a length of rope around his two wrists.

"A beautiful job, Absalom. No need to gag him, either—he won't be calling for help." Diamondstone tied knots expertly. "What was in your squirt gun that time, Absalom?"

"'Monia, boss. I just came out of the hall and looked in. There you was in trouble again. So I slung the squirt gun at you."

Diamondstone looked at his servant. Absalom was growing browner now that danger was past. Diamondstone chuckled. He looked at Kitty Marris. She was standing upright, looking well again.

"Absalom," he explained to her, "is scared stiff of firearms, but he packs a water-pistol and half a dozen assorted razors."

The girl gazed round-eyed at the man on the floor. "Wh-what are you going to do with him?" she asked.

"Put him to bed for the time," Diamondstone told her. "Things are fogging up considerably."

He nudged the bell-hop over on his back with the toe of one yellow shoe. The man's handkerchief had slipped down around his neck. Diamondstone commented that he quite looked the part of a disgruntled cowboy.

Tears from the bell-hop's eyes guttered down hard, black wrinkles. He whispered oaths between his clenched teeth. Absalom, interpreting his employer's thoughts, dragged the bound bell-hop into the adjoining bedroom.

"Y-you're not going to send him to jail?" asked Kitty Marris, somehow fearfully.

Diamondstone shook his head. "Not until I know what for. You see—"

A man came into the room. He was remarkably thin and dapper. He lifted a soft, grey hat from outstanding ears and leaned slightly forward on a satiny yellow walking stick. A white ribbon on his coat lapel was lettered in black: "WELCOME M.S.P."

His name was Norton Beams. He was president of a local chemical manufacturing concern and a bigwig in the Chamber of Commerce.

"I knocked," he apologized uneasily.

"Uh-hum," Diamondstone grunted. "And we were busy. Perfectly all right. I've considered your proposition. At first, guardian to a lot of old postage stamps didn't appeal to me. That was before I heard of the Cock-Eyed King. If the Midwest Society of Philatelists are going to exhibit their collections here tomorrow, I'll be only too glad to do what I can to protect owners of valuable stamps from thieves."

Norton Beams rubbed his hands. He smiled thinly. "That's fine."

"And will this famous Cock-Eyed King be exhibited?" Diamondstone asked.

Beams went into an angular shrug. "I don't know. I'm not a philatelist myself. But I've heard of the stamp. It's got such a rotten reputation we'll all feel better with a detective on the lookout. I'd like to know more about it—that Cock-Eyed King, I mean."

Diamondstone looked beyond Norton Beams. Kitty Marris was gathering up her purse. She straightened up, met Diamondstone's eyes, and flushed, angrily and resentfully, he thought.

"Miss Marris can tell us all about it," Diamondstone said. "She's a great friend of Dr. Meanwell, its owner."

Kitty Marris was backing toward the door. "No, really," she denied hurriedly. "I don't know anything about it. It's just a Siamese stamp. The picture of King Somebody-or-other on it is cross-eyed."

Diamondstone followed her. "Yes?" he urged interestedly. When he came abreast of her, he leaned against the door frame.

"Well," she went on, her eyes lowered, "the king really wasn't cross-eyed. It was just a flaw in the engraving."

"I'll bet his majesty was put out no end," said Beams.

"He had all the stamps destroyed," explained Kitty Marris. She was breathing rather rapidly now, Diamondstone thought. "Except one. One got through the mail. It's a freak. Worth a hundred thousand dollars. People who have it in their possession generally keep quiet about it."

Beams tucked his tongue into his sunken cheek until it looked as though he had just mouthed a quid of tobacco.

"I've heard about that," he said. "Its owners are almost always unfortunate. They lose things."

Diamondstone's red-gold brows raised. "What sort of things?"

"Their lives, generally."

CHAPTER II

TORTURE MURDER

RIGHT BENEATH his left vest pocket, Diamondstone had an odd, burning sensation. That was because of the bit of perforated, mauve-colored paper secreted in a hidden compartment in his cigarette case.

It was no longer a matter of wonder that Dr. Ralph Meanwell had sought him out early that day and begged him to take care of the famous and sinister Cock-Eyed King! But where did this girl fit in? He looked down at her, so small, so pretty, so worried. She would have liked to squeeze past him and get through the door.

Discourteously, he made her beg: "Really, I *must* be going."

Diamondstone shook his head. "Surely not." He put his hand out for her purse. "Just think, Mr. Beams, someone with malice aforethought must have slipped a capsule of cyanogen or something in this young lady's purse. It's beginning to look as though it doesn't even pay to *know* the owner of the Cock-Eyed King."

Kitty Marris got her purse behind her. Her breast beneath her trim, grey traveling suit was palpitant. There were angry lights in her large, dark eyes.

"Aren't you going to let me examine your pocketbook, Miss Marris?" asked Diamondstone smoothly. "I could have sworn that you were overcome at the very instant that you opened your purse."

"No need, really," she said, a frightened girl trying to act cold. "Must have been a coincidence. I felt faint all of a sudden."

A change came over Diamondstone. Suddenly, he was diabolically suave. He moved to one side, bowed slightly; smiled, but his open joviality was gone.

Kitty Marris caught her breath, muttered something and turned to go through the door. As she turned, she tried to bring her pocketbook around in front of her. As her left hand, holding the purse, swung around, Diamondstone made an effortless, perfectly-timed movement. Kitty Marris' purse was suddenly in Diamondstone's hand. He flicked back the flap, fingers darting into the interior.

Kitty Marris turned on him. "Damn you!" she whipped out. Tears not quite quenched the anger burning in her eyes.

"Look here, Diamondstone—" Norton Beams started to intervene.

"Don't crab my act!" Diamondstone snapped. His scowl vanished and the even more alarming suave smile was back as he looked over the flap of the purse at Kitty Marris. "Why damn me, now?" A sudden twist of the fingers and he almost turned the purse inside out. "See, there's not a thing in it. Not even that capsule of cyanogen I thought your would-be murderer had placed inside. Really, Miss Marris, you're in a bad state of nerves."

He closed the purse, the long fingers of his right hand finger-palming two small, mauve stamps; two stamps clean and new with the broad visage of the Cock-Eyed King staring out from their surfaces.

He handed the purse back to Kitty Marris. She took it venomously and walked briskly into the living room. Diamondstone was at her side with Norton Beams following.

"I say, Diamondstone, the committee will want to know—"

"To hell with the committee."

Diamondstone put a hand on Kitty Marris' elbow and guided her into the hall. She tried to jerk away, but the gentleness of Diamondstone's grip was all deception. She stopped, stamped her foot, bit her lip.

"Will you let me go?" she demanded spiritedly. "Must I call the police?"

"Well, must you?" he asked, smiling, urging her forward to the elevator. "You see, I know almost all the policemen. I used to perform at their benefits. And to be arrested for annoying a lady— Well, it would be humiliating." Diamondstone thumbed the elevator signal.

"What are you going to do?" she demanded.

"Take you to see your old friend Dr. Meanwell," he told her. "Odd, that we should have a mutual acquaintance."

"N-no. You mustn't. Please!"

The elevator bobbed to the floor. The safety gate opened. Diamondstone forced her into the car. Norton Beams followed.

"Next up," Diamondstone ordered.

"Look here, Diamondstone—" Norton Beams began again.

DIAMONDSTONE'S STEELY blue eyes flashed. "You still here?"

"Well, yes. The committee will want to know what consideration you will want. You see our budget—"

Diamondstone shook his head vigorously. "I never work for fees."

The elevator stopped, and he marched Kitty Marris down the hall. In front of Dr. Meanwell's room, they stopped. She looked up at him. Her eyes were glistening. Her soft lips trembled.

"Please!" she begged. "You couldn't. You don't know what you're doing. I—I— Oh, you haven't anything on me. You don't know—"

Diamondstone's red-gold brows came together. He was staring at the floor.

"Look at the toe of your right shoe, Miss Marris," he said in a low, even voice.

Kitty Marris looked. She uttered a sharp scream and sprang back a little. The toe of her right shoe left a dark stain on the grey carpet. Blood puddled beneath the door of Dr. Meanwell's room.

Diamondstone glanced over his shoulder. "Beams, make yourself useful. Just push the door open, won't you? And be careful. This isn't a nice murder at all."

Beams put his hand on the door knob, twisted it. He pushed the door open with his cane.

Diamondstone looked at Kitty. "You won't run away now, will you, Miss Marris, even if I let you go? You're obviously implicated in this Cock-Eyed King business for reasons that you and I know. If you ran away— Well, that would almost amount to a confession to the murder of somebody on the other side of this door."

"I—I didn't do it," she stammered. "I didn't even know he was dead."

"Neither does anybody else for that matter," Beams put in. "Look here, Diamondstone, Dr. Meanwell may have cut himself."

"Uh-hum. While shaving. Knowing the approximate blood contents of the human body, I feel pretty certain that no one could lose that much blood and still be alive."

Diamondstone thrust himself between Kitty Marris and the doorway. The room was dark, either because dusk had dropped swifter than Diamondstone had realized, or because the curtains were drawn.

Crack! Diamondstone swung around. His left arm out stiff was a mighty moving lever that knocked Kitty Marris' slight form back and flattened her to the hall floor. Diamondstone dropped to the floor just as someone charged through the open door and sprawled.

"You let me go!" a little man shouted, and kicked and squirmed to free his left ankle from the grip of Diamondtone's hand.

The little man was squeezing the trigger of a funny-looking, sawed-off gat that emitted sharp, terrier-like barks. When the gun stopped its clamor, Diamondstone stood up to stare down at an owl-eyed person who was losing his toupee and his temper along with it.

"Why, it's Mr. Jordan!" gasped Norton Beams.

The little man got up panting. "You're damned right! I've been robbed, swindled, tricked! I would like to have, at this very moment, the man in my hands who sold me that worthless bit of paper and made me believe— Bah!" He shook a diminutive fist at Diamondstone. "You tripped me, you big—" He saw Kitty Marris. "She—she—she—" he stuttered. "She was with him. They're in this together. A fine fool they've made of me—me, the secretary of the Midwest Society of Philatelists."

Footsteps tramped the hall. "What's going on here, anyway?" a voice bellowed.

Big Mark Guffy, the hotel detective, with his black hat tilted one way and his cigar the other. Little Mr. Jordan wilted, dropped his gun and tried vainly to hide it under his shoe. Guffy collared Jordan and snatched up the gun. Diamondstone tapped the detective on the shoulder.

"There's bigger game," he said, nodding toward Dr. Meanwell's room. Then he stepped inside and pushed the light switch.

"Ho-lee—" gasped the hotel detective as he followed Diamondstone.

THERE WAS a man back of the door. He had been stripped to the waist and his torso was criss-crossed with long, torturous wounds. Then there was one small wound that hadn't tortured, that had let life out suddenly. Diamondstone thought that the wound must have passed completely through the body.

The man had once been Dr. Ralph Meanwell, erstwhile owner of the Cock-Eyed King. The Menace had gone savagely at this butchery, knowing what he was after and determined to get it. Diamondstone felt the cigarette case, which contained the Cock-Eyed King, in his vest pocket. He was just a little uneasy.

Little Mr. Jordan came in. He was vigorously polishing the lenses of his horn-rimmed glasses with the tip of his tie. His eyes were weak and red-rimmed. His face was pale.

"You—you've got to believe me," he pleaded. "I'll make a clean breast of everything."

Mark Guffy took out his cigar and poked it at Jordan. Jordan jumped.

"You watch the guy, Diamondstone," Guffy growled. "I'm calling the police."

Jordan got his spectacles back in place. He blinked at the body.

"I swear I didn't see it when I came in. I noticed the door pushed hard. It was perfectly dark in the room. I called out to Dr. Meanwell. He didn't hear me—naturally." Jordan looked at the corpse, tried to laugh, then daubed at his brows with his handkerchief.

"What in hell was you comin' in here for anyway?" demanded Guffy from the stool where he squatted over the telephone.

"I—I wanted to see the Cock-Eyed King. Dr. Meanwell has it. You see, I had just purchased one also. There was always some doubt as to whether all the other Cock-Eyed King stamps had been destroyed. I had purchased one that seemed new and uncancelled, last night. And a pretty price I paid. A water-mark test indicated that the stamp was genuine. But later on, when I checked the perforations. I came to the conclusion that I had been properly fleeced by a counterfeiter.

"Naturally, I wanted to check with the original. I came up here, knocked, found the door unlocked, and walked in. I didn't see Meanwell until I stepped in the blood. Then I saw— I saw—" Jordan gulped. "I saw he was dead, just as he is now. I—I ran to the door. Then I was all panicky. I couldn't go out with that blood on my shoes. I ran into the bath, cleaned my shoes. When I came back, somebody was opening the door. Gentlemen, I saw before me, the electric chair. I, an innocent victim of circumstances—"

"Save the eulogy," Diamondstone cut in. "You tried to shoot your way out like a cornered gangster, eh?"

"No—no. I just wanted to scare you. I—I couldn't have killed you."

"Not with this gun, anyway." Guffy held up Jordan's stubby gat. "It won't shoot nothin' but blanks. It's just a scare gun."

"My wife always makes me carry it," Jordan told them.

"You look guilty as hell," Guffy said. "I gotta hold you for the police, Mr. Jordan."

Jordan groaned. "Oh, what will my wife say!"

DIAMONDSTONE, EATING peanuts, went over to the door. Norton Beams was there. He was leaning lightly on his cane. He looked worried.

"I say, Diamondstone, this is going to ruin the convention," Beams complained. "The secretary of the philatelists arrested for murder! Can't I go bail or something?"

Diamondstone shook his head. "Not on a murder charge. Jordan, what gave you the idea that the Cock-Eyed King stamp you purchased was a forgery?"

"W-e-ll," Jordan dragged out, "I just thought, what if it was? Then I read up on its history a little. That whole series of Siamese stamps was printed in America. The plates from which the Cock-Eyed King was made might still be in existence, making perfect counterfeits possible. When I thought I had been swindled—"

"Where did the real Cock-Eyed King come from in the first place?" demanded Diamondstone.

"That I really do not know."

Diamondstone sighed. A police siren wailed dimly. Diamondstone went out of the room, turned, and came back to pick up the peanut shucks he had dropped. For a very good reason, he thought it wise not to leave any evidence that the police might misconstrue. After all, somebody was going to find the hundred-thousand-dollar stamp missing, interpret that as the motive for the murder. And Diamondstone had the stamp.

CHAPTER III

THE MENACE MOVES

"**N**ATURALLY, I'M as interested in this amateur detective work as you gentlemen are," Norton Beams said.

Mark Guffy and Diamondstone both resented the word "amateur." Guffy cocked his cigar a little higher and grunted. Diamondstone only smiled. They were seated in one of the hotel lounges half an hour after the police had taken charge. The hotel was overrun with stamp collectors, all oblivious to the fact that in the Grand Atlantic was the Menace with his swift, cruel blade and his dogged determination to get what he wanted.

Beams put a cigarette butt in the ash stand where it smoldered among peanut shucks.

"Anybody got a slip of paper?" he asked.

Guffy had a worn notebook in his pocket which he offered, but Beams had found an envelope in his pocket.

"This will do nicely, thanks," Beams said as he flattened the envelope on the arm of his chair and took out a fountain pen. "Just where are we now?" Thoughtfully he poked his tongue into his left cheek.

"Well, we got one body full of holes—knife holes," Guffy told him.

Beams scratched notes on the envelope. "And our murderer is a collector of postage stamps. The police say the Cock-Eyed King is missing. Who but a stamp collector would want the thing?"

"Uh-hum," Diamondstone grunted. "But what can the murderer do with the stamp? Just look at it! You think anybody's bugs enough on the subject to kill a man for a stamp?"

"I read once where a man was killed for a painting by this Van Dine guy," Guffy said.

"Van Dyke," Diamondstone corrected. "But this is just a postage stamp."

"It's worth a hundred thousand dollars," Beams recalled.

"But what good is it?" Diamondstone persisted. "You can't sell it. It's too well known. Now that a man's been murdered for it, what sane person would buy the stamp? It's dangerous to mess around with stolen property."

"Jordan bought one, didn't he?" Beams made more notes on his envelope. "Even if it did turn out to be a fake."

"That's true," Diamondstone admitted.

Guffy shook his head. "You know boys, I'm not keen on stamps, but I sure would like to see this Cock-Eyed King."

Diamondstone reached into his pocket and brought out the two mauve-colored stamps he had filched from Kitty Marris' purse. He passed them over to Guffy.

"Feast your eyes on them," he said. "Those are two as pretty counterfeits of it as you'll ever see."

"Huh!" Guffy's eyes popped.

Beams leaned forward eagerly, then turned his dead-mackerel gaze on Diamondstone.

"Say, I wouldn't show those around if I was you. Where'd you get them? If they're counterfeits, you wouldn't stand in so good with the police. If you had an enemy you might find yourself faced with a charge of fraud or something."

Diamondstone nodded. "That's small change, Beams. Small change compared with a charge of murder. You're in the presence of the perfect fall guy for the Meanwell murder. I've got the real, the genuine Cock-Eyed King!"

"You—you've got what?" gasped Beams.

"Let's see it!" Guffy exploded.

Diamondstone shook his head. "Meanwell told me not to show it to a soul. It's just like those forgeries except you can hardly see his Siamese majesty because of the pen cancellations scrawled all over the stamp."

Diamondstone chuckled. He took hold of what looked to be about a three carat diamond ring on his third finger and turned it so that the setting was toward his palm.

"You mean that Meanwell gave it to you?" demanded Beams.

"Just to keep for him," Diamondstone explained. "He had the idea that someone would try to steal it. He was right. Someone did more than that. Someone tortured him, tried to make him tell where the Cock-Eyed King was; then, in a frenzy someone murdered Meanwell, determined to find the hiding place of the Cock-Eyed King himself."

"You mean this Meanwell went through hell and death rather than tell where the Cock-Eyed King was?" Guffy demanded, and added flatly, "You're nuts, Diamondstone."

"Probably," Diamondstone agreed. "But look at it this way: Meanwell was cornered, tortured, but he kept his head. What he figured was that his tormentor wouldn't kill him as long as he didn't divulge the hiding place of the Cock-Eyed King. If he told where the stamp was, his tormentor would have had to kill him to keep him quiet."

Diamondstone reached into his pocket and brought out a ring of iron about an inch and a half in diameter. Beams leaned forward on his cane and watched. Guffy smoked and watched. Diamondstone chuckled.

"One of the cleverest effects of the late Jardine Ellis," he told them. He leaned forward suddenly touched Beams' cane. "Behold!" He looked smilingly from Guffy to Beams. The iron ring had apparently passed onto Beams stick. Then Diamondstone had it off again and tossed it to Guffy.

"Perfectly solid. An absolute impossibility. The detective and the magician are kindred souls. One a maker of mysteries; the other devoting his efforts to unraveling them. Both sometimes accomplish the impossible." He stood up. "I'm going to bed to rest uneasily with the Cock-Eyed King under my pillow."

"What about the girl, Diamondstone?" asked Beams. "Miss Marris—wasn't that her name?"

Diamondstone looked blank. "Oh, Kitty Marris. I really didn't have anything on her. I told her she could go if she wanted to." He started toward the elevator.

CHAPTER IV

THE TRAP

WHEN HE arrived at his apartment, Diamondstone went directly into the bedroom. He noticed at once the total absence of Absalom's homely visage. Puzzled, he looked toward the bed. The bell-hop bandit lay there. Absalom's ropes crossed and criss-crossed him. But where was Absalom? There was not so much as a snore to indicate the servant's whereabouts.

Diamondstone went over to the bed.

"Still here?" he asked, his stone apparently surprised. "Ah, but I see you are."

"Dammit!" snapped the bell-hop.

Diamondstone leaned over the bed. He shucked a peanut. "You're not in a bed," he commented. "You're in a hole. Suppose I go to the police and tell them what you tried to pull off? They'll fry you for the murder of Dr. Meanwell."

"You mean he's dead?"

"Sort of. Now, you tell me your game. Unless, of course, you want me to bring in the police."

"You go to hell."

"Then I'll tell you." Diamondstone munched the peanut. "You thought you'd do a nice business selling counterfeit Cock-Eyed Kings to the suckers at this stamp collector's convention."

"They aren't counterfeits," said the bell-hop. "They're printed from the same damn plates that produced the originals. Only the perforation of the paper is a little different. I couldn't duplicate that."

"How did you know so much about it?" Diamondstone wanted to know.

"Why shouldn't I?" asked the man. "Wasn't I the engraver that made the plates for the original?"

"Why were you so anxious to get hold of the original Cock-Eyed King then?" Diamondstone asked.

"To duplicate the cancellation, you say. I didn't want to steal the stamp. Just wanted to borrow it for a while. I was watching Meanwell this morning when he came here. I had a hunch he'd brought you the stamp. I would have returned it to him as soon as I'd copied the cancellation. Now, you let me clear out of here. I'll leave town. You haven't even got proof that I intended to defraud. You don't know but what I would have sold the fakes as reproductions. Lots of people do."

Somebody gave Diamondstone a push from behind. His knees struck the edge of the bed. He lost his balance, fell forward. The bell-hop's hands came up unbound. A shot-sack whizzed and caught Diamondstone a blow on the head that made him groggy. Rope looped about his wrists and bit deeply. The bell-hop landed a blow on Diamondstone's jaw.

"Joe! Don't hurt him. Please don't, Joe!" Kitty Marris' voice, sounding far away. It was she who had pushed Diamondstone. "You promised you wouldn't hurt him."

Bell-hop Joe, who wasn't a bellhop at all, laughed harshly. He kicked Diamondstone off the bed and landed on top of him.

"Cut it, Kitty. When I get through with this guy, he'll be freight for the ambulance."

Ropes around Diamondstone's legs tightened. He kicked weakly, tried to see through floating red mist. Kitty was pleading. Maybe she remembered how Diamondstone had knocked her flat against the wall to protect her when little Mr. Jordan had burst from Meanwell's room with a blazing gat in his hand.

Diamondstone tried to say something to her. A gag was plunged into his mouth at the moment. More rope, now. He was as helpless as a mummy. He was dragged along the floor, kicked into a closet. The lock clicked.

"Joe, what are you going to do?" Kitty's voice.

"Find that damned stamp. Our little fraud scheme—"

"Your little fraud scheme," Kitty was heard to correct.

"Well, *my* little fraud scheme has gone haywire. But if I can get my mitts on that stamp we'll skip the country and sell it in England."

"I'm not leaving, Joe," Kitty Marris said, cold and desperate. "And you're not stealing any stamp."

"The hell I'm not!"

IN THE closet, Diamondstone was listening to them wrangle. And he was doing a lot more. He had chewed the gag and worked it out with his tongue. Somehow, he got to his feet.

The closet was lined with shelves. In his mind's eye, he could see the contents of those shelves—apparatus for hundreds of clever illusions. To his right was a shelf covered with neatly boxed gimmicks, pulls, and handkerchief tubes—all good on the stage, but not for a man tied hand and foot.

"I say you're not going to swipe a damned thing!" Kitty was laying down the law. "You're going out of here! I'm going to the police. We'll tell the whole thing. We'll take a rap if we've got to, but we'll come clean. I'm washed up with these lies and deceits."

Joe laughed. "A goody-goody girl, eh? Say, another crack like that and I'll iron you out!"

"Help! Pol—"

Kitty's scream was cut short by the blow of a fist. Diamondstone heard the crack and the creak of the bedspring as Kitty fell across the bed. Diamondstone boiled over. But it didn't get him anywhere. No further sound from Kitty. Joe's blow must have laid her out. Diamondstone felt himself going white. The trap he had planned was set. Its jaws were of steel. But good Lord, think of the bait!

He forced himself to think. Chemical magic—third shelf, right. He wiggled to the shelf. He flopped to his knees. He had nothing to see with but his tongue and nose. There wasn't even a string of light shining beneath the door.

Joe had left the bedroom and could be heard prowling around another part of the apartment. Diamondstone's nose found bottles and boxes. Ink illusions, phantom writing, water to wine—he ticked them off mentally. Where in hell had he put water to fire?

SOMEWHERE IN the apartment, he heard Joe's harsh whisper.

"Stick 'em up!"

Then it had come, Diamondstone knew. He heard a steely whisk sound. There was a small, surprised cry, the sound of a body falling, and a dull groan. Silence, then footsteps. It was the Menace in motion; not Joe. Diamondstone knew where the Menace would strike next. His big body shuddered.

Then his dry, dust-covered tongue encountered the round sides of a small bottle. That *must* be the substance for the water to fire illusion. Had to be. He knocked the bottle to the floor and listened to its roll. Then he groped for it with his knee, found it, kneeled on it.

Glass shattered, needling into his flesh. He squirmed down flat. His bound hands found the fragments, discovered that he couldn't distinguish the broken glass from the metallic potassium the bottle had contained.

He had to get down closer, feel it out with his nose.

Footsteps now in the bedroom, approaching the bed. Kitty Marris was there, lying on the bed in the dark room. The Menace would kill without warning; not knowing his victim, not caring greatly.

Diamondstone thought he had located the potassium. No time now. He kicked back against the panel of the door with his heels. It was a loud crashing sound. Footsteps stopped. Diamondstone spat on the floor at the spot of blackness where he thought the potassium was. Nothing happened.

Footsteps again. Toward the bed? Toward the closet? Diamondstone drew a long breath, forced himself to a calm. "Stop!" he said distinctly. "I have you covered from this closet."

Covered! That was a laugh. What had he accomplished by that bluffing? Delayed Kitty's death a few moments; insured his own. The Menace had only to open the door of the closet and plunge his blade into Diamondstone—unless he could find that potassium.

He spat again. This time a spark, a hissing sound as the saliva struck the potassium. He spat at the spark. It flared up with the intense flame of burning hydrogen. He squirmed around, thrust his bound wrists into the rapidly dying flame. There was spark enough to catch the dry hemp.

In the flickering light, he glanced around the closet. Ought to be some sort of weapon somewhere. His stage revolver was filled only with blank cartridges. But there was the stiletto he used for stabbing cards.

Under the strength of his straining muscles, the half-charred rope broke. Diamondstone had already marked the location of the stiletto. He hopped toward it, got it, stooped to saw through the ropes that bound his ankles and calves.

"Diamondstone," someone just outside the closet was saying, "don't try to shoot at me through the door."

Something slammed against the panel. Then came the sound of hands slapping cheeks, and a hoarse: "Snap out of it!"

A sharp, indrawn breath. A pitiful, quivering cry from Kitty Marris.

"The girl's up against the closet door, Diamondstone," said the Menace coldly. "So don't shoot through the panel. You forced me to shoot and the girl gets it first. You know what I'm after."

Diamondstone severed the last strand of rope. He gripped his dagger and moved swiftly to the door. Ear against the panel, he fancied he could hear Kitty's rapid breathing.

"Diamondstone, can't you hear me? I want the Cock-Eyed King. You're not ass enough to defend it with your life. You're no stamp collector. The thing is valueless to you. It's worth millions to me."

"Why?" asked Diamondstone. He was stalling, thinking.

The Menace, shielded by the girl, was impregnable as far as Diamondstone was concerned. Still, there *must* be a way. He thought of the gimmicks and handkerchief tubes. A tube of transparent celluloid flashed across his mind. He groped for it, listening to the Menace speaking coldly on the other side of the door.

"You remember six years ago a man died of injuries received during a mysterious explosion?" the Menace asked. "The newspapers said he died guarding a secret worth millions. He told one man that secret. I am the man. I am the rightful owner of the Cock-Eyed King. It was stolen from me by some ass of a stamp collector. I tried to procure it honestly. I've traced it the world over. I wanted to buy it from old Meanwell. He wouldn't sell, even refused to let me see it. I tortured him—as I will most certainly torture this girl if you don't hand over the Cock-Eyed King."

Diamondstone was thinking desperately. To hand over the Cock-Eyed King meant what? Certain death, for Diamondstone could identify the killer. So, probably, could Kitty Marris since she was now face to face with the man.

But would death be instantaneous or would the Menace first examine the Cock-Eyed King to make sure that Diamondstone had not deceived him? If Diamondstone could make the killer suspect trickery, if he could imply, by the very tone of his voice, some perfectly nonexistent, slight—

Diamondstone reached into his pocket and took out his silver cigarette case. It was something more than it appeared. Actually, it was an ingenious card-box with which he could cause playing cards to vanish or change at will. The Cock-Eyed King reposed in the secret card compartment; and unless one knew the secret of opening that compartment, it probably would never be opened.

"Suppose," said Diamondstone, and his voice was oily with craft, "suppose I do hand you the Cock-Eyed King. How do I know—"

"Don't try to bargain, Diamondstone," came the snapped reply. "Another moment's delay, and I'll let you hear this girl scream. Where is the Cock-Eyed King?"

Diamondstone ripped the celluloid handkerchief tube with his knife. He bent and straightened it until it was a thin strong film about six inches long.

"Open the door a little," Diamondstone directed. "I will pass out the stamp."

A MOMENT'S hesitation. Then: "I have my gun pressed against the girl's side. A hint of treachery, and I'll let her have it."

The lock clicked. The door opened perhaps four inches. Both of Diamondstone's hands came forward at once; the right hand, holding the cigarette case, concealed the movement of the left.

"The Cock-Eyed King is in the cigarette case," Diamondstone told the Menace. "One of my hands was wounded and I can't open the case. You need both hands. The stamp is underneath the false bottom."

The Menace snatched the silver case, slammed the door, turned the lock—*thought he turned the lock.* For with his left hand, Diamondstone had slipped the tough bit of celluloid between the bolt and its socket.

"Stand where you are, girl," whispered the Menace. "I can draw a gun faster than you can think."

Footsteps retreating to the other side of the room. In the dark, Diamondstone smiled. He listened intently. A metallic snap such as the spring lock of the cigarette case made when opened. Diamondstone gripped his stiletto in his right hand, drew back a little, and suddenly flung himself at the door.

CHAPTER V

MEET THE MURDERER

THE PANEL swept back, threw Kitty Marris to the floor. Across the room, a swiftly moving shadow of a man dropped a cigarette case and drew a gat. He fired hastily. The bullet keened by Diamondstone's ear.

But Diamondstone's stiletto was in the air, a brilliant, silvery bird that stopped suddenly against the angular silhouette of the killer's shoulder. The man dropped the gun, sprang toward the table, picked up something. There was that sinister, steely *whisk*, but it was only half sounded this time.

Diamondstone's left fist crashed to the point of the killer's jaw. The man reeled backward, then folded over Diamondstone's right to the body. He was out, then, probably, but Diamondstone added another left for good measure.

Mark Guffy came tramping in, brought by the shot. He saw Diamondstone with a big arm around Kitty Marris' slim waist. Kitty was weeping. Diamondstone was chuckling.

Across the room, Mr. Norton Beams lay groaning with a knife-hasp sticking out of his shoulder and his jaw beginning to look bloated. Beams' satiny cane was beside him, the handle separated from the rest of the wood casing by six inches or so of gleaming, blood-splashed rapier steel. The silver cigarette case was not far off. Inside was the sinister Cock-Eyed King, but no one would have known it.

"What you got here? A shambles?" roared the house detective. "One of our bell-hops is out there, bleeding to death. Your colored servant has a goose egg on his head. What the hell—" He stopped, as he saw Norton Beams.

"Meet the murderer, Guffy," said Diamondstone. "I felt pretty certain it wasn't a stamp collector who wanted the Cock-Eyed King. None of them would be crazy enough to kill for it. I figured the thing had some value besides just its scarcity. There was writing on it—writing that some of the philatelists took for a pen cancellation. Actually, that writing was part of a chemical formula developed by a man working in Norton Beams' plant a long time ago. The formula was for a new deadly explosive. In demonstrating the explosive, its discoverer was fatally injured. He lived long enough to recite his secret formula to Beams. Beams wrote it down on an envelope. In his haste, part of the formula was written across the stamp."

Guffy nodded his head. "I getcha. The formula wasn't any good without the part that was written on the stamp. Beams couldn't remember it."

Diamondstone nodded. "Then some stamp collector got hold of the envelope, recognized the stamp thereon as the supposedly destroyed Cock-Eyed King. He took off the stamp, leaving Beams the envelope. That stamp was the one Cock-Eyed King that got by the Siamese postal officials. I happen to know that Beams has a brother who's quite a globe trotter. The brother probably sent Beams the Cock-Eyed King on a letter, not knowing the value of the stamp."

"But after all, Diamondstone," Guffy protested, "Beams was a pretty important guy. How'd you guess he was the guilty party, the murderer?"

Diamondstone smiled. "After all, I'm a magician. But it all works down to this: It was Beams who was instrumental in getting the philatelist society to convene here. He was tired chasing the Cock-Eyed King. The convention brought the stamp right to his door. Then, you and I both saw that Beams has a habit of jotting down things on old envelopes."

"Lots of people do that," objected Guffy.

"Yes, but that made Beams a suspect. Then there was the cane. It never left him for a moment. A knife hadn't killed Dr. Meanwell. It was something longer than a mere knife, because the blade passed clear through the body and bit into the floor. Then the killer must have had a sword. It's a short jump from there to a sword cane."

Guffy was still puzzled. "How the devil did you know that there was a sword inside of it?"

"Downstairs in the lobby, I worked the Jardine Ellis ring trick on Beams. *Apparently,* I passed the solid iron ring onto the stick. Apparently, I say—but why spoil a good trick by telling you how it was done? The trick itself was only a bit of legerdemain to give me an excuse for bringing my right hand against the cane. On my right hand was a finger ring. There's a sensitive compass needle beneath the bit of glass. Magicians all use something similar in effects that depend on identifying hidden objects by the presence of steel embedded within the objects. I noticed that the little needle in my ring dipped because of the magnetic attraction of the steel inside the walking stick."

"Why the devil didn't you accuse him then?" demanded Guffy.

Diamondstone looked down at the small, pretty girl in his arms. "Because, I wanted to make sure there were no other people involved in the crime. Then, also, I like to trap my villains red-handed. That my trap didn't work, that I didn't get Beams just as he was in the act of swiping the Cock-Eyed King wasn't entirely my fault."

Police were coming in as Diamondstone spoke. In the next room, the hotel doctor was looking over the real bell-hop who had unfortunately met Beams on the way out. Joe, the masquerading bell-hop, got in a statement before death caught up with him. He was generous, dying. He told all about the fraud he had planned, but he kept Kitty out of it. He told how he had been surprised by Beams, how he had drawn his gun, how Beams had thrust him through with his sword cane.

Kitty Marris did a good deal of crying. She kept saying she ought to stay with Joe. He was her half-brother. He had been good to her, sometimes. She hadn't wanted to try the stamp fraud. She hadn't wanted to fake that faint in Diamondstone's study so that Joe could catch Diamondstone unawares and force him to give up the Cock-Eyed King. She really wanted to go to jail and come out straight.

Diamondstone told her there was no reason for anybody to go to jail but Norton Beams. He shucked a peanut with one hand, put the nut to his lips, then on sudden inspiration, popped it into Kitty's mouth.

"You can consider yourself kissed," he told her.

She choked, then laughed. Laughed with Diamondstone.

II

THE BROTHERS
OF DOOM

CHAPTER I

TAINT OF MADNESS

M ISS JACK LOWERY heard of Diamondstone from Miss Cecil Patterson.

"He adjusted a small matter for me, with dispatch that was perfectly staggering," Miss Patterson declared. "Not at all the type of detective you'd mind having around the house." This, of course, with a maidenly blush. "There's something mysterious about him. He used to be a magician, you know, and you've a feeling of wanting to see all around him at once."

Mrs. Jack Lowery found Diamondstone a great, golden-haired man, sitting on his desk, trying to evolve a trick that consisted of apparently passing peanuts through the solid bottoms of paper cups. After a moment, he sighed, deliberately spoiled his trick by cracking and eating one of the peanuts.

"It cannot be done, my dear Mrs. Lowery," he admitted, "for the sole reason that I generally eat all the peanuts before the routine is complete. Do have one." And he smiled so happily that Mrs. Lowery, who had always found peanuts along the road to indigestion, did not have the heart to refuse.

She sized Diamondstone up and was somewhat surprised to find that he wasn't fat; simply big. His shoulders looked as though they had been made for carrying ice. And no one who had seen his long, strong hands in action could have thought him awkward.

Diamondstone studied his visitor with a pleasant, though intense, blue-eyed gaze. Here was a woman, pretty in a washed-out way. A woman who clung grimly to a wadded handkerchief and stared vacantly at the peanut husks on Diamondstone's expensive carpet.

"It's about my husband," Mrs. Lowery began. "I have a strange persistent feeling that he is not the same man I married three years ago."

The slug clipped the man in the shoulder and sent him spinning around.

Diamondstone just managed to resist commenting that most wives made the same discovery after an interval of three days.

"I mean that literally," Mrs. Lowery continued. "He even says he's not the same man."

"Uh-hum," Diamondstone said with an air of magnificent understanding that was convincingly counterfeited. "Who do you suppose he is, then?"

"I—I don't know." Knuckles of the fist that held the handkerchief whitened. "The other day he was the man who reads the gas meter. Just this morning he greeted me with: 'Good morning, madam. I can highly recommend the alligator purses'."

Diamondstone's bright, gold brows crimped together. He regarded Mrs. Lowery from the left hand corner of his eyes.

"And you said?"

"I put my arms around him and said: 'Jack, what on earth is the matter with you?' And he took my arms away quite coldly and said: 'Please, madam, not here. The floorwalker might see us.' Then he went right on with his shaving."

This was all ludicrously funny to Diamondstone. Yet he hadn't the heart to laugh. There was something so utterly helpless and distraught about Mrs. Lowery.

"Perhaps," he suggested, "Mr. Lowery has been working too hard."

Mrs. Lowery shook her head. "He doesn't work. You see, I'm quite comfortably fixed."

Diamondstone heaved wide shoulders helplessly. "But my dear lady he has to do something! Doesn't he play golf? Anything?"

MRS. LOWERY shook her head. "I've been sending him to the Gun Club to take bridge lessons during the past year. I was in hopes he would become interested in cards. But he prefers reading. He only goes to the club to please me. He's really clever. Was clever I mean. But when he came home with those t-tin soldiers—"

And simply the mention of this phase of her husband's malady was too much for Mrs. Lowery. She began to weep softly. Diamondstone put an arm impersonally about her shoulders.

"You really ought to consult a psychiatrist. I am in no position to advise you. But there is Dr. Claude Westmore—"

"My—my husband's best friend," sobbed Mrs. Lowery. "I went to Dr. Westmore. He admitted that there was a taint of madness in my husband's family, and—"

Absalom, who was Diamondstone's sloven-lipped, colored servant, put his homely, spotted face around the edge of the half open door.

"You care 'bout seein' a Mr. Lowery?" he asked, his Southern accent negligible.

Mrs. Lowery ducked under Diamondstone's arm. "Quick! It's Jack. Where is he?" And she fluttered past Absalom and through the door.

Diamondstone followed, saw in his living room a tall, stooped man with horn-rimmed spectacles. His features were finely cut, his mouth and chin sensitive.

Mrs. Lowery faced her husband, her handkerchief stuffed in her mouth, her eyes frightened-looking. Mr. Lowery looked over his wife's head.

"Everywhere I go, women act this way with me. The penalty of being an ice-man."

Diamondstone couldn't say a word. He shucked a peanut, from force of habit, and nearly conveyed the shucks to his mouth after he had dropped the kernel on the floor. All of his attention was upon a nut of another species. For there couldn't be a doubt but what Mr. Jack Lowery had gone completely blah.

Lowery sighed, turned to Diamondstone's console radio, and put his arms about it.

"I am sorry about the ice-cream, sir. It isn't the policy of our firm to *make* anyone eat our ice-cream. This was so nice and new I did hope you'd like it."

Lowery grunted, strained, lifted the radio and started for the door.

"No, dammit!" Diamondstone cracked out. "Put that down!"

Lowery dropped the radio, rushed across the room and seized both of Diamondstone's hands.

"Then you'll eat it? How good of you. I know that if you'll try our ice-cream once you'll never have your car greased any other place."

Lowery whipped around, pushed the goggling Absalom aside, and raced out into the hall. Mrs. Lowery had completely given way to hysterics. Diamondstone got the woman to a couch, told Absalom to get a doctor.

"Do everything you can for the poor woman," he ordered.

Out in the hall, he found that the elevator had swallowed the mad Jack Lowery. Diamondstone took the stairs, plunged down four flights three steps at a time. In the hotel lobby, he floored a fat salesman loaded down with sample cases. He gained the street and had no trouble picking out the tall form of Lowery.

The madman was hurrying up Illinois Street, jerking his head around to see if anyone was following. When he spotted Diamondstone, he began walking backwards, bumping into people, attracting plenty of attention, but still making rapid progress.

At the corner of an alley, he paused, pointed toward the sky, and uttered an owlish screech. Then he turned and plunged into the alley.

DIAMONDSTONE AND everyone in the street got to the mouth of the alley. Somewhere, from behind the magician-detective, came a distinct *plop*. Diamondstone knew he should have turned around in an effort to see where that sound had come from, but at the moment he could only watch Jack Lowery.

Lowery pivoted on the heel of his left shoe. His right leg kicked upward. Then his bones seemed to melt and he crumpled down on the alley pavement.

The crowd lurched forward. A woman screamed. Diamondstone was first at the side of the fallen man. He knelt, saw a little blood curling from beneath Lowery's head. He moved the head slightly to one side, saw a neatly drilled hole where a bullet had passed completely through the occipital bone and entered Lowery's addled brain.

And Diamondstone saw something else that even the oncoming policeman didn't see. He saw it, and slipped it from Lowery's pocket into his own. It was a small wooden box, that had been sticking from Lowery's pocket. More like a crate than a box, for through the tiny slats, Diamondstone saw the contents.

It was the most insane patch on the entire crazy quilt, that thing inside that miniature crate. A little, highly decorated tin soldier mounted guard with a diminutive rifle that was topped with a glistening bayonet.

CHAPTER II

CLUE OF THE TIN SOLDIER

DETECTIVE-SERGEANT PROUT saw a peanut shuck outside the door of the office of Chief Markly. He forgot, for a moment, the nature of his errand, burst into the office, and strode across the room to pump Diamondstone's hand.

"Haven't seen you since you took the two dozen eggs out of my mouth at the police benefit party," Prout cried.

Markly looked up at his sergeant wryly. "A miracle which loses its mystery when you contemplate the size of Sergeant Prout's mouth."

Prout reddened. "Sorry, sir. Humpy Glomis, the hunchback from the Gun Club, is out in front. He's ready for that identity test."

Markly nodded. "I'll take him in a moment." He leaned forward with his elbows on the desk and squinted at a tall man who occupied one end of the oak bench where Diamondstone sat. This man was Dr. Claude Westmore, noted psychiatrist and the murdered Lowery's closest friend. "Tell me this, Doctor. Was Jack Lowery crazy?"

Dr. Westmore made a tent; of his index fingers for his pursed lips to play in. "No-o-o," he replied slowly. Then definitely: "No. Quite as sane as you or I."

"Then how do you account for his actions in front of Diamondstone?" Markly asked.

Westmore cleared his throat. "I shan't try to."

A moment's silence was broken by the snap of a peanut shell. "Was there ever any insanity in the Lowery family, Doctor?" Diamondstone asked thoughtfully.

"No. I—" Westmore coughed, stood up, and sat down gingerly. "I'm sorry, but I'm afraid I'm not going to be much help."

Diamondstone conveyed a peanut to his mouth and talked while chewing. "Interesting to speculate on how you would have answered the same question had Jack Lowery been alive at this moment." He turned abruptly to Markly. "Prout mentioned the Gun Club. Jack Lowery had been going there for about a year. What sort of a place is it?"

Markly took a deep breath, puffed his cheeks. Across the room, Prout whispered: "Here comes the blast." And Markly bounded to his feet, looking as though he were about to explode.

"That damned place!" he roared. "Filthiest spiders' nest in our basement. A gambling house we can't close. Raid it and what do we find? A lot of silk-stockinged people who are apt to make trouble for you. They'll be dancing decently, or taking a few drinks, or taking bridge lessons from a conceited ass named Hanson. You can't find even a poker chip. Operated by a guy named King. But find King! He may be nonexistent. But he sure is hell! Enough brains to run all the crime in the city.

"There's a hunchback called Humpy Glomis. Humpy stands out in front of the Gun Club and collects tips from the elite who scratch his back for luck. But Humpy's never been inside the joint. And you can't close the club just because they've a hunchback hanging around in front. Humpy looks like a beggar, but he's so well patronized that he doesn't do another thing except make a few tin soldiers. Lives all alone and works alone, he's so damned ugly.

"Last week there were five deaths traced to the Gun Club. A banker, who had spent depositor's money on gambling, committed suicide while driving his car at sixty per. That Juggernaut with the corpse at the wheel junked taxi and killed three more people. The same night a man whose pockets were bulging with money left the Gun Club and was murdered by a thug. Humpy Glomis saw the thug beat out the poor devil's brains. We'll get the thug because Humpy is our friend. But we can't even tickle King."

"Nobody could crack the Gun Club gang," Prout declared.

"Nobody but a magician," Markly added. Then, as he realized what he had said, he sprang at Diamondstone. "*You* can crack that Gun Club. You're not too well known around town. You could gamble King into the open. King would notice you—"

"Er—that's what I'm afraid of," said Diamondstone.

He rubbed the back of his head reflectively, got up hastily, left the office by the back door, and went around to the reception room to get a look at Humpy Glomis. The hunchback was ragged and as ugly as a

Tyrol witch. His nose was crooked and warty. His teeth were darkly-stained tusks.

"I'll see you later, Mr. Humpy Glomis, I'm afraid," Diamondstone muttered to himself as he left Headquarters to go to his hotel.

THE CRAZY trail that Diamondstone followed led to the Gun Club. There Lowery had gone to learn cards—a different kind of cards than his wife knew about. Lowery had lost money as all who went to the Gun Club must. And it had not been Lowery's money. Lowery was in a pitiful state of dependency upon his rich wife, something that must have cut Lowery deep, judging from the man's sensitive mouth and chin.

Had he seen a way out? Something so subtle that Diamondstone scarcely grasped it?

A few minutes later, Diamondstone sat at his desk and looked at the tin soldier he had found on Jack Lowery. Dumb and lifeless as it was, it might answer bothersome questions.

"It's made of tin," he muttered to Absalom whose homely brown visage was visible just beyond the door. "But the bayonet of the little fellow's rifle has the unmistakable glint of steel." He was about to touch the bayonet with his graceful forefinger just to see how sharp it was. Suddenly, he pushed back in his chair and said: "Oh, hum," quietly.

He directed Absalom to bring his longest wand from his paraphernalia closet.

"For I have a vague notion this man of tin should not be touched with anything less than a ten foot pole," he said. Diamondstone's necessarily keen eyes had detected a tiny hole in the side of the tin soldier's bayonet.

Absalom brought the wand and with it a word of warning.

"You better watch out for that contraption if it belonged to that crazy ice-cream man."

Diamondstone shook his head. "Please don't refer to Jack Lowery as crazy." He stood up and touched the soldier's bayonet with the tip of his wand. Instantly, a concealed spring thrust the bayonet half an inch upward. At the same time a greenish liquid fountained over the wand and spread droplets across the desk. Diamondstone began to smile. "Crazy? As a matter of fact, Jack Lowery's cleverness as a murderer transcends anything I have yet encountered."

"How come?" Absalom regarded the soldier fearfully. "I thought the ice-cream man was one that got hisself murdered."

"So he was."

"Mus' have been that little ol' soldier that done him in." Absalom wagged his head wisely.

"Hardly. The medical examination has properly squashed your theory. Lowery was shot through the back of the head. Things are fogging up at a remarkable rate, but as long as we progress, we're bound to come out in the clear. But why a tin soldier, of all things, for a murder weapon? It looks, Absalom, as if an immediate visit by me to the Gun Club is indicated." He arose and reached for his hat.

"A quiet place to play cards or dance to sweet music. A rendezvous for persons of refinement." That was what the advertisements, as modest and sedate as a physician's business card, had to say about the Gun Club.

It was housed in a grand old manor built by some Hoosier who had been impressed by someone's Southern accent. There was a flashing red sign atop its slate roof. Move it down on Indianapolis' Meridian Street and someone would have bought it for an insurance office. Or maybe an undertaking establishment.

"More appropriately, an undertaking establishment," thought Diamondstone on his arrival before the place, prepared for his invasion.

Humpy Glomis was the only bit of sincere atmosphere about the place. Monte Carlo boasted no better hunchback. Diamondstone was surprised to find the very people who would have looked upon scratching as vulgar tipping liberally for the privilege of scratching some luck off Humpy's luckless deformity.

"I declare," Diamondstone began innocently when there was a lull in Humpy's business, "I don't quite see the point."

They were standing in the shadows of the fir trees that surrounded the club. Humpy Glomis simply leaned against a tree, rolled cigarettes, and waited to be scratched.

It was not often that people spoke to Humpy Glomis. And here was Diamondstone, smiling good-natured upon a man whose visage generally provoked only shudders.

"They think that scratching our back brings luck," Humpy explained. "And we never say it don't."

"But what would one need luck for?" Diamondstone asked, his face remarkably dull.

"Some people need luck at cards," Humpy went on. His spiderlike eyes glittered like jet in the light of the club entrance.

Diamondstone frowned. "I was looking for a quiet bridge game. Of course, I wouldn't think of going in if there were games of chance inside."

Humpy sniffed. "Can't say. Never seen the inside of the place. Fine dressed drunks and little women are given the gate. Only the best people go there. Why even Gregory Francis Louis has scratched my back."

"You don't say!" Diamondstone pressed a five dollar bill into Humpy's grimy hand. "Who am I to pass up the opportunity of touching the precise spot where the great G.F. Louis has placed his fingers. Small wonder your back hasn't changed to gold!"

CHAPTER III

THE ROOM DOWN UNDER

ENTERING THE GUN CLUB, Diamondstone took in his surroundings wide innocent blue eyes.

"Uh-hum," he said to himself. "The place fairly reeks refinement. But somewhere down under—"

Then he spotted Hanson, the young bridge teacher to whom Markly had referred as a conceited ass. Diamondstone thought Hanson rather anemic. His oval face was pallidly white. His polished, black hair was neatly bisected.

This first visit to the Gun Club was purely for the purpose of reconnoitering. Diamondstone signed up for a series of Hanson's lessons. Then he acquired four decks of exclusive Gun Club cards while deftly misdirecting the attention of the serving staff.

Next he obtained evidence that Markly's suspicions regarding the club were not unfounded. He actually overheard the sleek Hanson subtly, suggesting that a white-haired couple might find more thrilling games than bridge beneath the roof of the Gun Club if they so desired.

This bit of eavesdropping Diamondstone managed from a remote corner of the room, for he was an adept at lip reading.

"I begin to understand," he mused on his way back to the hotel. "From the high intellectual level of the bridge table, patrons of the Gun Club are permitted to sink gradually lower and lower until Lady Luck has fastened her tentacles about them."

As soon as he arrived at the hotel, he went to work performing a number of major operations on the four decks of cards he had filched from the Gun Club. He scorned such obvious deceits as marked decks, but by the time dawn approached he had made undetectable changes in those cards in the way of trimming and stacking that rendered them positively uncanny.

HE WENT to bed and slept as though he never expected to lay his head on his pillow again.

The following evening, he introduced himself at the Gun Club as Carl Anthony. Then he began a series of card miracles calculated to ruffle the cold nerves of the mysterious King himself. Seated at the table with Hanson and two novices, he proceeded to whip Hanson into a rage by beating the bridge teacher to every trick. The substitution of his special cards and the use of numerous false shuffles accounted for that, but the result was that Hanson took him to one side.

"See here, Mr. Anthony," he said, "you seem to know quite a bit about cards."

"A gross understatement," Diamondstone said gravely. "I know *all* about cards. I'll bet that I can deal three sets of hands in a row and my hands alone shall hold all the honor cards."

Hanson became so stern he was almost convincing. "There is no gambling here, Mr. Anthony. No gambling of any kind. But for our more advanced players we have a separate club. If you would be interested—"

There was a room at the end of the ballroom to which Hanson had a key. It was a small, under-furnished hall with mirrors on the walls—mirrors, possibly, of argus glass which permitted hidden eyes on the other side to scrutinize those within the room. Diamondstone could have shuddered without resorting to too much imagination. Something sinister about all this. Something vastly dangerous about the face of the attendant who was in the act of putting a black blindfold over Diamondstone's eyes.

There might never be a maple tree on Maple Crest Farm. And never so much as a rain barrel on Lake View Addition. But there were guns at the Gun Club. One of those guns sagged the coat pocket of the attendant who was blindfolding Diamondstone.

"I declare," Diamondstone said. "Why all the secrecy? I can't see where I'm going. But I suppose that's the reason I'm being blindfolded, eh?"

"Exactly, sir," replied the attendant. "And figuratively speaking, this cloth is also about your mouth. Do I make myself clear?"

"Oh, quite."

No sooner had he been blindfolded than Diamondstone was aware that the floor beneath his feet was quivering. There was a sensation of going down and down until the moving room came to an abrupt stop. Diamondstone was then escorted along a circuitous path and eventually the blindfold was removed by the same gentleman gunman who had put it on.

"Straight ahead through that door, if you please," the attendant directed. And a moment later Diamondstone found himself in the room the police had doubtless been looking for—the secret gambling den of the Gun Club.

There *were* guns at the Gun Club. Two of them eyed Indianapolis' elite from slots in the handsomely decorated walls. In the center of the room was a beautifully designed roulette table. Near the walls were tables for cards.

Events that followed were carefully calculated to stand Mr. King on his head. Diamondstone attacked a poker game first and readily marked one of the men at the table as a professional card shark. Another, who wandered aimlessly about, signaled to his companion by means of long and short puffs on a cigarette.

A quick substitution of decks, which Diamondstone had never surpassed even at the height of his magical career, brought one of his prepared decks into play. There followed a series of astounding, whirlwind hands that left the poker players gasping over shrunken chip piles.

And all the while, Diamondstone kept an eye on the roulette table where he discovered that an innocent-looking blonde secretly manipulated a brake that stopped the wheel at the desired point. A few minutes later, he attacked the roulette game with equal vigor, secretly clipping the brake wire beneath the table while his right hand was busy placing chips. All things being equal for perhaps the first time in the Gun Club's noxious existence, Diamondstone's luck and playing sense had him well on the way toward breaking the bank.

"A most disgruntled and highly disturbed person is Mr. King by now," he thought, as he crammed his pockets with bills the cashier handed out.

When he had left the room down under, by the same blindfold route, he was met by pale Hanson.

"Er—Mr. Anthony, I've heard of your phenomenal luck this evening."

Diamondstone's red-gold brows raised as he regarded Hanson. "I beg your pardon?"

"Your luck." Hanson coughed. "I mean your evening here has resulted in some reward besides pure entertainment."

"It was worth about five thousand dollars, I imagine. I am glad I have found a place where I can play cards without fear of professional gamblers. You see, I don't gamble."

Hanson was amazed. "You—you don't gamble!" This man was obviously laughing at him.

"My dear Hanson," Diamondstone informed him, "when I sit in a game Lady Luck retires to the farthest extremity of the room." He started for the check room.

"Wait," Hanson whispered hoarsely. "I would like to speak with you alone."

He led the way across the card room into a small office. When they were inside the little room, Hanson closed the door. On a flat-topped desk were cards and more cards. Some decks were neatly boxed. Others spread fanwise across the table. There was a typewriter and some paper on one end of the desk. Hanson smiled frostily.

"EXCUSE ME for just a moment. These cards must go out by post tonight. I still have a little work to do on them."

Diamondstone sat down and frowningly watched Hanson as he divided decks of cards into four hands of thirteen cards each.

"Many persons play bridge by mail, you know," the expert explained. "Persons who have never seen the inside of our club. I'm making up mail-order hands now. A record of the cards is kept and the players mail us a record of how the cards ought to be played, in their opinion."

"How interesting." Diamondstone watched Hanson as he arranged cards in problematic combinations.

"And now for Mr. Brown's package," said Hanson. "Brown, poor fellow, must have his bridge problem every night. He's an invalid, you see. I have exhausted myself on him. Now it is Mr. King who makes up Brown's hands."

Hanson took a small card from the inside of his wallet. On it were names of cards and playing suggestions. He made up the four hands and typed the suggestions which he wrapped around the cards and inserted in an envelope. The envelope was addressed to "Max A. Brown, 4225 East New York Street, City." This done, the bridge expert turned to Diamondstone.

"I—I...." He looked nervously about and began again: "This is a matter of business. Mr. King has been watching you closely tonight."

"Really? I wasn't aware of it, except perhaps in that curious elevator room. The mirrors, I suppose, aren't what they're cracked up to be." It was a shot in the dark, but Hanson's brow suddenly became clammy with sweat.

"Mr. King sees everything. Everywhere. He wants to talk with you about taking up some card work here. I advise you—"

"Perhaps tomorrow night," Diamondstone said. He had an intense desire to see the sun again. Besides he had not written his will. Perhaps that should be attended to before he heard of King's proposition.

Hanson bobbed his head. "As you wish. May I count on you early tomorrow evening? We really need another card man downstairs."

"As I live," Diamondstone promised. "If I live," he muttered under his breath as Hanson walked with him into the card room.

Hanson locked the door of his office and made the mistake of putting his keys in his hip pocket where they remained less than a tenth part of a second before Diamondstone had slipped them out and placed them in his own pocket. He said good night to Hanson, wandered toward the bar to make a sharp detour as soon as Hanson was out of sight.

Then, heart in his mouth, he returned to Hanson's little office, unlocked the door, went in, and locked the door from the inside. He hurried to the steel cabinet where records of the mail order hands were kept. But on looking through, he found no records of bridge hands dealt to Max A. Brown. This, he decided, was extremely odd.

He went to the disk, searched among the packed decks ready for the mail, and found the one addressed to Brown. He took a duplicate envelope from the desk and addressed it to Brown on the typewriter. Then he ripped open the package and studied the instruction sheet enclosed. It read:

> August 6th. To be played at 9:30 P.M. West a clever player. Too wise, in fact. Trumps are lead. Play ace of spades to get West's heart.

Diamondstone fanned the enclosed playing cards. Nothing strange about the arrangement. But those instructions— They were not bridge; they weren't even sense.

"Damn!" he whispered. "Where's my spelling! The past tense of the verb 'to lead' is 'led', not 'lead'. Trumps are lead. Good Lord! He means lead, all right. Gun lead. 'Get West's heart', Gun lead through the heart maybe. But who's West? Does it mean the man 'holding the left side of the bridge table? And 'play the ace of spades'. That's the Death Card in fortune telling. I wonder—"

He packed up the cards and instructions, glancing about the room as he did so. Was King watching through some concealed peep-hole?

Diamondstone's heart pounded. His hands trembled. Things were shaping up into something far bigger than even Chief Markly had imagined.

Diamondstone slipped from the room and from the club unnoticed, he hoped. Tomorrow was August 6th. And he was definitely certain that King had scheduled murder for that date. Much had to be done. Diamondstone was deep, deep down in King's underworld. He felt that he should never sleep again until there was a good stand of sod blanketing the insidious King.

EARLY THE next morning found Diamondstone pacing in front of 4225 East New York Street. It was a dismal, flat-faced grey, house, smudged by soot and smoke. At nine o'clock, he went to the door, knocked, and met the grey-haired landlady, a woman quite as flat-faced and smudgy as her house. She wore a dust cap. She carried a waste paper basket under her arm.

"I'm looking for a Mr. Max Brown, an invalid living here," Diamondstone told her. "Is he in?"

"That he's not. Went out about an hour ago in his wheel chair for a bit of airin', poor man," the woman replied. "That's how it happens I was cleanin' up his room a bit, emptyin' his trash and such."

She waved the paper basket at Diamondstone. His keen eye saw that there were a number of playing cards visible among the waste paper.

Diamondstone tore a leaf from his note book, pretended to scribble something on it, sealed it in an envelope and handed it to the woman together with a five dollar bill.

"Just put this in his room, won't you? The fiver is yours for the trouble. I'll wait here a few moments in case he returns." He stepped uninvited into the hall.

The landlady's eyes bulged. She took envelope and bill, mumbled surprised thanks, and put down the paper basket.

"Won't take but a moment, sir." And off she flurried up the steps, leaving Diamondstone in possession of the paper basket.

He went through it like a vacuum sweeper and a little later walked out triumphantly with several small slips of paper that undoubtedly had come out of King's typewriter.

Those papers were apparently bridge instruction sheets, but their cryptic contents revealed worlds to Diamondstone. One read:

> To be played at 11:26 P.M. Make an effort to draw out South's diamonds as planned. Trumps are not led until absolutely necessary.

The note was dated August 2nd. And just a few days ago the newspapers had told of an important jewel robbery in which diamonds had been stolen. The subtlety of the secret left Diamondstone aghast. King, Napoleon of crime, was actually directing the city's underworld through mail-order bridge hands!

But the prize of all prizes was a sheet of instructions dated August 3rd, the very day Jack Lowery had been murdered. It read:

> Play ace of spades to take jack of clubs. Trumps are lead.

And this hand was to have been played at 4:00 P.M., the very hour of Lowery's death. Here was absolute proof. He needed only to find King—

Only to find King! Diamondstone grunted as he hurried along to his hotel. King was as illusive as the will-o'-the-wisp. And death always seemed so close, guarding King, snapping at those who would have betrayed him.

At the hotel, Diamondstone wrote a note which he addressed to Sergeant Prout.

> Dear Prout:
> I have convinced King that I am an indispensable accessory to his Gun Club. I shall meet him tonight, or else I shall have gone the way of all flesh.
> I have a premonition that on seeing King, life will take on new hazards. This thing is bigger than any of us supposed. From the Gun Club, I may be able to communicate with some watchful member of the police force familiar with Morse code. Watch the flashing red sign atop the Gun Club roof. Should its intervals of light and darkness become irregular, it will be your old friend Diamondstone doing a bit of broadcasting. Don't attempt a raid unless I tell you to. I'll have something you can sink your law-hound's teeth into, and I don't refer to beefsteak!

CHAPTER IV

MR. KING
DEALS DEATH

// THE ONLY thing wrong with that old adage about it taking a crook to catch a crook is that it can work both ways," mused Diamondstone as he selected equipment to take to the Gun Club that night.

He had spent some time in the afternoon learning about electric sign flashers. An electrician had hooked up a bit of wire, a telegraph key, and an electric plug which could be substituted for the flashing device. By means of the key he would be able to send Morse code from the flashing sign on the Gun Club roof, providing, of course, he lived long enough.

For a weapon he chose a baby hammerless .22 caliber revolver. One of those handy body-load clips that a magician frequently uses carried the gun, muzzle down, about two inches above the cuff and on the inside of his right trouser leg. Finally, he optimistically added a pair of hand-cuffs to his equipment.

At eight o'clock he descended upon the Gun Club apparently empty handed. Humpy Glomis was hopefully on hand outside the building. He greeted Diamondstone with a ragged smile.

"You like the Gun Club, then?" he inquired in as pleasant a manner as a man who is eternally conscious of his ugliness can muster.

"Yes. One meets such worthwhile people. Tonight I am to be introduced to Mr. King."

"Which Mr. King?" asked Humpy.

"Are there two of them?"

"Dozens in the phone book," replied Humpy. "There is one Mr. King who buys our tin soldiers. We make fine ones."

"Oh, a toy dealer?" Where there had been only blackness, there was a faint glimmer of light. Diamondstone repressed excitement with difficulty. King bought tin soldiers!

Humpy shook his misshapen head. "We make tin soldiers from authentic uniform patterns only for collectors. Mr. King has the finest collection in the country. His favorites come from our casting ladle."

"Interesting!"

King collected tin soldiers. Then a gift of a tin soldier would have been just the thing. Diamondstone's admiration for a murderer who had not lived to kill grew and grew.

"Does King come to the club frequently?" he asked.

"Don't know. Never seen him. Don't even know his address. He orders his soldiers through a servant."

"And did you ever make any soldiers for a Mr. Jack Lowery?" Diamondstone's arteries pounded audibly, he thought.

Humpy nodded. "He used to come to the club. Once he asked for a squad of Royal Scot Guards."

Diamondstone laughed. "Oh, yes. Little fellows with muskets and bayonets."

Humpy shook his head. "No bayonets. Didn't want 'em. A strange man was Mr. Lowery. He wanted his soldiers hollow and left open at the bottom."

Strange, perhaps, but not insane, thought Diamondstone. It was clear as a crystal now. Jack Lowery, hopelessly in debt to King, had decided that rather than bring disgrace on his wife he would murder King. Not an unworthy project, as Diamondstone looked on it.

LOWERY KNEW of King's passion for tin soldiers. So he had prepared a gift that King would have accepted eagerly—a new tin soldier with a spring-plunger poison needle for a bayonet. King would have fingered that bayonet just as Diamondstone had come close to doing. And King would have died.

Then came the clever part of Lowery's plot. As clever as his murder weapon was, he knew that it might be traced by the law hounds. So Lowery had feigned madness. His friend, Dr. Westmore, would have testified falsely as to Lowery's insanity. Thus Lowery would have escaped the death penalty.

But King had fathomed Lowery's scheme and had Lowery killed even before Lowery could mail that deadly tin soldier. How had King known of Lowery's plan? True, Lowery could have had an accomplice in Westmore. Was it possible—

Diamondstone drew a long breath, reached out and rubbed his knuckles on Humpy's back. If ever a man needed luck it was Diamondstone. Was he not to meet King who dealt death in cards?

"How odd that your misfortune is someone else's luck," he said.

"The way of life," Humpy philosophized.

Inside the club, Diamondstone met the pale Hanson. "Mr. King will see you in a half hour, Mr. Anthony," the bridge instructor informed him. "Can you amuse yourself until then?"

"Oh, to be sure. No hurry at all."

Indeed, Diamondstone felt that the distance between himself and the jaws of death was measured in terms of minutes between now and the time of meeting King. And there was much to do. Murder was scheduled for tonight. And beneath King's very nose, Diamondstone had resolved to communicate with the police.

DIAMONDSTONE WENT up the carved stairway. A man with a scar on his cheek was coming down. He eyed Diamondstone in a manner that was chill-provoking. But the magician went boldly on until he came to the men's lavatory on the second floor. There he met the janitor who was cleaning wash bowls.

"I say there," Diamondstone hailed the janitor pleasantly, "you know there are a couple of burned out bulbs in your sign on the roof? Hanson told me to have you fix 'em."

The janitor looked Diamondstone up and down. "Oh, you're the new card man here. Right. I'll look at the sign right away."

He left the washroom and started down the hall. When he opened a door leading to the attic stairway. Diamondstone was at his heels.

"You'd better not come up," the janitor said. "You'll look like a tramp afterwards."

He turned and plodded up the steps, but, Diamondstone followed him into a cavernlike attic and climbed up the ladder leading to the skylight. He gained the ridge pole and followed the janitor down the sloping slates toward the back of the sign.

"Globes burned out, you say?" asked the janitor.

"Yes. I'll show you how the lights go out."

The janitor waited behind the framework of the flashing sign, his form silhouetted when the sign was lighted, disappearing when it flashed off. Diamondstone took hold of the janitor's arm. During an interval of darkness, he started a long, powerful blow that ended, as the lights came on, at the back of the janitor's right ear. The man leaped and started rolling down the roof. Diamondstone sprang catlike, caught him by the ankle, and hauled him to a place of safety behind one of the sign supports.

Without any trouble, the magician found the fuselike flasher screwed into a porcelain socket at the back of the sign. He removed it. For a time, all was darkness until Diamondstone got his wire and telegraph key from the secret pocket inside his coat. Then he screwed in the plug where the flasher had been and depressed the key. The lights came on.

Crouching on the roof, Diamondstone sent Morse slowly so as not to attract attention of those persons who were entering the Gun Club. This was his message:

> Prout, pick up supposed invalid Max Brown at 4225 East New York Street. He is King's pawn. Brown will move to murder at 9:30. No other details available. Better raid club. King here at 8:45. Gambling den in basement. Diamondstone.

He then replaced the flasher, used the electrical wire to tie the janitor to the sign support, and hurried from the roof.

No sooner had he gained the card room than Hanson came striding toward him. He was patting his cheeks with a folded handkerchief. His forehead was dewy.

"Mr. King will see you, Mr. Anthony."

The words hurried from his lips. His voice had lost its usual degree of modulation. He nipped Diamondstone's arm and hurried into the hall and from there to the little elevator room. There Diamondstone was again blindfolded by the courteous gunman. The room descended slowly, stopped. Diamondstone was led once again through a world of blindness. Outside the gambling room, the blindfold was removed. Hanson guided Diamondstone past the roulette table.

Diamondstone jerked to a stop, instantly recovered himself, and became interested in the ceiling. For no sooner had the magician-detective put in his appearance than a man had pushed back from one of the card tables and stood up so quickly his chair had overturned. That man was Dr. Claude Westmore!

Diamondstone could feel Westmore's eyes studying him as he crossed the room. Westmore a gambler?

It seemed impossible that a great psychiatrist had succumbed to the lure of Lady Luck.

Through a door at the back of the room, Hanson led Diamondstone down a short hall. The bridge teacher rapped at a door that gave out the unmistakable ring of hard steel.

The door opened slowly. Hanson marched Diamondstone straight ahead, turned him to the right, and bowed low.

"Mr. King," he said, "may I present Mr. Anthony."

Diamondstone blinked. He seemed to be looking across miles of hilly country that joined an azure horizon. And up hill and down dale were hundreds of marching men in uniform. Many countries were represented—soldiers from every war, from brilliantly armed Crusaders to Hitler's storm troopers. Yet not a man of them moved.

The miles and miles of scenery extended only a few feet beyond the wall of the room. But the prospective in the niche was so wonderful and the proportions so perfect that Diamondstone had been dazed at first.

THEN HE remembered that King was the greatest collector of tin soldiers in the country. After realizing that, he could pay some attention to King himself.

King wore a long dressing gown of black satin delicately piped with white. A heraldic coat of arms adorned the breast pocket. King's head rose mountainous and hairless above a veil of white silk that concealed his features completely.

The vast army of soldiers, inanimate though they were, the embroidered gown, the regal bearing of the man himself told Diamondstone much of King's character. Here was an arrogant man who toyed with his fellows as though they, too, were tin soldiers. A man, perhaps, with an inferiority complex that had reverted to something akin to grandiose illusion. A man who had discovered power he had always dreamed of. And a man who had misused that power.

"Mr. Anthony, we have witnessed your extraordinary ability with cards." King had a thin, piping voice that was probably disguised. "It is our pleasure to extend to you the choice. You must either agree to join us, to obey our commands implicitly, or be killed. We need men of your talents. Your loyalty will be rewarded. On the other hand, every man in our organization is pledged to kill any of his fellows who should be indiscreet. Who might, for instance, try to sell information to the police."

Diamondstone's blood seemed sluggish, frozen stiff. Little wonder that Jack Lowery's murder scheme had failed.

It was little wonder that Diamondstone had failed. For he had failed, miserably. Yet he smiled, that suave magician's smile of his. Gently, he stroked the back of his head.

"There is hardly room enough inside my skull for both brains and bullets. You can deal me into the game."

King chuckled quietly. "Very good. You are one of us—one of the Brothers of Death as we call the men who serve us."

The door of the room opened and the armed attendant gave King a military salute.

"Mr. Brown is here, sir," he announced.

Diamondstone, at that moment, felt much like a man who reads his own name and epitaph on a tombstone.

The sensation it gave him was far from pleasant.

CHAPTER V

TRUMPS ARE LEAD

DR. CLAUDE WESTMORE marched through the door of King's sanctum, his lips thoughtfully pursed, his fingertips tapping soundlessly together. He was followed by a neckless, blue-jowled person wearing flannels and a beet-red shirt. King addressed Dr. Westmore.

"You understand why you are here?" he asked.

"Perfectly," replied Westmore, coldly.

"And you, Anthony, understand?"

Diamondstone nodded. "Someone is to die."

"Good. Then there should be no disillusionment. Hanson, you will search Anthony."

Hanson stepped over to Diamondstone. The pores of his face reeked cold sweat. He hastily patted Diamondstone's pockets and produced nothing but a pair of handcuffs. Diamondstone cursed himself for having brought the bracelets. Hanson didn't look at all surprised but took the cuffs and dropped them on King's desk.

King opened a drawer of his desk, waving his hand airily.

"You may sit in our presence, gentlemen."

They all sat down uneasily except the blue-jowled person and the courteous gunman who had previously blindfolded Diamondstone. King took out a heavy automatic.

"The work originally designed for Brown's silenced pistol," King began, "has been delegated to our newest servant, Anthony. I think we all know what is coming. One quick, painless shot, then a period in our lime vat for the gentleman who knows too much. There is no way you would rather die than by means of a bullet in the brain, Dr. Westmore?"

Westmore! Then Westmore was the "West" referred to in King's cryptic, bridge-hand message to Brown. The neckless person in the beet-red-shirt was Brown, the supposed invalid, and King's minion.

"It matters little," said Westmore coldly. "As a matter of fact, I have little idea why I am to die."

"The penalty of having gained the confidence of one of our enemies," King said haughtily. "You know that Jack Lowery owed something like ten thousand dollars to the Gun Club. Furthermore, you know how he intended to pay it back. You cannot deny that you urged Lowery to introduce you into our temple of chance for the sole purpose of spying on me."

"I do not deny it," Dr. Westmore husked. He was facing death bravely. Diamondstone hoped he could do as well.

"That matter settled," King said after the manner of a club chairman who has just allowed a bill, "we may as well proceed. Anthony, you will take this gun and put a bullet in Dr. Westmore's brain."

"One moment," said Diamondstone. "I am a gambler, not a murderer. Do your own dirty work."

There was a long, painful silence in which Hanson daubed at his pale face and sweating brow.

"You are gambling now with your life, Anthony," King finally said. "The jig is up. It has been for some time. I merely wanted to see how far you would carry this mad scheme of yours. Why are my enemies always madmen?"

"Possibly, it's just because of your point of view," suggested Diamondstone. He was bending far over in his chair, his chin resting on his hands. "A madman always thinks he is the only sane person. Trumps may be 'lead' and the ace of spades may take the Westmores and the Anthonys, but you've dug your own grave."

The veiled face jerked upward in surprise. "So, you have penetrated my communication secret."

"I know *all* about cards, as I told Hanson," Diamondstone remarked. "I know your mail-order bridge has been directing most of the crime of this city for some time. The only reason that the 'invalid' Brown is here tonight is that the police were just a moment late in catching him. You see, all these things are in the hands of the police. I have ordered a raid and told them to search the basement. If you had taken Hanson into your confidence a little more, I might not have learned this secret about the 'invalid' Brown. Surely he did not know of your communications system else he would not have told me of Brown. I—"

"Oh, yes," King cut in. "About that raid. We meant to tell you that the large-mouthed Prout and some of his men were digging around in the Gun Club basement. The raid is probably over by now. We do not know how you managed to call the police, for your every movement outside the club has been watched. At any rate, the information you gave the police was inaccurate."

Diamondstone said nothing. Was it possible that the gambling den was not in the basement of the Gun Club?

"Since Anthony refuses to kill Westmore, Brown will do the job. Westmore first. Anthony second. And quickly!"

King really had no right to say "quickly" for, up until Diamondstone made his next move, he hadn't the proper conception of the word. Diamondstone's long right hand snaked into his right trouser leg, seized the little hammerless revolver, pulled it from the clip, and beaded it on King. So swift and deft were these actions that they seemed blended into a single motion.

The roar of a shot dinned in Diamondstone's ears. His intense, blue gaze flashed to the numb, pain-shot fingers of his right hand. The revolver was gone, shot away. Hanson stood close by, pale, nervous, covering Diamondstone with an automatic. King jerked his head at Hanson.

"Where did Anthony get his gun?"

HANSON COULDN'T speak.

King picked up Diamondstone's handcuffs and tossed them to the neckless Brown.

"Put these on those card-sharping hands of his," King directed. "A man who picks a gun from empty air can't be trusted until he is dead."

Brown jerked Diamondstone's wrists together and clipped the handcuffs in place. Then he drew his automatic and approached Westmore. Hanson kept his gun within a foot of Diamondstone's heart.

"Just a minute, King," Diamondstone said. "I wouldn't try any more murder. Killing Westmore would not keep your head out of a noose. If you were to go up on the roof now, you would find the janitor tied to your electric sign by means of the device which I used to signal the police. You can go look. Or better, send Brown. He'll be arrested for murder as soon as he leaves the club. The police know all about him. I have written proof that he was ordered to kill Lowery. Some of your cryptic bridge instructions fell into my hands."

Brown's cheeks paled perceptibly. He turned to King and snarled: "You gotta protect me, King."

"A really fine position King is in to protect anyone," Diamondstone chuckled. "You see, I know exactly who he is."

"That's a lie!" King shouted. "No one knows me."

"And," Diamondstone went on unperturbed, "I know how Jack Lowery planned to kill you with a little tin soldier. And I know exactly why he failed and was removed before he could make another attempt. You can rest assured that that information will reach the police."

Suddenly, Diamondstone's head jerked to the right. His mouth opened, his eyes widened, as though he had suddenly got the shock of his life. For a split second, all eyes turned toward the blank wall that was evidently the source of Diamondstone's surprise.

THERE WAS never neater misdirection. Diamondstone brought his trick handcuffs down sharply on his left knee. They fell apart like magic, their secret catch released. At the same, time, his big body slammed straight at Brown. His right hand locked over Brown's gun wrist and gave it a wrench.

Hanson tried a shot that went wild. Diamondstone let Brown have a left to the jaw, swung around and dropped Hanson with a shot from Brown's gun. Diamondstone's blow had only staggered Brown. The blue-joweled gunman roared, sprang.

The weight of Brown's body threw Diamondstone back against the wall. But he couldn't have asked for a better shield than Brown who was attempting to crack Diamondstone's ribs in a grizzly bear hug. Diamondstone got his gun arm free and shot straight at King's armed attendant. His slug clipped the man in the shoulder and sent him spinning around.

Diamondstone's gun arm swung up. The butt of his automatic caught Brown at the back of the neck, a paralyzing rabbit-punch. Brown staggered backwards. Diamondstone helped him to the floor with a driving left to the belly.

Guns still yapped. Dr. Westmore was holding Hanson's gun in both hands and shooting inaccurately at King's desk. King was visible only split seconds at a time when he ducked around the desk to pop lead wildly at anybody. The arm was cracking. His empire was going to pieces. Flying lead had wrecked that elaborate array of tin soldiers behind him.

"On your feet, King!" shouted Diamondstone. "Next time you bop around that corner, I'll let you have one. Trumps are lead! I rubbed all the luck off your back tonight, Mr. Humpy Glomis, alias Mr. King!"

With a surprised oath, King sprang to his feet, turned his blazing gat on Diamondstone. Diamondstone kept his promise, shot once, but with amazing accuracy. King dropped his rod, clawed at his left shoulder, slumped into a chair. He tore down his silk veil, glared at them with his twisted, warty face, writhing with pain and terror. Never had Diamondstone seen a face more hideous than that of Humpy Glomis at the moment.

"You'll never get out alive!" Glomis shrieked. "We've signaled our men. They're coming down here. The police can't find this place because there's only one way down—the secret elevator room. The elevator shaft is concealed by the coal pile in the basement. There is no way the police could guess of the existence of this place *below* the basement."

"But," a crisp voice spoke from the doorway, "when the police see a lot of servants and bartenders dashing into a crazy room that contains no furniture, they get damned suspicious!"

Diamondstone glanced over his shoulder. Sergeant Prout and the police were crowding into the room. Prout grinned at Diamondstone.

"We were just about to call you a damned liar when we saw the stampede for that elevator room. Then we—" Prout's eyes swung on King. His lower jaw dropped. "Good Lord, Humpy Glomis' face! But where's his hump?"

"Faked," said Diamondstone softly. "Yes, King is really Humpy Glomis whose hideous face must have given him a terrible inferiority complex. But the worm so often turns. In his private dream-world he must have frequently thought himself a man of power. He would make those who had sneered at his ugly face squirm if that power became real. And he made it real! The inferiority complex became something like grandiose illusion.

"He built himself a criminal empire where he could be king. His passion for tin soldiers, his faked coat of arms on his clothes—all part of the dream-world of power that he made real. Yet he kept sane, fearfully sane." Diamondstone smiled at Dr. Westmore. "I guess I'm the only insane man in the room. I might just as well have told Glomis I was investigating Jack Lowery's death when I asked him about the tin soldier he made for Lowery.

"Lowery had made the same mistake, not knowing that King, a collector of tin soldiers, made his own soldiers. Lowery asked Glomis to make up a special tin soldier, planning to make it into a murder device to send to King. And of course Glomis knew Lowery's purpose. That's how he knew he had to remove Lowery or run the risk of being killed. Am I right in saying that Lowery was trying to escape from King's persecution because of gambling debts, Dr. Westmore?"

"Yes," replied Westmore. "I am ashamed to say I approved of Lowery's plan and agreed to help prove Lowery insane in case the police traced murder to him. It was with the idea of pleading insanity that Lowery put on that act for his wife and you, Diamondstone. I think you saw through our little scheme almost at once. I even obtained the poison Lowery was going to use."

"I see," Prout said. "And Glomis, real owner of the Gun Club, wore a fake hump on his back to give him an excuse for standing out in front and watching the people who went into the club.

"But, who in the wide world would have thought that Humpy Glomis was King? Nobody but a magician. A pretty lucky guess, I call it, Diamondstone."

Diamondstone looked amazed. "Luck? Guess? That's a great injustice! Haven't I been giving you a lesson in logic these past minutes? It had to be Humpy Glomis. And just as soon as I talked with King, I *knew* King and Humpy Glomis were one and the same person. Ever notice how Humpy Glomis rarely used the pronoun 'I'? He usually referred to himself as 'we'. So did the imperious King. Glomis played at being a king so much of the time that his identity as King sometimes carried over into his life as Humpy Glomis. Royalty always uses the so-called imperial pronouns 'we' for 'I' and 'our' for 'my'."

Prout addressed one of his men, thumbing at Diamondstone at the same time.

"Diamondstone would know about that. He pulled out six links of sausage from the pockets of the Queen of Roumania's riding habit once."

III

THE BUDDHA WHISPERS

CHAPTER I

MURDER IN
THE FUTURE

THAT WINTER, a young wife leaped to her death from a window in the maternity ward of a New York hospital. The woman, hardly more than a girl, had handed over the savings of a short lifetime to a man with a pinpoint mustache who had promised to double them for her. Money and man had disappeared. Death had seemed more attractive to the girl than the promise of poverty for her and the little one.

Tragedy, suicide that was indirectly murder, cried aloud from the tear-stained note she had left her husband. And over and above it all was an immobile, gargantuan shadow, awful in its impressive majesty; terrible in the evil it portended.

Westward stretched the shadow. Tragedy again when a bank clerk became an embezzler because he had listened to mutterings from brazen, lifeless lips. And for every crime that was marked by sudden death, there were dozens of others that ashamed dupes would never tell about—crimes in the shadow of the bronze Buddha of Bhutan.

Police knew of the Buddha. They could, and frequently did, run Buddha and Dal Rama, its "Blessed Guardian" out of town. But could police help it if Barnum was right? They could not!

"But for the love of heaven can't something be done about it?" asked Attorney-at-law John Wrenn of Diamondstone, that summer evening they sat together and talked in the lobby of the Plaza Hotel.

Diamondstone lazily shucked a peanut and regarded John Wrenn gravely. That was a bit hard, because Mr. Wrenn was a comical figure.

He was a pin-head, was John Wrenn, and to make the capital of his figure the more absurd, Wrenn had huge shoulders and thick arms and legs, and big, chapped-looking fingers. His claim to the appearance of intelligence rested solely on his nicely balanced pince-nez.

"Take it here in Meadow City, for instance," said Wrenn. "We've got a wealthy family by the name of Helm. The old man is around seventy and still likes his liquor. He's got his second wife, who's about a score of years younger than he. Got a son by his first marriage and a daughter by his second. Now, his wife is daft on things occult. Suppose something should happen to the old man. Mrs. Helm would hand the whole fortune over to this fortunetelling fakir. See?"

DIAMONDSTONE NODDED. "As long as the old man lives, the Helm money is safe, because, as I understand it Mr. Helm has no use for spirits except when they come in bottles."

"Look here," said Wrenn, "you're a detective. Why don't you tackle this Buddha business? You work on your own. You've got all the money you need, I've heard tell. You'd be unhampered by orthodox police procedure. I'd like to see you stir up some hell."

Diamondstone stretched long arms towards the ceiling. "My dear Mr. Wrenn—that is the name, isn't it?—may I ask you why you suppose I came to Meadow City? Obviously, it isn't for your climate. Detective I may be, but always remember, I am first of all a magician. We gentlemen of the abracadabra hate none of our fellow men save charlatans who employ trickery for the purpose of defrauding the innocent into believing that Aunt Nettie, speaking from the Great Beyond, can tell exactly what ought to be done with a Postal Savings account."

"Strike," screamed Isis. "Strike!"

And he shucked a peanut with the same vigor he would have liked to apply to the cracking of Dal Rama's vertebrae.

Thirty minutes later, Dal Rama, Blessed Guardian of the Buddha of Bhutan, faced his audience in the long-deserted opera house on Main Street. Turban included, he was every bit as tall as Diamondstone. He was not as broad; for without being anything like that Diamondstone was nevertheless immense from his light tan shoes to his golden-haired head.

Dal Rama was dark—a Mephistopheliain sort of darkness. His cheeks were a satiny yellow, his eyes about as expressive as porcelain doorknobs. His mustache and goatee were fragilely pointed with wax.

Diamondstone was in the front row of chairs rented from the local undertaker. Tonight, he had determined, he would have the exquisite pleasure of landing his huge fist in the approximate middle of the Blessed Guardian and also of tramping on the feet of clay that undoubtedly supported the Buddha of Bhutan.

Dal Rama's envelope switching, by means of which he retained the questions from the audience and at the same time seemed to burn them, was all clear to a trickster of Diamondstone's caliber, but it was also clear that the entire populace of the city was sold on Dal Rama, his medium, a large-nosed woman called Isis, and the bronze Buddha itself. For the benefit of those who sought the wisdom of the Buddha for the first time, Dal Rama explained that the Buddha communed only with the dead. It was therefore necessary for the Blessed Guardian to plunge a knife into the heart of Isis, his medium, before Isis could bring the audience's questions before the Buddha.

And here Dal Rama produced a slender-bladed, businesslike knife with an ornate hilt. The audience gasped, appropriately and Diamond-stone sat up a little straighter.

Off stage, a gong sounded thrice, curtains parted, and the lowly were permitted to feast their eyes on the Buddha of Bhutan, "or possibly Boston," Diamondstone added under his breath.

Squatting on bronze knees, the Buddha was still as tall as two men. The usual placid face was spoiled by a slightly open, infinitely hateful mouth.

After he had reverently salaamed before the image, Dal Rama com-mitted sacrilege by dealing the Buddha a number of lusty blows with a hammer, ostensibly to prove its solidity. Then he called for volunteers to come up on the stage and witness the execution and subsequent revival of Isis.

Diamondstone, of course, volunteered. Among the other five who joined him on the stage, was Mrs. Marcus Helm herself, wife of the town's wealthiest man, a comfortable, buxom matron of fifty whose faith in things occult could not have been shaken by the San Francisco earthquake.

Diamondstone walked all around the Buddha but detected no visible wires leading to it. Assuredly there were wires somewhere, because that polished black button on Dal Rama's lapel could be nothing but a lapel microphone. Some way, if Diamondstone didn't keep his keen blue eyes wide open, Dal Rama would manage to connect that microphone in circuit with a loudspeaker hidden within the Buddha's head.

Isis addressed the audience.

"Be not alarmed when Dal Rama, Blessed Guardian of the Buddha and member of the cult of Holy Assassins, plunges his knife into my heart. A believer cannot die. I go only to the realm of the dead in order that your troubles may be brought before the Buddha."

THUS PREPARED, Isis knelt before the image and Dal Rama, knife upraised, stood beside her.

"Are you ready with the knife, Dal Rama?" Isis asked.

"I am ready."

Muscles at the corners of Dal Rama's mouth tightened. If this were murder, here was the man to do it.

"Then strike!" screamed Isis. "Strike!"

The audience rose from its chairs like a single being. The glittering blade descended, seemed to plunge into the medium's back. Isis was prostrate, her whole body quivering. Mrs. Marcus Helm screamed, looked for a moment as though she would faint. Diamondstone took her arm.

"Easy, madam," he whispered. "It's all a fake. The knife blade telescopes into the handle. That stuff isn't blood. It's some sort of dye released by the knife."

Mrs. Helm stiffened, fixed Diamondstone with a frigid glance.

"Fake, indeed! I have seen this three times now. Dal Rama passes the knife for inspection directly afterward. Isis is dead. Truly dead!"

Dal Rama stepped to the edge of the stage and quieted the audience. But he didn't offer his knife for examination. He wiped it delicately and replaced it in his sleeve.

"From the vale of death you will hear Isis speak," he said. "Your questions, which you have seen destroyed, will be brought before Buddha. From the lips of this solid bronze image you will hear the wisdom of the ages. Those desiring more complete information should arrange for private hearings, for which a nominal fee of twenty-five dollars is charged."

In the audience, white, strained faces gleamed with sweat, waiting for the questions of the medium and the miraculous answers of the Buddha. But all the pale faces were not in the audience. Dal Rama was gradually turning the color of sifted ashes. For Diamondstone was laying down his gauntlet.

Smiling suavely, confidently poised, Diamondstone's big, well formed hand reached out and produced a cigarette, apparently from the air. He lighted it, while Dal Rama goggled. He put the cigarette in his left fist, only to open his left hand and show it empty.

Then he calmly pulled the burning cigarette from his vest pocket, vanished it in a twinkling, and pulled it out of his ear. And while Dal Rama watched, actually stunned to find a magician, and consequently a vowed enemy of all "spook crooks," on his own stage, Diamondstone's miraculous trickery moved on at a pace that the eye could scarcely follow.

Isis was speaking in a dreamy monotone:

"I wander in the vale of the dead, seeking the questions of the living. A girl named Flo wants to know when she shall wed. Speak, oh, Buddha."

Hysterical giggling in the audience. Dal Rama moistened his lips. Diamondstone's cigarette was driving him crazy. It was time for him to make the Buddha speak, but evidently he was too stunned to get to his microphone outlet.

Isis was desperately repeating her question and Diamondstone's blue eyes were brittle with laughter. The Buddha would not speak. It could not speak. It—

A cold draft played along Diamondstone's spine. His eyes turned from Dal Rama to the bronze image. For the Buddha was doing the impossible. The Buddha was whispering, a whisper that seemed to come from the grave itself.

"Murder," whispered the Buddha. "Murder." And that was all.

CHAPTER II

MURDER IN THE PRESENT

S CREAMING, ISIS came out of her trance. In the audience, two men were on their feet, struggling. One of them, heavy-jowled and purple in the face, was shouting:

"A fake! I won't have it! Clara, I forbid you—"

Then, in spite of the interference put up by Attorney Wrenn, with whom he struggled, the jowled old man pulled a gun. He fired twice, two slugs that glanced against the giant Buddha and buzzed off into the wings.

"Mr. Helm!," cried John Wrenn. "Please, Mr. Helm! Control yourself!"

And then Wrenn got a raw-knuckled hand on the elder man's gun and wrenched it away from him.

The buxom Mrs. Helm was wringing her hands in anguish.

"My husband!" she was whimpering. "Why did I insist on his coming!"

Dal Rama was at her side, solicitous and comforting. Diamondstone vaulted from the stage and got through the crowd to where Helm and Wrenn stood. Helm looked as if apoplexy were just around the corner.

"Half soused," Wrenn whispered to Diamondstone as he tried to bundle Helm toward the door.

"I am, am I!" shouted Helm. "Why, you popinjay lawyer, I'll show you my head's clear! We'll get home, by hell, and make out that damned will. We'll settle that greasy-faced fakir's hash!"

"Marcus!" cried Mrs. Helm in desperation. "For heaven's sake, be a gentleman."

Dal Rama was trying to quiet the crowd and succeeding in some measure.

"I think," he said smoothly, "inasmuch as there are so many unbelievers in our audience we'd better not risk incurring the displeasure of the great Buddha any more tonight."

"Uh-hum," said Diamondstone. "I think so."

Dal Rama gave him a black look, hurried to the front of the house and courteously bowed to every member of the audience as the people filed out, whispering, gasping, chattering. Diamondstone was the last to leave. Dal Rama stood stiffly in the door. His right hand was in the pocket of his coat.

"Listen, you mug," the Blessed Guardian whispered, "you've got four hours in which to tear out of this burg. Get me?"

Diamondstone put his hand in his pocket, withdrew it slowly to disclose nothing more formidable than a peanut. Nevertheless, Dal Rama jumped when Diamondstone popped the shell.

"Remarkable," Diamondstone said quietly, "how you can change from an East Indian to an East Side New Yorker with a mere twist of the tongue."

"No funny business," said Dal Rama. His hand came out of his pocket and there was a small, black automatic in it. "I'm giving you a chance to get the hell out of this town."

Diamondstone munched thoughtfully for a moment. "Damn generous of you, but suppose I choose to stay?"

Dal Rama's glittering teeth came together with an audible snap. "Then your life won't be worth a plugged nickel."

Diamondstone's red-gold brows went halfway up his high forehead. "Oh, that would never do. Dead, I might consult the Buddha of Bhutan and ask such questions as, 'What game is Dal Rama playing that is worth so much he would commit murder to win'?"

And with that he backed from the opera house.

A brown, dried leaf of a man was sitting in Diamondstone's big car. Absalom, Diamondstone's Negro assistant back in vaudeville days, was an accessory for which Diamondstone had never found a substitute, even after inherited wealth had made all the world his stage.

"You be needin' me tonight?" Absalom asked, sloven-lipped.

"You're indispensable," Diamondstone told him. "Keep your muddy eye on Dal Rama, understand? Your natural protective coloration was undoubtedly provided for the sole purpose of shadowing the Blessed Guardian. So, on your toes."

"D'rectly," said Absalom.

He got reluctantly from the soft cushions of the car. Diamondstone got in, drove back to the Plaza Hotel where he had taken a room two days before. There he lounged in a chair, absently munched peanuts and crunched the empty shells well into the carpet with his sizable tan shoes.

"Very bad," he soliloquized. "Clara Helm obviously a firm believer in Dal Rama or anything pseudo-occult. *If* old man Helm should die, we'd have one wealthy widow who'd be dope enough to sugar Dal Rama's purse with very little persuasion. To show the public that Dal Rama is a fraud is my job. He *ought* to be a fraud. But—hum! How did he make that hunk of bronze whisper?"

"Murder—Murder," the Buddha's whisper echoed in the caves of thought. Diamondstone, after musing for half an hour, pushed himself out of his chair. It would not be a bad idea to see just how the land lay at the Helm mansion.

A LITTLE later he arrived in front of a newly painted house that was on a ramble over a rolling lawn. Cupolas, bay windows, porches accurately chronicled each successive step in the building of the Helm fortune.

There was a ridiculously broad, pinheaded figure standing at the gate. As Diamondstone came up, he addressed the man.

"Mr. Wrenn? Ah, but I see it is Mr. Wrenn. What's going on?"

Wrenn pressed Diamondstone's hand.

"Just been helping old Helm with his will. He's smashed Dal Rama's hopes, anyway. His entire fortune, something close to a million, goes to his beloved wife providing none of it is used for any occult business. I just went down to the village for some witnesses so the old man can sign the will. They'll be along any moment now. But—"

Wrenn's hand moved up Diamondstone's arm. "Say, look at that!"

"What?" Diamondstone stared at the house. In an upstairs window, he could plainly see old Marcus Helm.

"The old duck is going to bed. He always takes a big peg of whiskey, undresses in the dark, then hits the bed like a log of wood. How in hell can he sign the will if he's asleep?"

In the window, Helm untied his tie, reached out his hand, and turned out the lamp. Wrenn grunted.

"He's been doing that for forty years, ever since I've known him. And, boy, will he be sore if we have to wake him up. Wrenn looked at his watch. "Let's go inside. You'd enjoy meeting Doris. She's a little up-stage, but nice looking."

Wrenn and Diamondstone went up the walk, crossed porch number one, and entered without knocking. A slim, short-skirted girl was in the living room. Dark-eyed, bronze-haired, and lovely, she acknowledged Wrenn's introduction of Diamondstone with the graciousness of a queen.

"Doris is really the only one who can do anything with Mr. Helm, he's that stubborn," Wrenn said.

"It would be a stubborn man indeed who would not comply with Miss Helm's slightest wish," said Diamondstone.

Doris accepted the compliment quite as if she considered it her due. Then they talked about nothing for fifteen or twenty minutes before a couple of townsmen who were to witness Helm's will arrived. Mrs. Helm came in, quite removed from the excitement of the evening and frigid toward Diamondstone.

"You gentlemen wanted to see Mr. Helm on business?" Mrs. Helm swept them all in with a cool glance. "Really, you'd better call in the morning. Mr. Helm has retired, I'm sure."

Wrenn squirmed uneasily. "It's about Mr. Helm's will. He was anxious to get matters settled tonight. I-I suppose I'll have to wake him."

"I warn you, he will not be particularly amiable," said Mrs. Helm.

"I know," replied Wrenn. "That's what worries me. Doris, I wonder if you and I could go up and awaken him gently?"

Doris nodded. "We can try." She got up, and with Wrenn at her side, went up the steps.

One of the proposed witnesses looked at the other and winked.

"Wake the old man gently," he whispered. "Imagine, when he's liquored up to beat—" He caught Mrs. Helm's frosty glance and tried to gulp back his words.

Diamondstone tried to fill an uncomfortable silence with a remark about the weather. Mrs. Helm sniffed. The witnesses reached simultaneously for the same newspaper to hide behind. Then Doris' footsteps could be heard coming down the stairs. She came into the room, ghost-white, her body swaying slightly. She went over to the telephone, picked it up, put it down again, burst into tears.

Diamondstone got up from his chair, started toward the girl. Mrs. Helm came between him and the girl.

"Doris, what ever—"

Doris buried her face against her mother's shoulder.

"Dad," she choked. "Something's happened. Dad—he—he's been killed!"

Diamondstone bounded into the hall and halfway up the steps where he bumped squarely into John Wrenn.

"Uh-uh-uh-uh," Wrenn stuttered. "Lord, this is awful!"

Diamondstone got by Wrenn, gained the top of the steps, turned into a lighted room and came to an abrupt stop. In a heavy, carved walnut bed lay Marcus Helm. His heavy face was placid, out of all accord with the moist, dark stain that spread across the bosom of his old-fashioned nightshirt.

Blood spread across the sheet, traced over the side of the bed, and pointed to a slender-bladed, scarlet-stained knife. Dal Rama's knife. Diamondstone recognized its ornate hilt instantly. And the blade was not the telescoping sort nor could the scarlet stain be anything but blood.

Murder! Murder in the shadow of the whispering Buddha.

CHAPTER III

DOPE

IN THE center of the room, Diamondstone turned around slowly. Nothing of the heavy luxury escaped him. It was like being in an undertaker's establishment. There was the body and all around it perfect order, clean, thick carpets, and a smothering, churchly hush with low sobbing sounds coming from below stairs.

There was a night stand beside the bed and on it a whiskey decanter and a half empty glass of liquor. Diamondstone sniffed the decanter and glass. On one corner of the stand was a manuscript of some sort.

"This the will?" Diamondstone asked. Then: "Ah, but I see it isn't the will. It's a manuscript for a radio play, 'Dark House of Terror', by J. Ivan Rhodes."

"Let's see." Wrenn came forward, looked down at the script. "That must belong to Jim Helm. J. Ivan Rhodes is the name Jim Helm uses in his radio acting. Writes and acts in plays. No wonder Helm was in such a huff today. That son of his is his pet peeve. J. Ivan must have been here today and walked off without his script."

Diamondstone's red-gold brows drew together. "Uh-hum. Now, let's see, was there the slightest sound from this room when you and Doris came up the steps?"

"Not the slightest. Mr. Helm was always a heavy sleeper."

Diamondstone nodded. "Tonight, he must have slept exceptionally heavy. Unwittingly, he drank a good size dose of knockout drops. You can smell the chloral in that decanter. That must have made death and murder a lot easier for both parties concerned. Now, tell me exactly what happened."

"Happened?" said Wrenn dully. "Why Doris knocked lightly on the door at first. Couldn't raise her father. She pushed the door open and pressed on the light. She was in front of me, and I could see nothing of the old man at first. Then Doris whispered: 'Blood,' in a tight little voice, and started toward the bed.

"I grabbed her shoulders, as soon as I saw what had happened, and told her to go phone the police. Since there was no one on the second floor but Doris and me, supposedly, I thought the murderer must be hiding. He could have got out of the room, as we came in, by slipping through the closet which connects with the room beyond."

Diamondstone went over to the closet. He produced a small flashlight and beamed it about. The spot of light paused on one yellow-papered wall. Next to Helm's bathrobe was an empty hook. Beneath the hook was a scarlet smudge on the paper.

DIAMONDSTONE TOOK his pocket knife, scored along the wallpaper, and deliberately tore off the piece that included the stain. This he slipped into his pocket. With Wrenn as a guide, he made a quick search of the upstairs rooms. Astonishingly perfect order every-where.

"Where was the will made out?" Diamondstone asked.

"In Mr. Helm's bedroom," Wrenn explained. "Then I took it down to the study. I was to procure witnesses and Helm said he would come down when the witnesses arrived. Didn't like to receive strangers in his bedroom."

"Modest, eh, like an old maid," Diamondstone said. "Even undressed in the dark. As long as the will isn't valid without the signature, suppose we go take another look at it."

They went down the back stairs, through the kitchen, and into a study built onto the back of the house.

"Right there," pointed Wrenn, "behind my briefcase."

Diamondstone went over to a chair, raised the briefcase. He ran long fingers through his golden hair, looked at Wrenn, and shook his head.

"Gone," he said.

"Why—why—"

Diamondstone slipped a peanut from his pocket.

"This is going to be a rather hard nut to crack, Wrenn. The case, not the peanut. Helm died intestate. That means one-third of his fortune goes to, his wife and two-thirds is divided among his children. Motives by the hundreds, or half dozens anyway. It wouldn't be coincidence if four or five people wanted to kill Helm this very night, because of that will."

Wrenn, picked up his briefcase and they started toward the front of the house. Outside the living room door, Diamondstone tugged Wrenn to a halt. Beyond the door, Mrs. Helm was speaking in a dry, firm voice.

"Everyone knows that J. Ivan Rhodes is an erratic madman. He was here this afternoon, quarreling with his father. As he left, I distinctly heard him say, 'And I'll get Dal Rama, too.' So I intend to warn Dal Rama."

Diamondstone plunged into the room in time to see Mrs. Helm raising the telephone.

"Madam," he said quietly. Then he gently removed the phone from the woman's hand and replaced it. "Allow the great Buddha to warn Dal Rama, if you please. Did you happen to overhear any of that quarrel between your husband and his son?"

Mrs. Helm lifted her head to stare along the ridge of her nose. "I did not. But they always quarreled about money. And I think—"

"Mother!" Doris Helm reproached, "You are prejudiced. Why, Jim is the only person in the world who *couldn't* have—have killed Father. Jim was due at the broadcasting station tonight to appear in his play. That's eighty miles away."

"Quiet, Doris," Mrs. Helm said haughtily. "And you, sir"—to Diamondstone—"you are an unprincipled charlatan and I would be delighted if you would leave."

"No doubt of that," said Diamondstone. "If the police want to see me, they may do so at the hotel."

As he left the front door, a shuffling shadow came from behind a clump of lilac.

"Boss." That was Absalom's voice.

Diamondstone paused, waited for the colored man to catch up with him. "Yes, Absalom?"

"That man with the headache I been followin'," began Absalom.

"Dal Rama? What about him?"

"Lots! Jest when the lawyer man left, the man with the turban on his head come down this way, me after him. He went to the back door where the missus met him."

"You mean Mrs. Helm met Dal Rama at the back door?"

"Posolutely. And he give her a bottle like a 'fumery bottle and told her to put the stuff in somebody's whiskey."

They walked down to Diamondstone's car.

"Queer," mused Diamondstone. "If the will had been completed she would have inherited the entire fortune. Now, two-thirds of the fortune will be split between the two kids, giving both Doris and J. Ivan Rhodes motive for killing their dad. Only I can't figure Doris as a knife murderer and J. Ivan couldn't have killed via radio. What do you think, Absalom?"

"The man with the headache," said Absalom.

"Uh-hum," Diamondstone said slowly. "Plenty of motive there. Helm had to die before that will was complete in order for Dal Rama to have a chance to get his hooks on Mrs. Helm's share of the money. By the way, where is Dal Rama?"

FROM SOMEWHERE out of the gloom, came the yap of an automatic. A slug slapped the windshield of Diamondstone's cab and converted it into a spiderweb. Diamondstone grabbed Absalom's scrawny neck and pulled him down behind the car.

"One way of answering the question of where Dal Rama is. He's not far off, Absalom, which means I can probably beat him back to that cottage he rented, and snoop around a bit. Keep your eyes open."

A red bulls-eye of light showed down the street.

"Cops!" said Absalom.

"Uh-hum," said Diamondstone softly. "Your constant terror of them must be a relic of crap game days, my friend. I think they've come rather opportunely. At least Dal Rama will hold his fire."

Diamondstone got into his car and drove off just as the representative of the police department pulled up to the curb. He went a block north and six blocks east. He stopped in front of the cottage which Dal Rama had rented, near the edge of town. The place was dark. Diamondstone went up the walk and creaked across the porch.

He tried the door, found it locked, but pushed that barrier aside by means of a skeleton key. His flat flashlight palmed, he sent a searching beam of light about the room. The light stopped jerkily. On the floor near a cobblestone fireplace was a long pine packing case smudged with dust.

"Not unlike a coffin," Diamondstone muttered.

He approached the box a bit warily. Nothing was inside the packing case. Diamondstone reached for a peanut, paused, wheeled slowly, his flashlight pointing toward the door.

"People who walk as softly as you, will eventually have their brains strewn over some nice cool sidewalk," he said.

DAL RAMA stood in the doorway—Dal Rama with his pistol and his thin-lipped, hellish smile.

"Sit down, won't you?" Dal Rama waved to a chair beside a cellaret littered with glasses and decanters.

"An invitation that is imperative, I should say." Diamondstone backed to the chair and sat down.

The Blessed Guardian closed the door and switched on a lamp. His knoblike eyes were inscrutable. "Now," he said, "we will talk like friends."

"We will talk, anyway," Diamondstone amended.

"Have it your way," said the fakir.

He picked up two small liquor glasses and a decanter and went over to the lamp. Diamondstone picked up a third glass, toyed with it, closed the fingers of his right hand over it, crushingly. He watched Dal Rama narrowly, and when the latter handed him a glass of whiskey, he took it in his left hand and transferred it, apparently to his right.

Dal Rama raised his glass. So, it seemed, did Diamondstone. The rim of the glass could be clearly heard as it clicked against his large, square teeth. Then he put the empty glass down, gestured with his left hand, fingers wide spread.

"Why all this hospitality?" he asked.

"Look," said Dal Rama, "how many times I gotta tell you to get out of this burg? I've warned you twice, once with a shot. Get this! If I'd wanted to do it, that slug would have been rattling around where your brain ought to be."

"Huh?" asked Diamondstone, dully.

Dal Rama's smile broadened. He brushed away a fly that buzzed about his face.

"When something gets in my way I flip it aside," he said. "You haven't the sense, to hear a warning. So I'm flipping you aside. I want you out of this town so damned bad I'm going to put you out."

Diamondstone moistened his lips. His eyelids flickered.

"What was in that drink? I feel funny."

"Laugh it off then. A double feature. It was good Bourbon with a Mickey Finn as an added attraction. You'll be asleep in a couple of ticks."

Diamondstone turned a drowsy head toward the fireplace. "Uh-hum. The box."

"Yeah, with you in it. Where would you like to be shipped to that's a couple of hundred miles from here?"

Diamondstone ran nervous fingers through his hair. "Now I begin to know how old Helm must have felt just before he was murdered."

Dal Rama's smile seeped back into his slit of a mouth. "Murder—" He took two steps toward Diamondstone. "Say that again, damn you!"

Diamondstone's broad shoulders went limp. His head wobbled forward. Dal Rama sprang to the chair, seized Diamondstone by the chin.

"Say that again, damn it! You pass out on me now and I'll kill you! Helm murdered? You're nuts! The Mickey went to your brain. What the hell?" He slapped Diamondstone's cheek.

Slowly, Diamondstone's eyelids peeled open. His formerly blank blue gaze brightened. Dal Rama stepped back, his jaw sagging. Diamondstone laughed outright, pushed out of the chair, and stood steadily erect.

"Honestly, if you could see your goatee when your mouth is open, you'd shave it off," he chuckled.

"You—you're not—"

"Not going to sleep? Well hardly. If you'd have taken a look at that liquor glass I put down, you would have seen it not only empty but clean. I simply switched an empty glass for the one containing the Bourbon and the knockout drops. I vanished the glass you handed me with my left hand."

Dal Rama's knoblike eyes explored the carpet around Diamondstone's chair. Not even a droplet of spilled liquor could be seen anywhere. He jumped at Diamondstone, seized Diamondstone's lapels.

"Whatcha do with that stuff, damn it? Out with it!"

Diamondstone's left fist balled, sank to the wrist in Dal Rama's middle. The Blessed Guardian doubled over, staggered backward, tangled with a stool, and sat down. His face turned the color of pea soup. He would have hauled out his gun had he not needed both hands to knead his belly.

"The doped whiskey is still in the glass and intact," Diamondstone told him, "if that's any comfort to you. But I see it isn't. No doubt the police will be interested in comparing it with the dregs of liquor found at the scene of the murder." He backed toward the door, eyes brittle with laughter. "Smooth," he said softly, "that Abbott method of vanishing a glass of liquid. I intended to use it to annoy you on the stage tonight. Glad I saved it, very glad!"

Dal Rama mouthed an oath. His yellow fingers started toward his gun. In the silence, the buzz of the fly's wings was thunderous. Diamondstone watched the insect, circling Dal Rama's turban.

"The fly is back, Dal Rama, or perhaps he never quite left. You'll have to do a little better job of 'flipping aside'."

And Diamondstone's big body moved with incredible speed. The door slammed even as Dal Rama got to his gun and taught it to talk. Two jagged slivers jumped out of the door and, from the other side, sounded Diamondstone's laughter, gently derisive.

CHAPTER IV

MAN MISSING

THERE WAS something decidedly stagey about Diamondstone's laughter. It was all right to worry a man as Diamondstone had worried Dal Rama, but Dal Rama had reached a stage of desperation in which he would no longer be content with mere threats. The fly must be properly squashed.

As a killer, Dal Rama had the deadly qualities of a rattler that had lost its rattle. Diamondstone knew he must tread warily.

In his room in the hotel, he dismissed the thought of impending danger and indulged in a little unscientific sleuthing. His microscope was a tumbler of water and with this he examined the piece of wallpaper he had torn from Marcus Helm's closet. Then he pierced his finger with the tip of a penknife and squeezed a little blood onto the paper beside the scarlet stain.

While he waited for it to dry, he reproduced the glass of doped liquor which Dal Rama had tried to get him to drink. This he placed on the dresser. With his improvised magnifying glass, he examined the stains on the paper again.

"Ingenious," he muttered. "Damned ingenious!"

Then he hurried down into the lobby to put in a long-distance call to J. Ivan Rhodes in care of the Ohio radio station with which Rhodes was associated. With Marcus Helm's son eliminated from the list of suspects the going would be definitely easier.

While waiting in the phone booth he asked himself why the local police hadn't taken in Dal Rama. Possibly, Mrs. Helm was using wealth and prestige to protect the fortune teller. If this protection was not voluntary, Dal Rama could have easily forced her into it. After all, Dal Rama had only given the drug to Mrs. Helm, suggesting that she put it in her husband's liquor. That made Mrs. Helm an accessory to the fortune teller's crime.

Ten minutes later, Diamondstone was talking to the program director of the radio station. He asked brief questions, hung up slowly. Instead of clearing up the mystery, the call had only doubled his trouble.

For J. Ivan Rhodes, radio actor and son of the murdered man, had not been seen about the radio studio that night nor the previous afternoon, for that matter. All efforts to locate him were fruitless.

HE TOOK the elevator back to his room, wondering if perhaps it wasn't time to have a talk with the police. On entering his room, he pulled up short and his red-gold brows started up toward his hair. A man in blue serge and gold braid was standing in the middle of the room. He was impatiently rapping thick thighs with a truncheon.

"You're lookin' at the law, brother," he said to Diamondstone.

"Oh," said Diamondstone, innocently, "is that what it is? I always thought the law consisted of calfskin-bound books that hold up the ceiling in a lawyer's office."

"None of your wisecracks brother. You're under arrest and the charge is murder."

Diamondstone frowned. "Uh—would it be too much trouble for you to explain whom I have murdered?"

"Marcus Helm, that's who. And I got the goods. See that chunk of wall-paper on the table? Well, it's covered with blood."

Diamondstone blinked. "The only blood on it is my own," he said.

"Maybe. I got no way of knowin'. But the wallpaper ain't your own. It came from the closet in Mr. Helm's bedroom. And that's only half of it. Mr. Helm was drugged, they say, before he was killed. And what do I find but this!" He pointed to the liquor glass which Diamondstone had obtained from Dal Rama. "It's got the same smell about it that that drugged liquor in Helm's room had."

"This, you mean?" Diamondstone mopped his brow returned his handkerchief to his pocket, and pointed at the glass of doped whiskey that the cop had transferred to the table.

"Yeah, that liquor," said the cop.

"What liquor?" Diamondstone's left fist smashed down on the table. At the same time, his right hand closed over the incriminating glass and squeezed. Then he exhibited both hands freely, back and front. And the cop goggled. There was no sign of the whiskey glass and not so much as a spilled drop of the liquid.

"Huh?" gasped the cop. "Here, you can't do that! That—that's exhibit 'A'!"

Diamondstone stepped back from the table. His big body crouched slightly. He smiled suavely, disarmingly.

"With almost everybody in town having a good motive for killing Helm, you pick on me, a perfect stranger with more money than he knows what to do with."

"It was revenge," said the cop. "Didn't Helm try to shoot you on the stage tonight?"

"He did not! Helm was a bit drunk. Furthermore, he was trying to kill the bronze Buddha. He didn't believe in things occult, yet the Buddha predicted the very thing Helm feared most—murder. Helm was afraid of Dal Rama, because Dal Rama had good motive to kill him. And he was afraid of his son, J. Ivan Rhodes, who had quarreled with him that afternoon. Ask Mrs. Helm why she drugged her husband's drink tonight. Find out what became of Mr. Helm's unfinished will. Find out why the Buddha whispered tonight. In other words, solve this murder before I beat you to it."

The cop took a threatening step forward. "I'm findin' one thing—that glass you just disappeared. I ain't a fool. Things just don't vanish."

"No," said Diamondstone, "I admit that. Things don't vanish. They just move a lot faster than the eye can follow—like this!"

His left hand came around from behind him and there was the whiskey glass and the unspilled contents. Another lightning move, and there was the glass, empty, with the whiskey dripping from the cop's chin.

"Exhibit 'A'!" cried Diamondstone, as the blinded policeman lashed frantically with his truncheon at the spot where Diamondstone might have been and wasn't.

"Exhibit 'B'!" And Diamondstone's right fist sent the breath exploding from the cop's lungs.

Then he closed in, knocked the cop back on the bed. He pulled bed clothes over the kicking form, rolled the cop up neatly, trussed up the bundle with a belt.

FEET WERE pounding along the hall outside his door. A whistle shrilled excitedly. Diamondstone bounded to the window, flung it open, sprang out on the fire-escape. Hereafter, he vowed, he would confine his sleuthing to cities where he was well known. He'd got himself into a pretty kettle of herring and might yet try his skill at a miraculous vanish from the county jail.

He clattered down the fire-escape and into an alley. He ran toward the street where his car was parked. He just missed meeting another policeman who was running into the front of the hotel.

As he sprang into his car, somebody hailed him. It was Attorney John Wrenn who came legging down the sidewalk, swinging his bulging briefcase.

"Diamondstone they're after you!" Wrenn panted. And he opened the car door and got in beside Diamondstone. "It's crazy," he said, "but it leaked out you were a magician and Mrs. Helm says magicians are no good."

"She should watch this one vanish!" Diamondstone said as he plugged at the starter.

"No! Think, man. You're alibied, don't you see? You and I saw Marcus Helm alive just before he turned out his light to undress. Don't you remember? I can testify to that. And you didn't go near Helm's room until the old man was dead. They haven't a thing against you. You run away—"

"Who's running away?" Diamondstone demanded. "I'm solving a murder. I can't stop to talk *habeas corpus* now. There's only one part of the puzzle missing—the answer to the Buddha riddle. When I know why the Buddha whispered tonight, I'll make some startling disclosures. Did you know that J. Ivan Rhodes never showed up at the radio studio tonight?"

"No!" gasped Wrenn. "But, good Lord, I've known that young man a long time. He wears a flowing tie. He's a bit cracked, but he's no murderer. That gyp fortune teller is the killer."

"Listen," said Diamondstone, "why didn't Dal Rama exhibit his knife tonight? He usually switches the telescoping one for a genuine article that looks just like it. What he does is pull a neat sleeve switch and hand out the genuine knife. Why didn't he do that tonight?"

"Hell," said Wrenn, "how should I know?"

"How should you," Diamondstone admitted. "It couldn't be that Dal Rama didn't have the genuine knife, now, could it?"

In a side street beside the opera house Diamondstone stopped his car and both men got out.

"I warn you," Diamondstone said as they stood at the stage door, "that Dal Rama is the top of America's scum. Furthermore, he'll kill if he gets a chance."

Wrenn's pin-head bobbed. "I'll just step inside the door and act as a rear guard while you're snooping. And don't worry about Dal Rama. I've an old revolver in my pocket and I'm not afraid to use it."

They opened the door; the lock, Wrenn explained, had been broken years ago. Diamondstone stepped into back-stage blackness and the door closed with a wheezing sound.

He beamed his light ahead, found the ramp leading to the stage, and strode quietly to the stage. Light fell upon the Buddha's gigantic side. Diamondstone paused, half expecting the image to turn its head. But the Buddha retained its attitude of serene contemplation.

He applied the test of the hammer that Dal Rama had used, to discover that striking the Buddha produced a convincing note of solidity only in certain parts. Others gonged resonantly, proving that there was a large cavity within the image. Diamondstone had guessed as much.

He went down into the orchestra pit, found the door which led beneath the stage. As he stepped through the door, an eerie chill rippled across his shoulders. His own breathing was audible, short and restricted, but there was no other sound.

He located the secret wiring system which led up into the Buddha and which was supposed to connect with Dal Rama's microphone. But Dal Rama had not spoken into his microphone that night, yet the Buddha had whispered: "Murder—Murder—"

The under-stage room itself was vaultlike. Canvas-wrapped stage drops looked like mummies of Titans where they lay on long shelves. In the ceiling, which was of course the stage floor, was a large size trapdoor closed by a spring latch. On the floor, directly beneath, was a white-ringed, greyish stain. Diamondstone dropped, scraped up some of the greyish stuff, and sniffed at it. It had a soapish odor.

Near by was a packing box, dust-covered. An iron wrecking bar, long in disuse, lay on the floor beside it. Diamondstone picked up the bar, kicked the packing case beneath the trap, and stood upon it. The spring latch of the trap worked easily. The door, extremely heavy, he allowed to drop down on his shoulder. His left arm explored the blackness of the secret cavity within the giant Buddha.

He closed the trap quickly, got down. His face was slightly pale. His heart drummed with the monotonous insistency of an African drum. He reached into his pocket for a peanut, cracked it, threw it away. If he never ate again, that would be all right.

In the corner near the door he found a brown bag of worn leather. Inside were some of Dal Rama's props—the knife with its telescoping blade and concealed dye duct, instrument of the mock murder committed nightly on Isis. He also found two bottles of the bloodlike dye and a new paper document, folded for the first time.

He opened it. It was Marcus Helm's will. Nothing illuminating about it. As Wrenn had said, it provided that all the Helm fortune should go to Mrs. Helm on condition she did not use any of it for occult experiments or for the support of any mystic or group of mystics. The will was unsigned, unwitnessed, worthless.

CHAPTER V

MURDER IN THE PAST

A **DOOR CREAKED** somewhere. Diamondstone's flashlight snapped off. Darkness sprang upon him like a black panther. He stood, nerves tense, muscles quivering. Footsteps, the pop of a light switch, and a dingy light globe became suddenly alive.

In the orchestra pit door stood Dal Rama, neat turban, black automatic and all. His teeth showed, but he wasn't smiling. His knoblike eyes flicked in the direction of his gun.

"This is a fly swatter," he said flatly. "Just had the pleasure of mashing Mouthpiece Wrenn in the head with it. I got a slug for you."

Diamondstone sighed, and took a firmer grip on the iron wrecking bar.

"I suppose you know you've made a sweet mess of things for yourself tonight," he said. "But before your slug crowds my brain, you'll have no objection to telling me how you made the Buddha whisper tonight."

"What the hell?" said Dal Rama softly. "I thought you did that. I thought it was one of your tricks."

Diamondstone shook his head. "My magical ambitions don't extend to wanting to make a Buddha whisper that way."

Dal Rama shrugged. "I don't get it. But you will. You've got to go, that's all. Mrs. Helm is up on the stage right now. She wants to consult the Buddha. She's going to be like putty in my hands and I can't have you messing things up for me. So I gotta kill you!"

"Drop that gun!" came a thick voice from the doorway.

Dal Rama whirled, fired. At the same time gun flame slivered the blackness beyond the door. Dal Rama dropped his gun to clap his fingers over his left biceps. Blood crawled between his yellow knuckles. His face was a furious, pain-furrowed mask. Yet his black eyes remained inscrutable.

The man who came through the door was grey-haired and portly. He wore a gold-braided uniform and carried a police positive in his hand.

"Your name Diamondstone?" he asked.

Diamondstone nodded. "And yours?"

"Wildeave, chief of police. You are under arrest for assaulting an officer of the law, for a starter. You're mixed up in this murder business some way. I'm going to get all of you suspects together and knock the truth out of you." He turned his head slightly. "Bring in Mrs. Helm and Doris Helm, Jerry."

Mrs. Helm and Doris came in without help. The cop Diamondstone had tussled with in the hotel was behind them. Mrs. Helm, on seeing the blood that drooled from between Dal Rama's fingers, uttered a faint scream. Doris had to support her mother for a moment until the elder woman had control of herself.

"Now," said Wildeave, "you're all here."

"No," Diamondstone contradicted, "we're not."

"You interrupted me," said Wildeave, "All here but J. Ivan Rhodes. He's disappeared."

Diamondstone's brows drew together. "Would you know him if you saw him?"

"Decidedly," said Wildeave.

"Good," said Diamondstone. His blue eyes flicked at Mrs. Helm. "Madam, did you know that in drugging your husband's whiskey tonight you were helping in a plot to murder him?"

White, tight-lipped, Mrs. Helm just stared through Diamondstone.

"What do you mean?" demanded Wildeave.

"Simply," said Diamondstone, "that I have a witness who can testify that Dal Rama gave Mrs. Helm something to put in her husband's liquor."

MRS. HELM drew a long breath. Her gaze shifted to Dal Rama.

"So," she said huskily, "it wasn't something to stop his drinking."

"Rather," Diamondstone explained, "it was something that would have stopped his drinking for all time had Dal Rama had his way about it. You see, Wildeave, it is positively not a coincidence that more than one person had a motive for killing Helm this very night. The murder resulted in Helm's dying intestate, so that his fortune would be divided into three parts. It was to Dal Rama's interest to kill Helm before that will was completed because he wanted to get his sly fingers on Mrs. Helm's part of the fortune."

"I see," Mrs. Helm interrupted. "He wanted me to donate money to build a fitting temple for the Buddha."

Diamondstone nodded. "He's worked that one with tragic results before. He gave you that drug, telling you it was something to keep your husband from drinking, and planned to murder Helm in his sleep. But Dal Rama did not kill Helm, damn it. All Dal Rama did was swipe the will, hoping to delay the signing of it until he could sneak in and murder Helm.

"All he accomplished by stealing the will was unknowingly to alibi himself. Dal Rama stole the will after Marcus Helm was killed, proving definitely that he didn't know that Helm was dead at the time. Had he known, there would have been no reason for him to steal the unsigned will. Therefore, Dal Rama is the only person who could not have killed Helm."

"Nice," said Wildeave. "But what about you?"

"I'm not going to alibi myself. Only a murderer has to do that. This killer framed evidence against Dal Rama, knowing that Dal Rama was bound to look suspicious because of his evident motive. In addition, the killer built up an almost impregnable alibi for himself.

"Except for a scarlet stain on the wallpaper in Helm's closet and the knowledge that Mr. Helm always undressed in the dark, the murderer could have almost got by with this. That stain on the wallpaper was not blood. It was Dal Rama's fake blood—a dye he uses in that trick knife of his. That dye was stolen when the murderer came in here and stole the real knife, a duplicate of the trick one, so that he could kill with that knife and thus frame Dal Rama."

"What about J. Ivan Rhodes?" asked Wildeave.

"You're out of order," Diamondstone said with a scowl. "But what about J. Ivan Rhodes? Motive, of course. And in addition, he was heard to quarrel with his father. Furthermore, he cannot be found. Still furthermore, on leaving the Helm house he was heard to threaten: 'I'll get Dal Rama, too.' Later, when Helm was killed, it seemed logical to suppose that the other half of that threat included the threat to kill his own father.

"But, you can't always fill in missing words that easily. J. Ivan might just as well have said: 'I'll get a case of Scotch and I'll kill Dal Rama, too.'"

"So what?" said Wildeave.

"Seeing that grey-white stain on the floor here, knowing that J. Ivan did threaten to get Dal Rama, knowing that Doris Helm did not discover her father's body, but actually discovered her living, breathing, though *sleeping*, father—all that tells pretty quickly who killed Marcus Helm. The murderer, Chief Wildeave, is the man with the other nightshirt. The man who—"

Wildeave clawed at his head. "Are you a raving lunatic? What in hell has a nightshirt got to do with this?"

DIAMONDSTONE STIFFENED. "Look behind you, Wildeave," he said softly, "and you'll damn soon find out!"

Wildeave, Dal Rama, everybody swung toward the door. A man stood there. The glint of his polished revolver was one threat. His two eyes were two more threats. His tongue was a fourth threat as he said:

"Back! Back against the wall, all of you. This isn't going to be clever murder, but it's going to be thorough."

"John Wrenn!" gasped Mrs. Helm.

"Do as he says," Diamondstone ordered. "He's a killer. Look at his knuckles. They're rough as though chapped. Actually, he wore his skin off scrubbing up the blood he spilled on the floor here. Wildeave I want you to meet the other half of J. Ivan Rhodes' threat. Rhodes must have known that Wrenn was misappropriating funds of the Helm fortune. Rhodes tried to convince his father of this, I believe. Failing in that, he threatened to get evidence that would expose Wrenn. Also, he intended to expose Dal Rama who was duping Mrs. Helm even as Wrenn was duping Mr. Helm."

"Back against the wall—all of you!" Wrenn repeated.

And one by one, they backed. All except Diamondstone. He stood perfectly still in the center of the room, arms at his sides.

"Up with, your hands, Diamondstone. None of your tricks. You get it first, because you're too damned smart."

Diamondstone smiled unpleasantly. "You ought to have stuck to clever murder. Something tells me you're going to make a mess of this Juggernaut variety." And Diamondstone raised his hands but he raised the wrecking bar, too.

"Drop that bar, Diamondstone!" Wrenn warned.

Diamondstone dropped it, but not until the hook at the end of the bar had found the latch of the trapdoor above. The door swung down. Diamondstone ducked under it. Something twisted and black, and horribly stiff, dropped through the opening, struck Wrenn on the back.

Wrenn went down, squirmed under the weight of the man from above, fired three shots into his perfectly dead opponent before Wildeave and Diamondstone could get the gun away from him and the bracelets on his wrists.

Diamondstone had never seen the dead man on the floor, yet he was not at all surprised when Wildeave gasped:

"That's J. Ivan Rhodes, Mr. Helm's son!"

Diamondstone nodded. "Murdered right here by John Wrenn. Remember that J. Ivan threatened to get Dal Rama. He came to the opera house with that purpose in mind, found Helm down here swiping Dal Rama's knife and a bottle of red dye. J. Ivan evidently precipitated the trouble by accusing Wrenn of getting sticky fingers into the Helm fortune. Wrenn knifed him, supposed that he was dead, stuffed him into the Buddha.

"After that, he cleaned up the blood with scouring powder, skinning his knuckles in the act. But J. Ivan wasn't dead. He regained consciousness before he died. Inside the Buddha, he tried to call for help, got out the word 'murder' before he passed away. That's why the Buddha whispered tonight."

"But," Wildeave objected, "how could Wrenn have killed Helm? He and Doris discovered the body. Up until the second time he entered the Helm house, Helm was alive."

"That's it," Diamondstone explained. "Helm wasn't dead when Doris and Wrenn entered the room. Helm was asleep. The front of his nightshirt was covered with Dal Rama's bloodlike dye. The dye was dry enough when Helm put the nightshirt on so that Helm wouldn't have noticed the moisture. Or perhaps Helm was too far under that sleeping draught to notice.

"You see, Wrenn knew, like most of the rest of you, that Helm always undressed in the dark. In darkness Helm wouldn't have noticed that fake bloodstain on his nightshirt. Once soundly asleep, clad in a nightshirt that seemed to be covered with blood, any one discovering the body would have thought the worst.

"Wrenn arranged it so that Doris and he discovered the body. Then he sent Doris to phone the police, calmly stabbed Helm, tossed the knife to the floor, took off the gloves he had undoubtedly put on for the purpose, and walked out of the room.

"The stain on the closet wallpaper gave the plan away. It looked like blood but it didn't turn brown on drying as blood does. The stain got there from the artificial bloodstain Wrenn had put on the nightshirt. The dye wasn't quite dry and it had to be up against the wall so that the fake bloodstain wouldn't show. But for that stain, Wrenn's alibi would never have been broken.

"How he substituted the nightshirt on which he had faked the bloodstain for the one Helm had hung in its accustomed spot, so that he could find it in the dark as was his custom, is simplicity itself. After he had helped fix up Helm's will, he left the bedroom through that connecting closet, took the nightshirt out of his briefcase that he had dyed and substituted it for the one hanging in the closet.

"THUS, BY falsifying the time of murder, he alibied himself for a murder he had to commit. Rhodes was wising up to Wrenn's manipulation of the Helm estate and Wrenn feared it was only a matter of a short time before Helm would call for an accounting. With Helm dead, Wrenn felt he could fox Mrs. Helm and Doris quite easily."

"Why," asked Wildeave, "would Helm go to bed when he had not signed the will yet?"

Diamondstone smiled. "Yeah. That was the first slip Wrenn made. Helm never intended to sign that will tonight. He would have attended to it tomorrow morning. Wrenn simply went out to get the witnesses for the sole purpose of having a legitimate excuse for returning to commit the murder."

Diamondstone crossed to the door where Wrenn had dropped his briefcase.

He opened the flap of the case, felt inside.

"Chief Wildeave, you are about to witness the remarkable production of a nightshirt—the one Wrenn took when he substituted the dyed one. As for you"—he whirled on Dal Rama—"if it hadn't been for you and your Buddha, Wrenn would have never thought up such a hellish scheme. I think I'll give you something to remember me by."

"Nix," said Wildeave, as Diamondstone began rolling up his sleeves. "I'm going to vanish that Blessed Guardian to the jail along with Wrenn. I think his attempted murder of Helm will put a stop to the Buddha's whispering for some time."

IV

THE LEFT-HANDED LEGACY

CHAPTER I

MURDER BELOW

S INCE TIME immemorial, millionaires have been eccentric. And one has only to read a little to discover that one of their eccentricities is their ability to become involved in murder; not infrequently playing the part of that pitiable object, the *corpus delicti*.

It was because he was a detective rather than because he was a magician, that Diamondstone was in Detroit to prevent the wealthy and eccentric Milton Markland Paget from becoming what the newspapers callously indicated by a black "X" inked onto a photograph. When Diamondstone considered that he did not know Mr. Paget; that apparently no one in the United States, including his two heirs, knew Mr. Paget, his task assumed enormous proportions.

The liquor-witted Stewart Lahern was one of the heirs of the unknown Mr. Paget. At approximately midnight, Lahern leaned out of his hotel window to give a thick-tongued, mushy-voiced imitation of a police announcer. An updraft of air from one of Detroit's busiest streets sucked the mushy voice into Diamondstone's window and gave Morpheus such a vigorous kick that Diamondstone gave up his sleep-wooing altogether.

"Calling all cars!" sang out Lahern. "Calling all cars in Maine, New Hampshire, Vermont, Mash—Mashashoosetts—"

And having floundered over Massachusetts, Lahern did not stop until he had called all cars in all the states, concluding with Alaska and Dependencies.

"Oh, hum," said Diamondstone disgustedly as he stretched pajama-clad legs over the side of the bed.

Possibly because he was a magician, he located his slippers without turning on the light. He crossed the room. The bigness of his body blotted out the flicker of the colored lights that passed through the open

window. Looking down, he could see Mr. Lahern waving his arms out of the window directly below.

While Diamondstone had a sense of humor that had endeared him to audiences the world over, when his magical act had trouped the vaudeville circuits, his good nature did not extend to Lahern's noisy geographical recitation. He cut short the second parade of states in the middle of Colorado by deluging Lahern with ice water from a handy carafe.

Lahern retaliated with a deluge of epithets that was soul-shocking even when aired on Detroit's worldly darkness. And then he all but fell out of his window in heaving an empty whiskey bottle that arced up and crashed the top sash of Diamondstone's window.

A man of Diamondstone's physical proportions had no intention of putting up with such treatment from a man like Lahern. As soon as he had shaken fragments of window glass out of his tousled, red-gold hair, Diamondstone pulled on trousers and coat over his pajamas and went out into the hall where he thumbed for the elevator.

The cage came up at the New Regent's usual leisurely pace. A grey-haired, sad-eyed man of about fifty years of age slid back the safety gate. A slow smile pushed aside some of the wrinkles that lined his thin cheeks.

Diamondstone's fist connected
with Marcini's chin.

"Troubled with insomnia, Mr. Diamondstone?" asked the elevator operator, a man generally known as Charley.

"Other people's, Charley," Diamondstone said. "Other people's insomnia and my dreams."

Charley, Diamondstone reflected, was a long way out of his element in the New Regent's shabbiness. Charley was a man of refinement, a sentimentalist, too, judging from the copy of Mrs. Browning's poems that lay on the velvet padded stool where Charley spent most of his time. Also, there was a gold-framed picture of a handsome and sedate woman, hanging directly above the elevator control where Charley could watch it during the slow hours of the night.

Charley's smile faded as slowly as it had formed.

"According to Cobbe," he intoned, "the frequent immoral character of the unconscious mind as indicated by our dreams, in which we commit all sorts of crimes without compunction, tallies with the Kantian doctrine that moral will is the true *homo noumenon.*"

Diamondstone's intense blue eyes flickered slightly. "Uh-hum," he agreed with an air of magnificent understanding. "Be that as it may, kindly lower me to the next floor. I dreamed of punching a man's head and I greatly fear I shall not be able to inhibit the unconscious urge."

The key to Room 31 was in the lock and on the outside of the door. Diamondstone entered, slipped out of his coat. The loose drape of his pajama top emphasized the immensity of his shoulders. It seemed impossible that a man of his size was capable of the swift dexterity of movement which his reputation both as a detective and as a magician attributed to him.

A MAN he presumed to be Stewart Lahern was stretched out on the bed, face down. He wore golf knickers and a Shetland sport coat. On his head, a plaid cap bulged enormously.

"Mashashoosetts," Diamondstone gravely addressed the man on the bed, "I have come to bury my fist in a portion of your anatomy. Have you anything to say for yourself?"

The golfer, if he had anything to say, kept it to himself.

Diamondstone strode over to the bed. His long, strong fingers seized the man by the shoulders and then turned him over.

"Playing dead, eh?"

Then all that was intense and alive went out of Diamondstone's blue eyes, leaving nothing but the glassiness of surprise. He drew a long breath.

"And," he whispered, "doing an excellent job of it, too."

For if ever he had looked into the face of a dead man, he was doing so now. The thin nose, the pointed chin, were features that not even death could soften. The eyes were pinched shut by the sweatband of the plaid cap which, when removed, disclosed a folded towel that sponged up blood from a gunshot wound in the head.

Oddly enough, Diamondstone's usually deft fingers had quite some trouble unfastening the man's coat. And when he felt for a heart beat he encountered only the chillness of stone.

Little wonder that liquor-witted Lahern had resorted to calling police cars. Lahern had evidently returned to his room after a grand party to discover this stiff, cold corpse where ordinarily Lahern would have encountered nothing more alarming than a fancied pink elephant.

But who was the man on the bed? Diamondstone drew his red-gold brows tightly together. Chills started to scatter across his back. There was something strange about the corpse on the bed—something that worried the magician-sleuth a great deal because he did not know what that something was.

Intuitively, Diamondstone realized that unknown wrongness. It was something more than the eye could reach. Then, knowing full well he would inevitably get into trouble with the Detroit police, he searched the dead man's pockets. They revealed nothing more enlightening than a handsome gold-plated cigarette lighter, new, and carrying the embossed initial "P."

Diamondstone sat down on the bed, momentarily oblivious to the corpse.

"Oh," he said quietly, "Oh, my!"

Then he thrust the lighter back into the pocket of the corpse and turned to an examination of the man's hands. They were tightly clenched into fists, and he observed that the right hand held a golf scorecard, and the left, a stub of a pencil such as are handed out at golf clubhouses.

He was far less interested in the pencil than in the score-card which he finally extracted from the death grip. The names of two players were simply indicated by the letters "S" and "P" respectively. And it was quite obvious that Mr. "P" had rather badly beaten Mr. "S."

Diamondstone was trying to wedge the card back into the right hand exactly as he had found it, when he noticed that the right forefinger was slightly blistered on the inside, between the first and second joints.

Suddenly he jumped to the foot of the bed, where lay a leather golf bag well stocked with clubs. He pulled out one and tried to swing it. Unfortunately, he was poised so, like a Titanic Bobby Jones about to tee off, when the liquor-thick voice of Mr. Stewart Lahern sounded in the hall.

"By what right, Offlisher, by what right has this guy to come in here and—and die right on my bed?" Lahern demanded. "Thash what I want to know. An' I called all the poleesh in the country and none of 'em heard me. Thash gratitude, with me paying taxesh all these yearsh."

Diamondstone turned his head slowly and looked over one big shoulder. Lahern, a large, soft-looking man of forty, was hanging on the lapels of a short, heavy-set man whom Diamondstone took to be the house detective. The house officer had an extremely wide face that was sawed off flat at the bottom by a tight, stiff collar. He had shrewd, piggish eyes that Diamondstone didn't like; eyes that didn't like Diamondstone, judging by their suspicious appraisal of the magician-sleuth.

AND NO wonder. The house detective was meeting Diamondstone at a disadvantageous moment, with Diamondstone wearing pajamas posed in a golfer's stance at the foot of a bed wherein lay a murdered man. On the bed was the best possible evidence of homicide. And, to the house detective, Diamondstone might have appeared very much the homicidal maniac.

The hotel detective lumbered out from Lahern's grasping hands and approached Diamondstone warily. Another man who had remained in the hall came into the room; a tall man whose bald head rose to a shiny and intellectual pinnacle. Lahern fastened himself on the newcomer, this time with the tenacity of a barnacle, calling him "Porter" and jittering inanely.

Diamondstone summoned a smile that he felt to be definitely stagey. He thrust the golf club into the house detective's unwitting hands. The hotel detective looked down to see what his own hands were doing and announced:

"Golf club."

"Left-handed golf club," Diamondstone amended. "And look—" He pointed to the hands of the corpse. "He's got a pencil in his left hand. Score card in his right."

It took the hotel detective a little while to grasp it all, or perhaps he only grasped at it, for he said:

"What of it?"

"Huh?" Diamondstone said. But of course he couldn't expect the hotel detective to realize the tragedy to its fullest extent. And perhaps it was just as well that he remained a little in the dark. "I simply pointed out that the corpse is left-handed," he said.

Stewart Lahern, one hand still clutching the goggling bald man, tacked unsteadily toward the bed. He held one hand over his eyes and peeped through slightly spread fingers.

"Does he look like he came from Australia?" whispered Lahern. "If thash sho, poshibly I'm a millionaire."

The hotel detective steadied Lahern.

"Seen him before?"

Lahern shook his head. His eyes dulled on the bald man's face. "You sheen him, Porter?"

The bald man shook his head. "Never in my life. Is his name Paget?"

"Very likely," said Diamondstone. "There's a "P" on his cigarette lighter."

"Well, if he'sh a left-handed millionaire from Australia," said Lahern, "and very eccentric, he's my Uncle Milty—Milton Markland Paget!"

"My client!" Porter groaned.

"My uncle!" gayly from Lahern.

As Diamondstone viewed the corpse on the bed, he began to feel the least bit futile. Diamondstone had come to Detroit for the sole purpose of protecting Milton Markland Paget from the possibility of being murdered!

CHAPTER III

THE SINGING
CORPSE

IT WAS fortunate for Stewart Lahern that he had an alibi, one that accurately chronicled his sins of the evening and saw that they gave him no opportunity for murder. The alibi draped herself over the arm and around the back of Lahern's chair and addressed him affectionately as "Stewy." The alibi was a luscious, dewy-eyed blonde who managed, magically enough, to hide her age by wearing a gown that hid little else. She gave her name as Dulcy Madden.

Detective-sergeant Sundeen of the Detroit police was trying to interrogate Lahern but found that the answers to his questions invariably fell from Dulcy's pouting lips.

Finally Sundeen exploded.

"Look here, is your name Lahern?" and he thrust a finger into Dulcy's face.

The blond woman put her face down on top of Lahern's sleek hair and made a face at Sundeen. "Not yet, but it soon will be, won't it, Stewy?"

"Huh?" Lahern sat up so straight, all of a sudden, that he nearly dislodged Dulcy from where she twined on his chair.

"I said we're going to be married, aren't we, Stewy?"

Lahern looked at Sundeen's glowering face. Then he looked across the hotel manager's office, where the police inquisition was being held, and smiled in a rather sickly manner at Attorney Oscar Porter. Porter refused to return the smile. As a matter of fact, that bald gentleman took a savage bite at a cigar and turned to Diamondstone who was leaning against the wall shucking peanuts and munching noisily.

Finally, Dulcy's attitude demanded an answer and Lahern, brow beaded with sweat, acknowledged that he and the blond Dulcy were to be wed.

Sergeant Sundeen gritted his teeth, turned around, glared at Diamondstone.

"Damn those nuts, Diamondstone! Get through with them, can't you? You're being damned offensive!"

"Oh?" Diamondstone said, mildly surprised. "Excuse me, but you know you've really not touched anything yet."

"I am not here to entertain an amateur sleuth, Diamondstone," said Sundeen acidly. Then he fixed his eyes on Porter. "How does it happen that Mr. Paget's two heirs, his attorney, and his supposed protector, Mr. Diamondstone, turned up in his hotel just about the time Mr. Paget was murdered?"

"Mr. Paget wrote letters from New York asking us all to meet him here some time this week," Porter said, in dignified tones. "These were evidently written the day of his arrival in the United States from Australia. I don't have mine, but perhaps Mr. Diamondstone has his."

Diamondstone brought out a piece of blond paper from his inside coat pocket and handed it to Sundeen. It was a letter concluded with the left-handed signature of the left-handed Mr. Paget.

Sundeen perused the letter slowly. While he was reading, the door of the office opened and Charley, the fifty-year-old elevator boy, entered and stood meekly at the sergeant's right.

"What do you want?" asked Sundeen, without looking up.

"I beg your pardon," said Charley quietly, "but I was under the impression you sent for me."

Sundeen thrust a glance over at Charley. "Oh, yeah. You sit down." Then he returned the letter to Diamondstone. He slapped a pile of clothes on the office desk. They were the golfing garments which had been removed from the body. "The man was Paget, all right. We've looked for laundry marks and found his initials inked on. As to his being left-handed, Diamondstone, no reason to place any emphasis on that."

Diamondstone fingered the shoes the victim had worn, and his brow drew into a red-gold scowl. The toe of the right shoe was badly scuffed from golfing. Also, the sole of the left shoe was worn at the ball of the foot. That was odd. Extremely odd.

"And there are only two heirs to the Paget millions," Sundeen said. "Mr. Lahern and a girl. Where is the girl? What was her name?"

"Miss Violet Devon," Porter supplied. "Shall I ask her in?"

"Yes," Sundeen sighed wearily. His eyes encountered Charley's deep, sad eyes. "Oh yes, I wanted to ask you something. According to the desk clerk, the victim, Mr. Paget, was brought into the hotel in an apparently drunken state at about nine o'clock this evening. He was more than half carried by a tall, thin man with a glass eye."

AT THE mention of the glass-eyed man, Diamondstone's scowl deepened.

"And," Sundeen continued, "the glass-eyed man asked for the key to Room Thirty-one. Paget was wearing these golf clothes and the tall man was carrying Paget's golf bag. Paget's head was muffled in a silk scarf so that the clerk couldn't see his face. The clerk thought that Paget was Mr. Lahern, simply because of Paget's supposed drunken state, and because the tall man had asked for the key to Thirty-one. The clerk thought that the tall man was simply putting Lahern to bed after Lahern had got himself pickled. Nothing unusual. Afterwards, when the real Lahern came in, the clerk was a little confused. He told Lahern that he had already given him the key. Lahern was too drunk to deny this. Now you took Paget up in your elevator?"

Charley nodded. "Yes, sir. Both the inebriated gentleman and the person with the artificial eye."

"And you didn't see Paget's face, either?"

"No, sir."

"And it never occurred to you that he might be dead?"

"Of course not, sir," declared Charley. "The man you say was Paget was singing drunkenly while the tall man was begging him to desist."

SUNDEEN, ADDICTED to scratching his head, had good provocation to indulge in his habit now. For, he said, according to medical opinion, Paget simply had to have been dead when he was brought into the hotel. And a corpse doesn't sing.

Diamondstone's intense blue gaze shifted from Sundeen's puzzled face to something much more charming that appeared in the office door. Violet Devon, the other heir to the Paget fortune, struck Diamondstone as being a rare combination of beauty and common sense. Her dark hair was arranged in a becoming coiffure that was simplicity itself. Her dark eyes were neither timid nor bold. Her makeup frankly admitted a few freckles that bridged her straight nose. She was rather small and was trimly tailored. She did not shrink when Sundeen whirled on her.

"Miss Devon?" snapped Sundeen, "You are the other one who benefits by the death of Milton Markland Paget?"

"I suppose so," she said quietly, "if you care to put it brutally. Naturally, neither my cousin, Mr. Lahern, nor myself could be expected to feel particularly cut up over the death of a man we've never seen. As to the inheritance, I've never thought much about it. I always understood that Stewart Lahern was to have the bulk of the money because Mr. Lahern was left-handed. I understand my uncle favored left-handed people."

"Thash me," shushed Lahern. "I'm left-handed."

Diamondstone fished a cigarette from a package, thrust it between his lips. He turned to the bald Porter and asked for a match. The attorney handed him a book of paper matches containing half a dozen matches on the right side of the book. Diamondstone lighted his cigarette, pocketed the matches. In the depths of his blue eyes was the merest flicker of amusement.

He went over to where Violet Devon had seated herself. The girl was toying with a lacy handkerchief which Diamondstone, much to her amazement, borrowed.

"What's eating you?" asked Sundeen, eyeing Diamondstone suspiciously.

"Eating me? Well, er—yes, I suppose something is eating me," Diamondstone said mischievously. "Has it occurred to you that except for laundry marks, an initialed cigarette lighter, a set of left-handed golf clubs, and the fact that the corpse held a pencil in his left hand, we have nothing to identify the body as that of Mr. Paget? Paget was an extraordinarily left-handed person. But before Mr. Lahern can enjoy his left-handed legacy, oughtn't we to think a moment?"

Diamondstone accomplished two rapid and clever vanishes with his cigarette.

"What's that for?" demanded Sundeen.

Diamondstone smiled. "I was thinking that it was rather odd that the shoes worn by the victim should have the right toe scuffed and the left sole worn, indicating that when he played golf he pivoted on his left foot and scuffed his right toe on the follow through. Try that with left-handed golf clubs, Sergeant. It simply can't be done unless you hit the ball with the reverse side of the club. Not considered good form in the best circles. Now, if it had been the toe of the left shoe that was scuffed—"

"By damn! You too?" roared Sundeen. "One of the medicos has the same complex. Only he goes in for blisters instead of scuffed shoes."

"Exactly," Diamondstone smiled. "In spite of planted evidence to the contrary, the murdered man in Room Thirty-one was not left-handed— because he played golf right-handed. Not only was this indicated by the scuffed toe of the right shoe, but also the fact that he had acquired a blister on the forefinger of his right hand. Supposing that he had used the approved overlapping grip when he played golf, had he been left-handed the right forefinger would have been locked over the left little finger and therefore couldn't have been blistered. Therefore the corpse didn't use the left-handed clubs. And therefore he couldn't have been Milton Markland Paget."

Stunned silence while Diamondstone's deductions permeated every head in the room. Then Sundeen roared:

"Who the hell is the victim, then?"

"I haven't the foggiest notion," said Diamondstone. He put his glowing cigarette butt into Miss Devon's lacy handkerchief, rolled up the handkerchief, and held it in his hand.

Sundeen bounded to the door. "I'm going to check with the medical examiner on that!"

"Here, take this a moment," said Diamondstone.

He extended Miss Devon's handkerchief to Porter. Wonderingly, the lawyer took it cautiously in his right hand. And almost at once, the handkerchief burst into flames. Porter dropped the burning cloth with an oath. Unfortunately, it landed in a waste paper basket where it immediately ignited some paper.

Diamondstone stood back at the door, eyes wide with astonishment, while the excited lawyer drew a cupful of water from the cooler, carried the cup in his left hand, and sprinkled the flames into a smoldering ash. From the debris, he resurrected Miss Devon's handkerchief. In the center of the burned cloth was the "vanished" cigarette.

"Smart guy!" Dulcy Madden raucously jeered the chagrined Diamondstone.

"The trick never failed before," Diamondstone said sorrowfully. He turned to Miss Devon. "My dear lady, I can't imagine how it happened."

"I think I can," Violet said in a low, sweet voice. "And I think you're a very clever person."

CHAPTER III

VOICE OF GUILT

THE ASSISTANT medical examiner, an enthusiastic golfer, was certain that the corpse was not that of Mr. Paget. The medico subscribed to a golfing magazine and had seen Mr. Paget's name listed among the foremost Australian golfers. And a good golfer would not have blistered his fingers on either hand. And this bit of light on the subject only served to emphasize the impenetrable darkness surrounding the death of the man in Room Thirty-one.

Near the elevator shaft, Diamondstone was talking to the telephone operator. Rather, Diamondstone's money was talking. He slipped the operator a twenty-dollar bill and a list of names: Dulcy Madden, Stewart Lahern, Oscar Porter, Violet Devon.

He directed the operator to make a record of all the calls that came in for these four persons and also any calls they might make from the hotel. Then he joined Charley in the elevator and asked to be taken to his room on the fourth floor.

"What do you make of it all, Mr. Diamondstone?" asked Charley anxiously.

"What I make of it," Diamondstone declared, "is the sort of fog the citizens of London would thrive in." He yawned. "Three A. M. Don't see how you stand these hours, Charley."

Charley's slow smile ironed out some of his wrinkles. "All in getting used to it. I have been reporting for service every evening at eight o'clock and working straight on till six in the morning for the past two years. It is all in establishing the habit."

Diamondstone left the elevator and took slow, lengthy steps to the door of his room. As he unlocked the door he was musing:

"It is conceivable that a left-handed millionaire might have a left-handed nephew. But it is hardly conceivable that a left-handed millionaire would—"

HE STOPPED. In the center of Diamondstone's room, bending over Diamondstone's suit case was a thick, squatting figure that spun around like an awkward dervish to confront Diamondstone. The squatting man was the house detective. He was holding a pasteboard box in his hand. His piggish eyes were squinting accusingly. He opened the cardboard box without taking his eyes from Diamondstone. Inside were golf balls.

"Golf balls," he said, as though it were most significant.

Diamondstone nodded. He went over and took the box from the house detective's hands. Apparently he removed one of the golf balls. His blue eyes had the chilly sparkle of chipped ice.

"Oh, for the privileges of a house detective," he murmured. "Golf balls. What of it? Your deductive sense dictating that these are left-handed golf balls taken from the left-handed golf bag found in Room Thirty-one? Highly inaccurate deduction, my unpleasant sir. These are magical golf balls."

"None of your lip!" The house detective's voice was so low that the vibrations of his vocal cords were almost countable. He stood up.

Diamondstone surveyed the man from top to toe.

"Remarkable specimen of bulldog!"

"I've had my eye on you, Diamondstone," the house detective growled. "And I think you and I will take a little trip to the station house. A one-way trip for you."

"What have I done?" asked Diamondstone innocently.

"I think you killed a man!" the thick-bodied detective thumped out. "I was standing out in the alley about the time the murdered man was brought in. It was dark back there. I couldn't see much. But I did hear a window on the third floor open. A man came sneaking down the fire-escape. When he got to the alley, I was all primed to collar him. But he must have seen me, for he said to some one: 'There is a man standing over there. We'll have to beat it.' I tried to nab him, but he gave me the slip."

"How very awkward of you," Diamondstone said.

He held the golf ball at arm's length, flicked his finger, and suddenly it became two balls. Then without his hand even approaching the body, he flicked his fingers again and there were three golf balls. It was a little confusing to the house officer, for just as he was about to decide that this was accomplished by means of half shells, Diamondstone tossed the three balls from hand to hand, proving their solidity.

"Don't be funny," snapped the house detective grumpily. "Because you were the guy who sneaked from the fire-escape. I recognized your voice."

Diamondstone stood like a statue, right hand outstretched, three golf balls held between widespread fingers.

"Uh-hum," he said, his voice silky. "My voice. And I suppose there is nothing I could do to convince you that I was not in the alley and that I did not come down the fire-escape? Ah, I see there isn't."

"You're damned right there isn't! You came out of the window of Room Thirty-one and I'm taking you up for murder!"

The detective's right hand went to his pocket to obtain either gun or handcuffs. Diamondstone didn't bother to find out. His blue eyes shifted suddenly toward his outstretched right hand. With tantalizing slowness, his fingers flexed and the hotel detective saw four golf balls where there had been three.

Then there was something like an explosion. All the volcanic energy in Diamondstone's big body seemed vented at the same time. The house detective received a close-up of the golf balls that left a lasting impression as hand and balls connected with the side of his face. The blow sent him reeling backward, but not far because Diamondstone's left foot was curved behind his ankles. He tripped, sat down heavily, then flattened to his back as Diamondstone landed on top of him.

All the oaths in the house detective's system were corked in by a golf ball that wedged in between his jaws. It was small wonder that he didn't swallow the ball, for a left hook to the temple drove him into the realm of all things black.

Five minutes later Diamondstone had the man bound and gagged in a manner that would have defied the efforts of an escape artist. Then he lugged the house detective to the closet and locked him up. And all this he carried out with smooth precision that displaced scarcely a single red-gold hair.

"SO," SAID Diamondstone almost angrily, "I was in the alley, eh? I was sneaking down the fire escape, was I?" And he plunged across the room and out into the hall.

Charley's elevator dropped Diamondstone to the lobby. He strode across to the phone operator to discover that his twenty-dollar bribe had borne fruit. Dulcy Madden had called the desk every five minutes to see if there had been any calls for her or any messages from a man named Smith. And there had been no messages, and no calls and Dulcy had resorted to calling the operator names.

Oscar Porter, the bald attorney, had received a phone call from a man with a crackling voice. The phone operator had gathered that the man with the crackling voice was rather angry with Mr. Porter. And, the operator said, if Diamondstone hurried he might be able to catch Mr. Porter who had just that moment gone out of the front door.

Out in the street, Diamondstone saw Porter's shiny dome tinged from the red of a neon sign in a shop window. The man was walking along with swift, jerky, furtive steps. He turned at the corner and kept right on going for about seven blocks. At the mouth of the alley, he stopped, looked around. Diamondstone jumped into a doorway, so there was nothing more alarming than a milk truck in the street. Porter entered the alley.

Diamondstone followed, saw Porter unlock the door of a small private garage. Inside was a queer, top-heavy appearing coupé. Diamondstone sprinted to the door of the garage, waited until Porter was in the act of getting into the coupé, then sprang to the wood-railed trunk rack on the back of the car.

The height of the queer coupé was a boon to Diamondstone for, as he backed the car out, it made it impossible for Porter to see the magician-sleuth's big body.

Once out of the alley, the old coupé roared down the street and cut across town with many a crazy twist and turn that threatened to dislodge Diamondstone at any moment.

The car slowed up and pulled toward the curb in a shabby, narrow street. Diamondstone bounded off the luggage carrier, sprang to the sidewalk and tried to conceal himself behind a lamp post.

Porter got out. He didn't look around this time, but plunged desperately into the gruesome task ahead of him. He pulled open the rumble compartment of the car, stood on the fender, tugged and strained at something that was cramped within. He got the something to the edge of the rumble, got down off the fender, hauled the something to his square old shoulders. Staggering beneath the weight of his burden, he approached the door of a dingy lodging-house.

Diamondstone took a long breath that whistled softly. For Porter's burden was very like the body of a man.

Diamondstone started down the sidewalk as soon as Porter had disappeared. He passed the old coupé, paused, turned around and stared at it.

"Left-handed," he muttered. "One of those old British cars with the steering-wheel on the right side. And no wonder!"

He crossed the street toward the door that had swallowed Porter and his dead and dangling burden.

CHAPTER IV

MURDER BY MISTAKE

DIAMONDSTONE BEGAN mounting the steps of the lodging house, his violin case-sized shoes making unbelievably little noise in the grey light of the upstairs hall, he saw Porter knocking at a door with one hand while he clung to the dead thing with the other hand.

Before the door opened, Diamondstone sprang up behind Porter. Porter half turned. His eyes glazed with fright. His burden slipped from his shoulder to flop disjointedly to the floor.

"Pick it up," ordered Diamondstone.

"No—no! You don't understand. It—it—it's—"

Diamondstone stooped, seized a fleshy-feeling arm of the figure on the floor and pulled it upright. He looked down into the face of the thing—a face that was startling with the bright, happy expression cleverly painted on its wooden features. For the figure was a life-size dummy, beautifully proportioned and weighted by one of Europe's cleverest craftsmen.

The door of the room opened. Clinging to the knob was a man whose proportions approached those of a toothpick, he was that thin. His face was smudgy-looking, narrow; his features sharply defined. His single live eye clashed with Diamondstone's blue gaze. He uttered a chain of oaths that required scarcely any movement of his thin lips.

"Go in," Diamondstone ordered Porter. Then he followed the frightened bald man, dragging the gay-faced dummy along with him.

Porter dropped wearily into a chair and patted his perspiring head with a handkerchief. Diamondstone and the thin man glared at one another over the head of the dummy.

"Marcini, the Great Gabby," said Diamondstone quietly. "You gabbed too much when you imitated my voice in the alley after pulling off that gruesome stunt in Room Thirty-one of the New Regent."

"You two know each other?" Porter gasped.

Diamondstone nodded gravely. "I've known Marcini, the ventriloquist, for a long time. We were in vaudeville together. We had an act once until various members of the show discovered that someone was looting their dressing rooms. Marcini was doing the looting, but his uncanny ability to impersonate my voice came near to bringing me to take the rap Marcini should have had. But it looks as though I am going to square things up a bit now."

Diamondstone tossed the dummy to the floor. Its carved face showed no resentment at such treatment.

"Now," said Diamondstone, "talk. Because if you don't, I will. And I'll do my talking to the police."

The glass-eyed man sprang at Porter. "I didn't have anything to do with this, hear me, Diamondstone? This guy did it all! He tricked me into doing his dirty work. He said he wanted to borrow my dummy and use me to play a joke on a friend. What he said he was going to do was take my dummy, put enough lead shot in it so that it would weigh about what a human would, dress it up in some different clothes, and muffle its face. Then I was to take the dummy, as if it was a drunk guy, to Room Thirty-one of the New Regent. He said his friend would think the dummy was a corpse when he tried to move it. And I'm damned if that wasn't what it was—a corpse!

"This guy drove me and the stiff I supposed was my dummy right up to the front door of the hotel. Then I got out with the supposed dummy and that damned golf bag on my back. He gave the car the gun, and there I was."

The glass-eyed man looked as though he was on the point of bursting into tears.

"You know that dummy of mine, Diamondstone. It's almost human in form. And I supposed this guy had weighted it down. I went into the lobby, lugging that damned body, thinking it was the dummy, honest to Gawd. And this guy was going to give me five hundred berries for the joke. I was to act like this dummy was a drunk friend. I double-voiced it; made it sound as though the thing I was lugging was singing. By the time I reached the elevator, there was cold sweat all over me. I'd got a glimpse of the thing's hands. And then I knew it wasn't a dummy, but a damned stiff. I liked to have a fit, but what the hell could I do?"

"Um-hum," said Diamondstone. "You were in a nice fix. You had to get rid of the corpse, and the best way was to carry out your instructions. You dumped the corpse and golf bag in Room Thirty-one and slipped out the fire-escape. Thought you were going to be caught by the house dick, so you 'double-voiced' again—imitating my voice, because you knew that I was at the New Regent. That was a rat's way out!"

Diamondstone turned to the bald man who was shriveling down into the chair. The magician-sleuth's blue eyes darted like rapiers of lightning. He was speaking rapidly now and all the softness had gone from his voice.

"It's conceivable that a left-handed millionaire might have a left-handed nephew. But it takes a long stretch of imagination to bridge the gap between a left-handed millionaire in Australia and a left-handed attorney in Detroit. A short time ago I discovered that you tear paper matches from the left-hand side of the book. That indicated left-handedness.

"Later, I created a little bonfire with Miss Devon's handkerchief. You were careful to take the handkerchief in your right hand, thus concealing your left-handedness. But when the handkerchief burst into flames you became excited. Then it was your left hand that served you best in drawing water to put out the fire. Eccentric as Mr. Paget might be, I don't think that he'd insist on employing a left-handed man as his attorney in far-away Detroit. So I think you've a lot of explaining to do, Mr. Milton Markland Paget!"

The bald man gulped air like a beached fish. When he at last could speak, it was in a husky, old-man's whisper.

"YOU'RE RIGHT. I am Paget. But I haven't killed anyone. I have been in Detroit two weeks. Realizing that I was in the same town as my two heirs, I used an assumed name, discarded everything I thought might be used to identify me, except my old car. You may have noticed it has the steering wheel on the right side. I have driven that type car so long I simply could not change to another type. But to avoid being identified by that car, I kept it in a private garage.

"I always feared that as soon as I returned to the United States I would be murdered. I was deathly afraid of my two heirs. They would, by killing me, become wealthy. And one of them"—he pounded on the arm of his chair—"is a murderer! One of them did attempt to kill me, but killed my golfing companion by mistake. You realize how this might have happened, since neither of my two heirs had ever seen me, but might have identified me by my car."

Diamondstone's brows knotted. "Who was your golfing friend?"

Milton Paget pounded furiously. "Immaterial! I met him at golf this afternoon. We played until nearly dark. I said I would give him a lift back to town. He, out of curiosity, said he'd like to drive my foreign-made car. I told him he might. Just outside the golf grounds, I discovered I had left my wallet back at the clubhouse.

"Realizing the difficulty of turning such a large car around in so small a compass, I told him to wait while I went back on foot, recovered my wallet, returned to find another car, which had been standing beside mine, speeding off down the road. I found my companion slumped across the steering wheel, dead. I knew instantly that some one had mistaken him for me.

"I should have summoned the police, but that meant revealing myself and thus indicating that I still lived, which would only have exposed me to the killer's gun. I remembered that Marcini person I had seen on Jefferson Avenue, putting on a ventriloquist act in the street in order to sell some pitchman's catchpenny device. I had marveled at the lifelike qualities of Marcini's dummy. I contacted Marcini and asked him if he wanted to earn five hundred dollars. He was willing. He has told you how I tricked him into placing the corpse in my nephew's room.

"I concealed the body in the rumble seat of my car. In the garage, I dressed it in a suit of my clothes, added the cigarette lighter which I had never used, put a pencil in the left hand and added the left-handed golf clubs, all with the idea that the body might be mistaken for mine. Having thus established my own death, I thought myself in a better position to discover the identity of my would-be murderer."

"And why put the corpse in Lahern's room?" asked Diamondstone.

"Because Lahern has the best possible motive for killing me," declared Paget. "Lahern is in a tight jam. Lahern has a wife in Chicago. That

Dulcy Madden is roping him in; intends to obtain blackmail money from him under threat of revealing everything to Lahern's wife. I thought surely when Lahern discovered the body of the man he had killed, now moved to his own room, he would do something to reveal himself. I am still convinced that Lahern's drunkenness is merely an act to hide emotions that would reveal him as my murderer."

"Please," said Diamondstone, "you are not quite dead, yet. And it has never occurred to you that Dulcy can't hope to collect much hush-money from Lahern unless Lahern inherits your fortune. So you can't limit your suspects to Lahern and Miss Devon. Dulcy Madden had as good reason as anyone for wanting you dead. And, in all probability, since Dulcy is a blackmailer, she has a male crook in cahoots with her. That's the way that racket is worked."

Diamondstone slid a slow glance at Marcini. Marcini's thin right hand flicked into his pocket and jumped out again. There was a heavy revolver in his fist.

"DON'T LOOK at me, Diamondstone! I didn't have a thing to do with this, but you'd frame me for the whole business. I'm getting out of town. Stop me, and I'll kill you, so help me."

"So help you?" Diamondstone looked worried. "Would you need help? Ah, but I see you would, judging by the way your hand is trembling." Diamondstone extended his right arm. With his left, he apparently tugged up his coat sleeve a little. "You are about to witness the marvelous production of a golf ball, Mr. Paget."

But the production of one of those golf balls he had taken from the hotel detective was for the sole benefit of Marcini who had doubtless witnessed the trick before. Nevertheless, Marcini had never expected it to conclude the way it did.

No sooner had the golf ball materialized at the tips of his fingers than Diamondstone threw it with something like bullet speed straight at Marcini's head. And scarcely slower than the ball, Diamondstone's big body was launched at Marcini. While Marcini ducked the ball, Diamondstone closed in, seized Marcini's unsteady gun wrist and wrenched the revolver from his grasp.

At the same time, Diamondstone's left fist connected with Marcini's pointed chin. Marcini reeled backward, clutching at things. Nothing but the wall of the room prevented him from going down on the floor.

"Now, my lads"—Diamondstone waved the revolver—"back to the New Regent where undoubtedly Sergeant Sundeen will welcome you with open arms. Or should I say open handcuffs?"

CHAPTER V

THE SECOND
DEADLY ERROR

WHEN **DIAMONDSTONE** marched Ventriloquist
Marcini and Milton Paget across the lobby of the New Regent
Hotel, Sergeant Sundeen pointed a finger at Marcini shouting:

"The thin man with the glass eye!"

Then, without so much as a thanks to Diamondstone for delivering
Marcini into his hands, Sundeen set off to the manager's office, bent on
grilling his new catch.

Diamondstone would have been in on the grilling if for no other
reason than to annoy Sundeen by crunching peanuts had it not been
for Violet Devon. The girl spied Diamondstone almost as soon as he
entered the door, and came toward him with quick, firm steps, a worried
frown spoiling the smooth beauty of her face.

"You want to see me?" Diamondstone asked. "But I see you do."

"Please. Somewhere where we can be alone. This is dreadfully important."

Diamondstone took her arm and guided her across to the coffee shop,
deserted this early hour of the morning. He noticed her slight nervous
flutter as they entered the room. He drew out a chair for her, then seated
himself at the other side of the table.

"This will only take a minute," she said, digging into the depths of a
plain handbag. She took out an envelope and placed it in front of Diamondstone. "Open it," she urged.

Diamondstone did as he was told. Inside was a pencil-printed message:

> Meet me in Room 69 at 5:30 A.M. and you will learn something
> about the Paget money.

There was no signature. Diamondstone gave the sentence, the paper,
and the envelope his closest attention. He said: "Damn it!" quite sharply,
then looked a little sheepishly at the girl.

"Don't apologize," she said, "I said damn it, too. It looks as though
it were written by a left-handed person, doesn't it?"

Diamondstone's face went blank. "Why?"

"That smudge up in the right-hand corner of the paper. It looks as though some one held the paper down with the right hand while writing with the left."

Diamondstone shook his head. "That isn't a thumb print. It's just a smudge. I don't know whether that means anything or not. But did you notice this envelope? It's been opened, then glued shut again. Who else has read this message?"

"I noticed that," the girl said. "I found the envelope sticking under my door. A good half of the envelope was out in the hall, so any one might have picked it up, opened it, resealed it."

Diamondstone looked at his watch. He got up.

"What are you going to do?" demanded the girl.

"Keep your appointment for you before somebody else does. It's five-thirty now."

He entered the lobby and strode to the elevator. Violet Devon was running to keep up with him.

"Charley!" Diamondstone seized the operator by the shoulder. Charley was propped up on his padded stool, stealing a few winks of sleep. He opened his withered eyelids and peered up at Diamondstone. He slid from the stool. "Third, sir?" he asked.

"No, Charley. Sixth."

"Sixth?" Charley looked from Diamondstone to Violet Devon. "But the rooms on the sixth are being remodeled. There's no one up there."

"Possibly not," Diamondstone said. "But possibly the murderer. Hurry!"

Charley leaned over on the starting lever. The cage began its creaking, rheumatic crawl upward. Somewhere, the elevator signal buzzed.

"DON'T STOP at any floor," Diamondstone ordered. "Straight to the sixth!"

The cage crawled past the third floor. Then the fourth, where one of Sundeen's detectives yelled for it to stop. Then halfway between the fourth and fifth floors, the cage jerked to a stop that sent Diamondstone and Violet Devon lurching into one corner.

"Matter, Charley?" Diamondstone rapped.

"Stalled, sir. Somebody must have cut the power!" Charley leaned over the control, jammed at the lever. Then he turned his wrinkled face toward Diamondstone. Fear enlivened his usually dull, sad eyes. "We— we can't go up or down, sir. Stalled. I—"

From the upper reaches of the old hotel building came a roar like that of a cannon, and echoing it came a shrill cry of agony. The elevator signal buzzed impatiently, seemingly from all floors at once. Police whistles skirled. Doors slammed. Women shrieked hysterically. On the floor below, the police detective was cursing fluently.

Violet Devon wrung her hands. "Can't you do something? We're caught like rats in this cage. Won't it start down if it won't go up?"

Charley jammed at the cranky lever again. A jerky throb of power surged through the car. It groaned, then worked into a steady climb to bounce to a stop at the sixth floor.

Diamondstone sprang out with Charley and the girl close behind him. There were no lights in the hall. He jerked out a flash and sent its white beam glancing from painters' ladders to scaffolding. Dodging around workmen's materials, Diamondstone gained the end of the hall and Room Sixty-nine. The door was open; the flashlight beam misty with acrid gun smoke. And on the floor—

Diamondstone whirled. His flashlight beam picked out the faces of Charley and the girl. He seized Violet Devon and thrust her into Charley's arms.

"Get her out of here!" he whispered tensely. "This isn't a nice murder at all!" Then he turned and entered the room.

Lashed to a piece of scaffolding about four and a half feet above the floor, was a sawed-off shotgun of large gauge. Diamondstone's keen eyes saw the length of cord attached to the trigger; saw where the cord ran through steel screw-eyes to connect to the door.

Centering a rapidly growing pool of blood was the body of a woman, lying face down. Diamondstone knelt, rolled the body over slightly. A sensation of nausea passed through his big body as he saw a bleeding, shot-torn breast and the look of agony death that had frozen on the face of Dulcy Madden!

Beside the woman was a handbag. Diamondstone picked it up. His ever-deft fingers rifled it, crammed the contents into his pocket. He took another quick look around the room, backed through the door.

Diamondstone swung his light on the girl and Charley. Their lips formed silent questions.

"Dulcy Madden," Diamondstone said softly.

"Dead?" whispered Charley.

"Dead," said Diamondstone flatly. For a moment, he stood there, listening to the pounding of feet on the stairway and the continual buzz of the elevator signal. Then he pulled from his pocket the contents of Dulcy Madden's handbag—compact, change purse, handkerchief, a crumpled piece of paper, a little photo frame.

"Then—then," Violet Devon stammered, "it must have been Dulcy Madden who—who opened that note intended for me. She must have come here before we did. And she met the—the death intended for me!"

Diamondstone jerked a nod. He turned the photo frame over. Beneath the glass was the picture of a man and a woman locked arm in arm, smiling as they had smiled in life and never would smile again. For the woman was Dulcy Madden. And the man was the *unknown*—the unknown corpse of Room Thirty-one!

Hastily, Diamondstone returned the picture to the bag. Then he unwadded the crumpled bit of paper. His blue eyes were shining, seeming to look through and through the maze of mystery.

"We're beginning to get somewhere," he said softly.

For the paper in his hand was a copy of the typewritten note that Violet Devon had found beneath her door. Exactly alike were the two notes that had named the deadly rendezvous, except that the note he had taken from Dulcy's handbag had an inked notation at the bottom: "Burn this!"

Diamondstone pushed the note, the compact, the handkerchief and the change purse back into the murdered woman's handbag. He started toward the elevator.

"Where is—No! Wait!" He stood there poised on his toes, his right forefinger pointing stiffly toward the ceiling. Then his finger, his whole body relaxed.

"Oh, hum," he sighed. "I'm afraid we aren't beginning to get somewhere. I'm afraid we have arrived!"

CHAPTER VI

THE MISTAKEN MURDERER

DIAMONDSTONE LEFT the elevator at the fourth floor. Violet Devon was directly behind him, though he scarcely paid any attention to the girl.

His jaws moved slowly, thoughtfully, grinding peanut kernels. He went to the door of his room, opened it. His eyebrows drew slightly together as he entered the room.

Sergeant Sundeen was there. There, too, was the house detective, rubbing ankles gone stiff from Diamondstone's bonds, and working his swollen jaw painfully. Sundeen was using the phone. He hung up when Diamondstone came in.

Diamondstone stood aside for Violet Devon to enter.

"Quite a reception," he said. He looked from Sundeen to the house detective. And he smiled his one-sided, secretive, magician's smile.

"The boys are going to bring up Mr. Paget, Mr. Lahern and Marcini for more grilling," Sundeen said. "This business isn't going any further. I suppose you know the Madden woman was killed?"

Diamondstone nodded.

"I thought you would know," said Sundeen. He examined Diamondstone out of the corners of his eyes. "Diamondstone, I've been listening to Ruckle, here." He indicated the house detective. "And I think we've got you right where we want you. You were seen in the alley—"

"I beg your pardon," Diamondstone interrupted. *"Heard* in the alley. Didn't Marcini explain how he had tried to frame me to keep his own nose clean?"

"No," said Sundeen, "he didn't. Anyway, it's going to take a lot of explaining to clear yourself of assaulting Ruckle."

"Well, he was very much in my way, for one thing," said Diamondstone. "If you think you have evidence against me, bring it into court. Right now, listen to this:

"Miss Devon received a note which asked her to come to a room on the sixth floor where a set gun was waiting to kill the first person who entered the room. A note, mind you, that seemed to have been tampered with—tampered with by Dulcy Madden, since it was she who kept the appointment with the murder machine. Apparently, here was another murder by mistake, since Dulcy was killed instead of Violet.

"The whole thing seems to have been a series of mistakes. Paget made a grave mistake when he claimed the murderer was after his money. You made a mistake by accusing me. We have all made mistakes—all except the murderer; for there has never been a shadow of a doubt in his mind as to what he wanted to do. And he did it!

"Apparently, the first murder was a mistake. It seemed that a man, mistaken for Paget, was killed. But that appearance of error was fabricated by Mr. Paget, himself!"

"Good Lord!" gasped Sundeen. "You mean—"

"Wait," Diamondstone interrupted. "Since we were all ready to believe that the first victim met death by mistake, the murderer tried to make it appear that the second murder was also a mistake, thus leading us further and further from the real motive of both crimes. The note the killer sent to Miss Devon he first sealed in an envelope, then broke the seal himself to make it appear as though someone—the 'mistaken' murder victim—had tampered with the note.

"Then the killer sent a second copy of that same note to Dulcy Madden, to make absolutely certain that Dulcy did what, *apparently,* someone wanted Violet to do. But the killer requested that Dulcy Madden burn the note. Why? Well, if Dulcy had burned the note, we would have deduced that it was Dulcy who had opened Violet's note, gone to Room Sixty-nine, and been murdered by the set gun which was intended, apparently again, for Violet. Actually, that note attracted Dulcy more than it did Violet, simply because Dulcy Madden *was* after the Paget money, via the blackmail route."

"I see," said Violet Devon. "And with two murders, one which looked like a mistaken effort to kill me, and the other looking like a mistaken effort to kill Uncle Milton, the blame would probably have fallen on Stewart Lahern, his motive being an attempt to control the Paget fortune."

"VERY GOOD," said Diamondstone, smiling at her. "Now, Sundeen, having come to the conclusion that the murderer killed the two people he wanted to kill, Dulcy and her partner, the man found in Room Thirty-one, thanks to Mr. Paget, things clear up at a remarkable rate. Dulcy's partner we'll call Smith, since that is the name of the man she had been trying so fruitlessly to contact.

"Dulcy and Smith were blackmailers. Dulcy was laying ground for blackmail by getting Lahern fogged up to make violent love to her, when Lahern had a wife of his own. At the same time, Smith was cultivating Paget's acquaintance, because it had to be through Paget that Lahern obtained the money to pay the blackmailers. Smith may have recognized Paget by means of a picture in some golfing journal, or simply through that gentleman's left-handed eccentricities."

"Say," Sundeen mused, "that's a new angle. That gives both Paget and Lahern motive for killing the blackmailers to get rid of them."

"I doubt if the blackmailing had reached such a point that murder was necessary," Diamondstone said.

Looking across the hall, Diamondstone saw the elevator door slide back. Out came Lahern, looking as though his head ached. He was followed by his bald uncle, Milton Markland Paget, and Marcini, the glass-eyed ventriloquist. They were accompanied by several police.

"What is the, meaning of this?" demanded Paget.

Diamondstone chose to look over the millionaire's head. He called the elevator operator.

"Just wait a moment, Charley, because we'll all be going down in a minute—with our murderer. No, on second thought, I wish you would step in here a moment."

THE WRINKLE-FACED elevator operator crossed the hall to stand wonderingly in the door.

"We're in something of a quandary," Diamondstone went on. "We have in this room a murderer who makes intentional mistakes to delude us. And it's all a bit difficult to separate the intentional mistakes from the unintentional ones, especially inasmuch as our mistaken murderer's last mistake was to save a life and insure another mistake. Er—am I being too obscure? But I see I am. The thing is, two people are about to be badly disappointed. Mr. Paget will be disappointed to learn that his money was not the motive for the murders of Smith and Dulcy Madden. And the murderer will be disappointed to know that he's apprehended.

"The murderer who took advantage of mistaken ideas we had concerning the first murder, to fabricate evidence that would make it appear as though Dulcy Madden was also killed by mistake, spilled his pot of beans when he insured the fact that Violet Devon could not possibly fall into his murder trap even though it appeared to have been set for her.

"To insure Miss Devon's safety, and consequently Dulcy's death, the murderer simply suspended Miss Devon halfway between heaven and earth in a brass-barred cage, canary fashion. By that I mean that when the murderer saw Miss Devon walking into the trap he had *apparently* set for her but had *actually* set for Dulcy Madden, he simply stalled his elevator between floors until the roar of that set-gun announced Dulcy's death! At which time, Charley, your elevator miraculously toiled on its weary way upward."

Charley wilted over against the door frame. He looked white and sick.

"You mean my money had nothing to do with this?" Milton Paget said.

Diamondstone nodded his head. "I am afraid your heirs are not up to murder, Mr. Paget. I frequently remarked that Charley seemed a man above his station, as indicated by his education and cultured speech. If I were to do a bit of guessing, I would say that the blackmail team of Madden and Smith brought Charley quite a way down the social ladder years back, by some insidious scheme. Right, Charley?"

Charley's body stiffened. His right hand moved with a speed such as even Diamondstone seldom surpassed. And in that hand was an automatic that threatened everyone in the room.

"Don't move, any of you!" Charley whispered. "I can use this with deadly accuracy, as the death of Delmar Smith would seem to indicate. I am not through yet. Down in Joliet Penitentiary is the third member of the Dulcy Madden blackmail group. I want to live to kill that third member, even if I have to kill him in prison. And I will surely kill anyone who tries to stop me." Charley's eyes were shrewd pinpoints gleaming in squinted, wrinkled eyelids.

"My wife," he said quietly, "was the victim of their rotten scheming. I need not name her. You have all forgotten her name by now, but once it gleamed in lights above the finest theaters in the country. Dulcy Madden and her two associates held information that would have plunged my wife's name in a slough of scandal. God, it was a rotten game they played! They forced her into retirement, bled both my wife and me of every penny we had. Poverty killed my wife! Is it any wonder that I pay them back in their own bloody coin?" Charley's eyes flashed to Diamondstone. "No tricks," he warned.

Diamondstone had removed a white linen handkerchief from the breast pocket of his coat and was daubing at his perspiring forehead. He smiled disarmingly.

"Just blotting up some of the excretion of agitation, Charley. You see, you promised to shoot any one who moved, and I'm just afraid that sooner or later I'm going to move."

Diamondstone's right arm extended full length and on the palm of his extended right hand the linen handkerchief peaked. With the tips of the fingers of his left hand, he took hold of the handkerchief at its peak and whisked it into the air.

It would have taken more self control than Charley had, not to follow that soaring handkerchief with his eyes. What he should have discovered was that in the palm of Diamondstone's right hand, where there had been nothing, was a diminutive automatic, produced quite simply from a concealed pocket in the white linen handkerchief.

So it was that when Charley shot at Diamondstone, he heard the roar of his own shot a split second after the terrier-bark of Diamondstone's little gun. Diamondstone's bullet tore into Charley's right arm. But Charley seemed to have drilled a more vital spot, for Diamondstone's big body fell forward at full length. Yet there was much life in the magician's long arms, for his hands cupped behind Charley's knees, came jerking forward, and tumbled Charley to the floor.

And then it was all over. Handcuffs welded the hands that had killed. Police held that thrashing, vengeful body. And there was really nothing left for the killer to fight with except oaths.

Diamondstone picked himself up, his pleasant face distorted with a grimace. He was gripping his right side as though in agony.

Sundeen and the hotel detective jumped forward simultaneously to lend aid to the magician-sleuth.

"Hurt, Diamondstone?" asked Sundeen solicitously.

"Did you," Diamondstone groaned, "ever fall flat on a nest of golf balls?" He raised his coat slightly, and for half a minute, golf balls rained steadily from the edge of his coat and bounded over the floor.

The hotel dick grunted in disgust.

"So that's where you got all them golf balls. Humph! Nothing to it."

Diamondstone smiled. "The most wonderful part of all fearful and wonderful things is that very element of simplicity."

V

THE MURDER OF
THE MARIONETTE

CHAPTER I

DEATH WRITES
A LETTER

THERE WAS something about the quality of the voice on the
phone that recalled to Diamondstone a newly painted park bench,
for it was both cordial and forbidding.

He stood at the window of the Palms Hotel and listened intensely
to its musical gruesomeness.

"Furthermore," it said, "I don't think you'll like it here at Mayfair
Beach at all. Allow me to extend the invitation to leave Florida on the
next train. There are, Mr. Diamondstone, *two* universal tragedies: one
is living too long—and the other is dying too soon."

Diamondstone popped the shell of a peanut with his right thumb.

"Uh-huh," he sighed. "In your opinion, if I remain in Florida I am
not apt to experience the first of these two tragedies."

"Precisely. Should you decide to stay, as I hope you will not, you can't
escape us. Even now our all-seeing eyes are upon you. You are in your
shirt sleeves. A pair of blue braces is cutting into that too, too solid flesh
of your shoulders. With one hand you are cracking peanuts—"

Diamondstone's knees hinged. His powerful body struck the floor
hard enough to threaten the plaster in the room below. Yet he managed
to retain both phone and peanut.

The blue blaze of his eyes was focused on the window pane. A small
neat bullet hole had appeared there like a sinister eye, staring at what
would have been, a split second before, a vital portion of Diamondstone's
anatomy. The red-gold brow over his left eye raised quizzically.

"So," he muttered to himself. "The all-seeing eye is located in the
window of the hotel across the street." His firm lips curved into a suave
smile that was wasted on the transmitter of the phone.

"My!" he exclaimed. "What extraordinary hailstones you have in
Florida." His blue eyes became brittle with laughter as he thumbed his

Diamondstone moved swiftly,
grabbed for the gun.

nose at the telephone. "If your all-seeing eye can see what I'm doing now—"

Thunderously, the connection was broken. Diamondstone, avoiding the window, got over to the light switch and turned out the light. He went back to the window in friendly darkness to watch two men hurry from the front of the hotel across the street and get into a car. Two men—the one who was proficient with a silenced gun, and the other who had been speaking after the manner of a newly painted park bench.

"And I'm damned if I'm not going to put my finger into the paint just to see how much of you is bluff," Diamondstone soliloquized, as he picked up the telephone which had begun to jangle again. In another moment the phone whispered tensely in the voice of a frightened woman.

"MR. DIAMONDSTONE! Thank heaven you are safe!"

Diamondstone, with a glance at the bullet hole, remarked that he was thanking heaven most fervently.

"Come up, Miss Chartis. Hotel lobbies have bigger ears than small pitchers," he suggested.

Miss Niki Chartis drew a breath that was like an audible shudder.

"Then I'm right? It really is a murder plot!"

"Decidedly," Diamondstone murmured. "Though these killers are a little confused as to whom to kill."

He left the phone to put on his tan Palm Beach coat. He surveyed that portion of his bigness which the door mirror could handle, buffed the toes of his yellow-tan shoes, and put a little oil on the troubled waves of his red-gold hair. He then considered himself fit to meet Niki Chartis.

It had been a letter from Niki that had brought him from Indianapolis to the Florida resort city of Mayfair Beach. Niki Chartis was the younger sister of a juggler Diamondstone had been acquainted with when he had trouped in vaudeville as Diamondstone, the Great Magician. Niki's letter had been filled with bad dreams, a woman's intuition and inexpressible fear of a murder plot in the hatching. When she entered the door of his room Diamondstone was firmly convinced that hysteria was no ingredient in the delectable concoction of Niki Chartis.

She had short, fine-spun, wavy brown hair that was tucked back over her ears. Her eyebrows kept within bounds without the aid of tweezers.

She had a babyish brow, brown eyes, a nice nose. Her lips were firm and determined, her chin cut in decisive lines. She was long-legged, yet well-proportioned. There was just a hint of golden orange in the pink of her soft cheeks.

Niki Chartis was evidently a bit puzzled with Diamondstone. His height and muscular development suggested that he possessed the grace of a steam shovel, yet when he walked to the door to meet her the impression of awkwardness was at once forgotten. His stride was catlike. The slightest motion of his long-fingered hands suggested power and suppleness. And that secretiveness that made the girl want to see all around him at once was offset by the amazing frankness of his intense blue eyes.

He asked her to take a chair. "But not near the window. I find the night air particularly unhealthy."

Heedless of his warning, Niki hurried to the window where Diamondstone immediately joined her to draw her back.

"Look," she whispered. "Down there in front of the drugstore. See those men?"

There was a dark-faced, roly-poly sort of man who carried a yellow walking-stick and twirled a silken mustache.

"Louis Lheureux," said the girl. "The elderly gentleman with the pipe is Dr. Curtis Polk. And that tall, blond young man—he has the pinkest eyelids you ever saw—he's Ben Consadine. He's quite nice and artistic."

"They don't look at all like the unholy three to me, though the Frenchman is a bit devilish in his appreciation of ankles as the ladies stroll by."

"They're all staying at Hospitality House," Niki said. "They may have followed me into town."

Diamondstone was unimpressed. He could have given a number of reasons, none of which was murder, why men would follow Niki Chartis to the ends of the earth.

NIKI SAT down and crossed her knees. "I'm sorry I brought you here," she said, regarding him steadily. "I'll never be able to afford to employ a detective like you."

Diamondstone sat down on the writing desk. He picked up a four-inch square of paper, held it in both hands, and exhibited it back and front. He smiled broadly.

"Gratifying to know the aura of magnificence surrounding me," he said, as he deftly fashioned the bit of paper into a cone. Holding the cone at its tip, he gave it several smart flips with his forefinger. A bit of brightly colored silk blossomed from the top of the cone, seemed to grow until it became a beautifully embroidered Chinese silk handkerchief. Still smiling, but albeit somewhat mysteriously, he tore the empty paper cone into bits which joined the peanut shucks that littered the floor.

"Something from nothing," he explained as he handed her the handkerchief. "My services are like that. I'm disgustingly wealthy and the opportunity of serving you will increase my riches."

Niki smoothed the gay piece of silk across her knee. "It's lovely," she said in a husky monotone that Diamondstone thought would never become monotonous to him. "And you're awfully nice. I suppose there's no dissuading you."

"None whatever."

"Then I may as well tell you that about a year ago, being out of work, I noticed an ad in a paper. Men and women who were utterly alone in the world were urged to apply. Both my brother and I applied, though he used a different name and address, so that none would suspect that we were not without family connection. Both of our applications were accepted, and we went to work for the Continental Distributors Company, which sells nationally advertised products from door to door and at greatly reduced prices."

Diamondstone's red-gold brows raised, but he said nothing.

"We had good luck. The products were just about everything the consumer needs—soaps, groceries, medicines, silk hosiery, underwear, kitchen aids, even fur coats. It sounds crooked, but those who bought received plenty for their money.

"Before our applications for jobs were accepted, however, we were given rigorous physical examinations. Then, some time later, we were approached by a man whom Buddy soon discovered to be a life insurance agent."

"Er—did he have a voice like a park bench?" Diamondstone interrupted. "Ah, but I see you don't understand. Go on."

"Well, it seemed that the concern gave their employees bonuses in the form of annuities which were to make them independent in their old age. Details of these annuities were kept pretty well covered, but a man isn't apt to ask questions if someone simply requires his signature to make him financially independent in his old age.

"But my brother—you know how quick he was—caught a paragraph in the annuity contract that struck him as queer. It seemed that if the insured died before he reached the retirement age, a lump sum of thirty thousand dollars went to his beneficiary."

Diamondstone's voice was soft. "And the beneficiary was the Continental Distrib— Ah, but I see it wasn't," as Niki shook her head.

"No, Buddy had never heard of the person whose name was written in the beneficiary space. You begin to see possibilities, don't you? Well, that's exactly what happened! Several months later, while in Philadelphia, my brother was struck by a car and killed. The driver was not considered at fault because evidence pointed to the fact that Buddy was drunk." The girl shuddered.

"And that," she said with an air of finality, "made it murder. Buddy never touched a drop of liquor in his life. I read in certain books on poisons that there are a number that might have been mistaken for alcohol. So I think that Buddy was poisoned, thrown into the street, and deliberately run over for the sole purpose of collecting on the annuity-insurance policy that the firm had given him."

"And I suppose the beneficiary was an agent of your Continental Distributors, eh?"

The girl nodded. "I think so. But I couldn't bring myself to go to Philadelphia to speak to the police. First, such a move on my part would have turned the eyes of the crooked company on me and possibly have shortened my allotted span of life. Second, I was afraid of the police, because I am convinced that I have actually been peddling stolen goods. Goods stolen by my firm, of course." She grimaced.

"Hm-m. Undoubtedly. Behind the company you'll probably find the biggest fence in the country. But what brought you to Florida?"

Niki Chartis' trembling fingers opened a gaily colored purse. She took out a typed letter bearing the heading of Continental Distributors. She handed it to Diamondstone, who held it to the light.

> Dear Employee:
> You have been selected as one of those lucky salesmen to receive our extra bonus of two weeks' vacation in Florida, all expenses paid.
> When you consider that there are nearly a hundred salesmen in our employ, this is indeed an honor.
> You will be my guest at Hospitality House, Mayfair Beach, Florida. Our house party begins not later than midnight, December 10th.

The note was signed by the president of the company in a curious ink scrawl. Diamondstone's brows drew together in a scowl.

"Ever meet this president or any other official?"

"No. I have received frequent communications, all signed in the same way. But don't you see what it is? Under pretense of giving us a vacation, we will be gathered together so that we will be so much more easy to murder. After all, if we're each worth thirty thousand dollars—dead, that is— But what do you make of the signature?"

Diamondstone squinted and studied it. "It looks like 'M. Ort.' Or possibly just 'Mort'."

Some of the soft, sweet coloring left the girl's face. " 'Mort,' I think. You know, that's French for 'death'."

CHAPTER II

SHADOW ON THE WALL

THE TALL iron gates of Hospitality House closed with a clang that had about it all the quality of hopeless finality which distinguishes an interment. Diamondstone was inside those gates, fully conscious of his loneliness and of the festoons of Spanish moss which swayed lightly from the twisted tree branches like ghosts of old gallows birds. Yet the subtropic night had for him the charm of an exotic woman. It was both intoxicating and dangerous, the very qualities that lured him on.

A narrow balcony, edged with a low iron rail, belted the large, yellow brick house at its second story. The balcony extended on the south side to become a roof garden over a glassed-in porch, and there were lanterns and radio music, and the tinkle of ice in tall glasses. The house party without a host was in full swing. Here the star salesmen and saleswomen of the Continental Distributors Company were enjoying their reward, oblivious to the fact that they were worth thirty thousand dollars apiece, dead!

Diamondstone strode up the steps to the front door. The door was open and the screen unlocked. Beyond was a small hall, inadequately lighted; with its single chair. A spiral of steep walnut stairs extended to the upper story. Without preliminary, the magician-sleuth entered, a suitcase in each hand.

From the hall he went into the living room. Here was darkness unbroken, save for a square of light thrown on the wall at the south end of the room, and this square of light came from the door of the adjoining room. Diamondstone put down his bags to grope for the light switch, then paused as into the square of light on the wall stepped the shadow of a man.

Gargantuan, this shadow, and hideous in its threatening attitude. The head was a shapeless blob, except for the chin. Either the man wore a pointed beard, or the lower part of his face was masked by a triangle of handkerchief.

Diamondstone started down the long living room toward the shadow. Inadvertently he ran into a coffee table, upset it with an alarming crash. Instantly the shadow moved; an arm went up, fingers clenching about a gun. The gun clubbed down once. Then the shadow was gone.

Diamondstone kicked up with his right leg and jerked the little automatic from its clip beneath his trouser leg. Gun in hand, he entered the room where the prowler had been. Curtains of golden damask waved beside open windows. Beyond was darkness and the swaying ghosts of Spanish moss. Diamondstone ran to the French windows, stopped, turned quickly, blue eyes incredulous. Here, in this small lighted room, was the maddest of crimes he had ever witnessed. It had no *name*.

"Unless," the magician-sleuth muttered, "you could call it puppet-cide."

LYING ON the floor was a huge collapsible suitcase, wide-open. In the top of the suitcase was a collapsible miniature stage. In the bottom, on beds of cotton, reposed a number of dolls about twelve inches in height, the heads artificially fashioned of some sort of plastic material. The dolls were marionettes, for fine black threads were attached to arms, legs and heads so that they could be manipulated by a puppet master.

On a polished walnut table, one of the puppets had been stretched out, the plastic head smashed into three parts by the blow of a gun-butt. Was Diamondstone's imagination getting away with him, or was the broken head with its plastic features similar to the face of one of the men Niki Chartis had pointed out to him from the hotel window—the dark-faced, roly-poly man she had said was a Mr. Louis Lheureux? To one plastic remnant was glued a long silky mustache that certainly caricatured the fat Frenchman.

"Diamondstone—"

The magician-sleuth's eyes swerved from the table and the mangled puppet to the long stretch of damask curtain beside the French window. The curtain breathed with a muffled male voice.

"Diamondstone, you have been warned. Yet you persisted in coming here. Very well. You and I shall be playing a most dangerous game. You are going to die. Everyone within this house is to die, one after the other.

You may be the first or the last. The order is of no consequence. After the first death, possibly the police will be here. No matter. The victims shall not meet with murder. Only 'accidental death,' in the eyes of the law. And whosoever shall find it murder won't live to tell about it," the voice sneered.

"Is this a challenge?" Diamondstone grated. His gun swung toward the curtain.

"A challenge. Your skill against mine, with the reward for your victory being certain death. I advise you to lose, Diamondstone."

Diamondstone massaged the back of his neck thoughtfully. "Suppose I put an end to the game by shooting into the very center of that curtain. True, I have some slight compunction about damaging such fine damask—"

"That would be a grave mistake, Diamondstone. For it would only mean another death by accident. You would not care to be the instrument of that accident, would you?"

A shrill woman's cry keened through the mutterings of the muffled voice. The curtain billowed out into the room. The lithe form of Niki Chartis was flung from behind the curtain into Diamondstone's arms, hampering the shot he might have chanced at the shadowy figure of a man springing lightly through the open window and disappearing into the gloom.

Niki checked her scream, looked wide-eyed into Diamondstone's face. Her cheeks were pale. Red lipstick had been smeared about her mouth by the hand that had held her gagged behind that curtain.

"You saw him—saw his face?" Diamondstone whispered.

Niki shook her head. "His face was covered with a cloth. I was just going out in front to watch for you when I saw someone prowling about in this room. I slipped in behind the curtain, saw him take out that puppet of Ben Consadine's and break it there on the table. When you came in, he ducked behind the curtain. Oh! I was terrified—too terrified to scream. And then I thought you would shoot—"

"Hush," Diamondstone whispered, "someone's coming."

That someone fell over Diamondstone's suitcase, cursed softly. By the time the magician-sleuth had found the light switch in the living room, the man who had encountered the suitcase was sitting in a chair, rubbing his shins, blinking, peering up at Diamondstone through spectacled, close-set eyes.

DIAMONDSTONE SMILED placatingly. "I'm sorry to be late, Mr. Mort," he said.

"No," said he of the barked shins. "No, I'm not Mr. Mort. Just Mr. Wood, Mr. Mort's secretary." He had a futile sort of voice. "Mr. Mort has not yet arrived."

"Hm-m. I can't be too sure," Diamondstone muttered.

Wood asked to see Diamondstone's invitation. Diamondstone had the typed letter Niki Chartis had given him, and this seemed to suffice; for as the others of the house party drifted down from the roof garden, he was introduced. The name of Diamondstone seemed to arouse no suspicion and no comment. But Mr. Mort knew why Diamondstone was there, and Mr. Mort seemed to worry very little about his presence.

Diamondstone met Ben Consadine, a blond young man with pink, sore-looking eyes. It was Consadine who made a hobby of puppets. Then there was Dr. Curtis Polk, pipe-smoking Dr. Polk, who was white-haired and benevolent. He went to great pains to explain that he was not in Mr. Mort's employ, but simply a friend of Wood's.

"A very strange party," remarked Dr. Polk. "Where *is* our host? Not even Mr. Wood has met him."

"Probably Mr. Wood's very good fortune," Diamondstone muttered as he turned a curious eye on Louis Lheureux, the rotund Frenchman with black-bean eyes that threatened to disappear in mobile mounds of fat every time the man opened his mouth. There was not the slightest doubt but what the murdered marionette successfully characterized the Frenchman's face. Why? And why had Mr. Mort taken the pains to smash the puppet's face? Lheureux was fairly pushed out of the way by a sprightly little man named Morris Greenbush. Greenbush grasped Diamondstone's hand.

"Well, well, well," he said nasally, and gave the magician-sleuth's arm a pump with each "well." Then he darted off, after the manner of an uncertain honeybee, to buzz at an unattractive young woman with red hair.

Then there was Mrs. Belle Fotos, fragile in her middle age, who broke down all barriers between herself and Diamondstone with her first words.

"I'm a widow lady," she said mournfully, and this no doubt accounted for her love of sorrowful purple. Her dress was all purple, unrelieved by any ornament save knobby silver buttons marching in a soldierly line on her bosom, the third button from the top missing. She was creating something with knitting needles from yarn that was the same unhappy shade.

The unattractive redheaded girl came up to cover Diamondstone with jumps from her pale brown eyes. She gushed, the type of woman who labors to give birth to her personality. Her name was Stella Moore.

"Oh, *Mister* Diamondstone," she fluttered, "have you met our Mr. Greenbush?"

Greenbush was the honeybee man who came buzzing up again.

"Well, well, of course. Just shook hands a minute ago," he beamed. He brought his lips up into a grin that formed a U about his long, crooked nose. He was even fuzzy like a bee, for there was nothing on his head but black fuzz, contrasting with the whiteness of his scalp.

Greenbush was seeking pink-eyed Ben Consadine in his busy, uncertain manner. And when he found Consadine, he whispered in the latter's ear. Consadine lowered his head and strode into the small room where Diamondstone had conversed with the unseen Mr. Mort. A moment later, Consadine gave vent to such a remarkable selection of oaths that Mrs. Belle Fotos dropped her knitting to cram her fingers into her ears.

GREENBUSH ROMPED to the center of the room, gesticulating with his hands.

"Someone has smashed one of Mr. Consadine's dummies," he announced.

"Puppets," protested Stella Moore. "That's what they're called."

Greenbush shrugged. "So there's a difference?"

The secretary, Wood, went to look at the damage. Diamondstone heard his futile voice saying something about calling the servants and investigating.

"Investigating?" shouted Consadine, as he exploded from the little room. "My God!" The glance of his red-rimmed eyes struck like an arrow at the rotund figure of Louis Lheureux, and, like an arrow, quivered there a moment before the angry man dashed into the hall to go up the steps.

Over his shoulder, Consadine called a warning. "When you do any investigating, it will be murder!"

Then there was an immensity of silence in which all, perhaps, were vaguely aware of the unseen presence of Mr. Mort, even as Diamondstone was. Stella Moore chose to hug her thin, bare arms and complain of the chill of the air. Or perhaps she was cold with fear conjured up by the gruesome tone of a clock chiming midnight.

"Morrie," she appealed to Greenbush, "would you go up to my room and get that little jacket?"

"Sure," Greenbush said, with his U grin, and left the room. Diamond-stone approached the sweet loveliness of Niki Chartis. The others were crowding around Wood, who had just summoned a Japanese cook and a tottering old butler. Wood was asking futile questions about the broken marionette.

Diamondstone spoke behind the back of his hand. "What did Con-sadine bring his puppets for, Niki?"

"It's his hobby," said the girl. "He said he had a very special puppet show he had written for the occasion. Queer, though—when he talked about that puppet show, it wasn't as though he was offering us a treat. Something more like a threat."

Diamondstone's blue eyes wandered toward the fat Lheureux, who had detached himself from the others and was being pursued by Stella Moore and her personality. It required all of Lheureux's continental gallantry to suppress a yawn. Finally, he muttered something to the redheaded girl, broke away, and came over to where Diamondstone and Niki were standing. Lheureux was sorry to withdraw from such charm-ing company, he said, but he was going to bed.

"So early?" Diamondstone was pleasantly surprised.

"So sorree," Mr. Lheureux said, as he consulted his watch. "Seven minutes pas' midnight. Pas' my bedtime. So I muz toddle off to bed, as you say."

"Waddle is the word in your case, my fat friend," Diamondstone muttered, as he watched Lheureux move toward the hall. He whispered to Niki: "You and I know that puppet of Consadine's was smashed as deliberately as though the smasher had contemplated murder. What's the answer? From what you've told me of your brother's death, I hardly think Mr. Mort needs practice at murdering. Besides, he'll contrive accidents. Think of the potential wealth Mr. Mort has in his hundred employees, at thirty thousand a head—"

"I'm going to bed," Stella Moore announced loudly.

DR. POLK yawned comfortably. "At ten after twelve? Indeed, we'd all be wiser if we did. Odd our host hasn't showed up."

"Say, the night is still young," declared Morris Greenbush, as he came flying into the room with Stella Moore's jacket. "How about a game of cards, Doctor? And you, Mr. Diamondstone?"

Diamondstone smiled mysteriously. "Hm-m. I don't think you'd care to play with me."

"Well, if you insist, Morrie," Stella Moore tittered, "you and I could have a game of double solitaire."

Mrs. Belle Fotos sniffed disgustedly. Then she and her knitting got up and tramped to the stairs. Dr. Polk had retired. Wood had dismissed the servants and was on the point of going to his own room. Niki followed Diamondstone into the small room where lay the broken marionette.

"Niki," the magician-sleuth said, "you'd better go to bed. Don't undress. Lock your door. Scream at the least provocation. Not that there is apt to be provocation. Every death that Mr. Mort engineers will have to appear accidental. Otherwise, the insurance company holding the policies on his employees is apt to get suspicious. Run along, now. I've got to think."

"Can't you think when I'm around?" she asked coyly.

Diamondstone looked down into her lovely face and wordlessly shook his head. Something in his intense blue gaze brought a warm flush to her face. She felt the flush and retreated toward the stairway in an attempt to hide it.

Diamondstone went over to the table and studied the pieces of the broken marionette. Joining the pieces roughly, he made absolutely certain that the puppet's face represented the face of Lheureux, devilish mustache and all. Then he closely examined the other puppets in the suitcase. There was not the slightest similarity between the faces of these other puppets and the present occupants of the house.

Then he sat down to the methodical eating of peanuts, scowled at the wall, and listened to Stella Moore's irritating laugh and Morris Greenbush's chatter coming from the next room.

"That man Greenbush," he commented, "has more 'wells' than an oil company."

It was half-past one when Diamondstone was aroused from what threatened to be a doze by the whisper of slippered feet. There was no other sound in the house. He raised his head, eyes sharpening on a shapeless figure in—Diamondstone groaned inwardly—a purple bathrobe.

"Mrs. Fotos?" he said. "Ah, but I see it is."

She shuffled toward him, gulping her breath like a beached fish.

"I—I can't sleep," she gasped. "Just such a shock as this, the doctor said, would kill me. I—I've just come out of the hospital. A very, what you might call touchy operation. I'm not apt to stand much more of this." She withered into a chair. Diamondstone got up and put a sympathetic hand on her shoulder. There was a jarring pulse visible in her thin throat.

"Shock?" he prompted.

"Yes. I was awakened from a sound sleep by a splash. It was horrible! I knew what had happened. There was no other sound. Just that horrible splash. No floundering. The splash— And I lay there, my heart shaking the bed, too frightened to move. What Mr. Consadine said about murder got me all upset. And then the splash in the silence of the night—"

"Splash?" Diamondstone prompted.

"Yes; noise water makes when you fall into it. It's that swimming pool at the back of the house. It's right under Mr. Lheureux's window, and when I first laid eyes on it I felt something terrible would revolve around it. Don't you ever have uncomfortable hunches?"

"Uh-huh. Multitudes of them." Diamondstone started for the door. "Don't come out. I'll have a look at the pool. When did you hear this—er—this splash?"

"Oh, it seemed like hours ago. I just lay there until I couldn't stand it any longer. When everything's dark, time doesn't matter, does it?"

Diamondstone went into the hall and out the front door. He trotted silently around the house, looking up at the girdling balcony as he ran. At the back was the pool, a long oblong of water, distorting a reflected sky of quivering stars and a smeary moon. Directly above the pool, the iron rail of the balcony had been torn loose and dangled from the corner, where metal rivets persistently held it.

Then he looked down into the pool; looked beyond the rippling reflection. Down there in the cool depths was another vague moon that was motionless—the face of a human being.

CHAPTER III

THE INVISIBLE HOST

DIAMONDSTONE, STRIPPED to his shorts, stood on the edge of the pool and drank deep lungfuls of the exotically perfumed air that had somehow lost its charm. He was as dripping wet as the limp body that repeated dives had enabled him to bring to the surface.

The waterlogged corpse was that of Ben Consadine, the tall, blond man who was the fashioner of puppets. His corpse, in the cold eyes of Mr. Mort, was thirty thousand dollars in insurance money.

As soon as he had his breath, Diamondstone knelt and examined the contents of Consadine's pockets. There were the usual articles a man carries, but nothing to indicate robbery. Nothing, for that matter, to indicate murder. But then, Mr. Mort didn't murder; he arranged "accidents."

Consadine's watch, which was fully wound but not running, found its way into the magician-sleuth's pocket as soon as he had pulled on his clothes. It was when he was putting the watch away that he discovered his little automatic was missing. Diamondstone's blue eyes shifted about the moonlit area around the swimming pool.

"So," he whispered, "Mr. Mort paid my clothes a visit while I was in the water. I must be very careful to avoid anything that has the makings of an 'accident' about it."

As he hurried away from the pool, Diamondstone caught sight of a grotesque figure rounding the corner of the house. It was Lheureux, ridiculous in bathrobe and nightcap. He all but bumped into Diamondstone, who caught him by his fat shoulders. Lheureux went into gestures and a babble of French.

Diamondstone steadied the man. "Could you," he asked, "get all that frog out of your throat and start in again?"

"Mon Dieu! I have come out for a breath of air. Is not that Stella Moore enough to take one's breath? I could not sleep. I come out for a walk—"

"In your nightcap?" Diamondstone's eyes were laughing. "Were you afraid someone would see you?"

"Non, non. That was not it. I heard a splashing sound in the pool. I was wondering—"

Diamondstone pointed to the break in the iron railing of the balcony above their heads.

"I AM very much afraid this is a bad night for sleeping. Consadine, however, solved the problem of insomnia permanently. He splashed— he was not splashing—in the pool."

"Consadine? Ooh! *Mon ami, vous*—"

"Stop blubbering! Did you know Consadine?"

"Mais oui! Like three brothers—Consadine, Saunders and I. We were all in this business—from door to door selling. We were all in New York. Naturally—"

"Saunders?"

"You have not heard of Saunders? He was with our company. *Mon pauvre ami!* Saunders, he kill himself with a revolver, six, no, four months ago!"

"Hm-m. Thirty thousand dollars," Diamondstone muttered. And if Consadine and Lheureux were like brothers, Consadine's glances at Lheureux that evening had very little fraternal affection in them.

Diamondstone took Lheureux by the shoulder; took, perhaps, Mr. Mort by the shoulder. Together they returned to the front entrance of the house, where Diamondstone had had to comfort Mrs. Belle Fotos.

"And do not inform the others of the accident," Diamondstone warned. "I am going to notify the police."

"Poleez!" Lheureux squealed. His eyes fled back into the mountains of fat that socketed them.

Diamondstone, a cautioning finger on his lips, picked up the hall phone and called the Mayfair Beach police, to announce simply that one of the guests had fallen into the pool and drowned. Then he hung up and hurried up the winding staircase behind Mrs. Belle Fotos, who was whispering to the walls that her heart would never, never get over the shock.

"Which is Consadine's room?" Diamondstone asked of the French-man, who had pattered thunderously up behind him. Lheureux pointed out the room.

Diamondstone opened the door, found the room lighted, the bed undisturbed. He went through the room swiftly and into the adjacent bathroom. Then he turned to the closet where was hung Consadine's "other" suit. His long, graceful fingers searched the pockets and produced a folded manuscript, neatly typed.

"A play," he murmured. "Presumably a puppet play. The title: 'Was It Murder?' And in the cast of characters a Mr. Mort and a Joseph Saunders."

"Saunders," whispered Lheureux. "Our frien'!"

Diamondstone hurried over the script, found at its conclusion the line:

Detective: And so the suicide of Joe Saunders wasn't a suicide at all.
I arrest you, Mr. Mort, as his murderer!

"Mr. Mort!" Lheureux said in a shocked whisper.

Diamondstone's eyes rested shrewdly upon the fat man. "You are not surprised, then, that it is herein indicated that Saunders was murdered."

"But yes—" protestingly.

"Yet you are surprised that Mr. Mort was his murderer."

Lheureux pawed Diamondstone's shoulders and sputtered excitedly a moment before he could translate his thoughts into English.

"But of course, there is certainly some doubt when a man kills himself. But Mr. Mort, our employer—why would *he* do this thing?"

Diamondstone shrugged quite as eloquently as Lheureux. "We have no facts. Just Consadine's suspicions. Consadine thought Mr. Mort murdered Saunders. And—shades of Hamlet—that was why Consadine brought his puppets. He planned to put on a show here that would enable him to accuse Mr. Mort of murder through the lips of his puppets." He looked one-sidedly at Lheureux. Was the Frenchman laughing at him?

Consadine had seen opportunity for murder, as well as motive, in the life insurance contract that Mr. Mort's employees had signed. Was it that Consadine had suspected Lheureux as being the mysterious Mr. Mort? "Mort" is French for death, as Niki Chartis had said. Lheureux had been in New York at the time of Saunders' death. And if Consadine had wanted to accuse Mr. Mort of murder in his puppet play, and if he believed Lheureux to be Mr. Mort, then that explained why one of Consadine's puppets had been fashioned to resemble Lheureux—the puppet which was to play the part of Mr. Mort.

BUT DID that explain the attack on the puppet-image of Lheureux? Diamondstone didn't think so. Aloud he spoke. "No, Mr. Mort is much more thorough."

"But I do not onerstan'," Lheureux objected.

"Who," asked Diamondstone, "does?"

The magician-sleuth ran fingers through the dankness of his red-gold hair. He went to the casement windows and stepped out on the narrow balcony. He examined the iron railing. It was so rusty that it might easily have been broken by accident. And the fact that the balcony encircled the house was not helpful in eliminating suspects. Anyone might have stepped from a second-story window, got Consadine out on the balcony, and pushed him through the rusty railing and into the pool. Diamondstone stepped back into the room.

"You think this could be something—something very ugly?" Lheureux whispered at him.

"Very ugly," Diamondstone said. "But," as he recalled Mr. Mort's warning, "it is a very ugly 'accident', of course."

Below stairs the doorbell rang insistently. Diamondstone stepped out onto the front porch and closed the door behind him. Outside was a man in plainclothes and a uniformed policeman.

"Where's this fella you said was drowned?" demanded the man in plainclothes. "I'm McArthur, chief of police at Mayfair Beach."

Diamondstone pulled out a card that identified him. The chief glanced at the card.

"A private detective, eh? Anything phony about this drowning?"

Diamondstone's lips lifted at the corners. "Who am I to venture an opinion before the law has its inning? Please don't consider me as a detective at all. I am merely Mr. Mort's guest."

"I get you," said the chief. "And who is this Mort guy?"

"Considerable confusion exists as to that point," Diamondstone said. He directed them to the pool behind the house. Then he went back into the hall. Niki Chartis was coming down the stairs.

"Is something wrong?" she asked.

"It would be folly to limit the wrongness to 'something'," he said, unsmilingly. "First a marionette is murdered. Then the marionette's master—"

"Ben Consadine?" Niki came down the last of the steps quickly to stand beside him, looking very small and frightened.

Diamondstone nodded. "And when you understand the reason for smashing the puppet—well, then you don't understand it at all. Here are facts," and he ticked them off on his fingers.

"Consadine suspected that a friend of his named Saunders, also associated with this crooked concern, was murdered by Mr. Mort. Furthermore, he suspected that Mr. Mort was Lheureux. So, borrowing a plot from Shakespeare's *Hamlet,* Consadine created a marionette show in which a puppet resembling Lheureux was presumably to play the part of the villainous Mr. Mort. Consadine was counting on watching closely Lheureux's actions toward the accusations in the play to substantiate his suspicions—that Lheureux was Mr. Mort, and that Mr. Mort was a murderer.

"Now, if Mr. Mort smashed the puppet modeled after Lheureux, then Consadine couldn't put on his play. But in smashing the puppet, didn't Mr. Mort practically admit to Consadine that he, Mort, was Lheureux? He did. But in preventing Consadine from putting on his show Mr. Mort might have thought to keep the incriminating information to himself and Consadine, killing Consadine before the latter could spread it around that Mr. Mort was Lheureux."

"I UNDERSTAND now," Niki said.

"Pardon the contradiction, but I don't think you do. Because if Mr. Mort was Lheureux, wouldn't he have either stolen the puppet or destroyed it beyond recognition? I'm inclined to think that the puppet smashing was, magically speaking, misdirection."

"What do you mean?" she asked, puzzled.

Diamondstone took a cigarette from a pocket case and held it under Niki's nose.

"Let this be Mr. Mort. My left hand"—he showed it empty and then balled into a fist—"represents Lheureux; and resembles the general rotundity of his body, incidentally. Now, keep your eye on Mr. Mort, represented by the cigarette."

With great deliberation, Niki saw Diamondstone put the cigarette in his closed left fist. His right hand, fingers wide spread, dropped to his side. He shook his left fist, flourished the fingers apart, and exhibited his left hand back and front.

"The cigarette's gone," Niki marveled.

Smilingly, the magician-sleuth shook his head. The fingers of his right hand gesticulated, produced the cigarette from a thumb-palmed position in his right hand.

"That," he explained, "was misdirection. You weren't watching the cigarette; you were watching my left fist. You were watching Lheureux instead of Mr. Mort, just as he intended me to do."

"But," Niki objected, "if Lheureux was wrongly suspected by Consadine, why should Consadine be killed? More misdirection?"

"More murder," Diamondstone corrected. "Are you forgetting the awful motive behind this house party? Mr. Mort nets thirty thousand dollars for every death occurring among his employees. And, of course, if killing Consadine heightened my suspicion of Lheureux, Consadine ought to be killed first, shouldn't he? And all this misdirection is for our benefit.

"You and I heard Mr. Mort say that he was going to commit murder. We can go to the police and say: 'Mr. Mort murdered Consadine.' The police, first of all, are going to wonder how we can prove it was murder. Then they're going to ask the embarrassing question of who Mr. Mort is."

Diamondstone's voice was grim. "And we're not able to tell them anything more definite than that Mr. Mort is someone in this house. No, the misdirection is for you and me; to get us to look elsewhere while Mr. Mort is up to more hellishness."

Chief McArthur pushed open the hall door then. "Well, the guy, simply leaned too heavy on the rail up there and fell into the pool. Where are the rest of the folks? I got to see if any of them witnessed the accident."

"Upstairs," Diamondstone told him.

McArthur turned to his subordinate. "Get 'em all down here. Too bad. But it'll only take a minute."

Diamondstone turned, entered the living room, removing Consadine's watch from his pocket as he did so. The hands of the dead man's watch had stopped at ten minutes past midnight. He put the watch down on an end table and dropped into a chair beside it. So engrossed in the contemplation of the dead man's timepiece was he, that he did not notice that McArthur and Niki had followed him into the room.

"SAY, WHAT'S all this mystery?" McArthur said.

Diamondstone's head jerked up. "Mystery? Oh. I wonder if you'd have any consideration for the wish of a dying man. Hm-m—I think you would. If something happened to me, if I should disappear, commit suicide, or be unable to get out of the way of a steam roller, my dying wish, would be that you do certain things, McArthur. First, I'd want you to find out if the dead Mr. Consadine had any relatives or friends, so-called, who might cash in on a life insurance policy amounting to thirty thousand dollars. I'd like you to check with every life insurance company and nab the man or woman who makes the claim.

"There's a man in this house who isn't exactly nice. He assaulted a marionette, he stole my gun. Back in your fair city he took a potshot at me, or maybe had someone do his shooting for him."

"In Mayfair Beach?" gasped McArthur. "Why, that town's as clean as a pin."

"People," Diamondstone said dryly "have been known to get lockjaw from the prick of a pin. You'd be rather surprised to know that I believe a large business concern devoted to the disposal of stolen goods has its headquarters in your town." Diamondstone picked up Consadine's watch and started to put it in his pocket.

"What are you doing with Dr. Polk's watch?" Niki asked him.

"Dr. Polk's?" Diamondstone exclaimed.

"Look here, Mr. Diamondstone," McArthur was objecting. But all of Diamondstone's attention was on Niki Chartis.

"That watch," the girl said. "Isn't it Dr. Polk's? Anyway, he has one just like it."

Diamondstone's red-gold brows drew together. "So," he hissed.

A thumping, bumping, crashing sound came from the hall. Diamondstone sprang to his feet to give McArthur an utterly new conception of speed. A straight-arm push in the chest shoved McArthur out of the way. Then Diamondstone was gone—through the living room, around a corner, into the hall.

At the foot of the steps lay a mound of purple—inert, pitifully huddled. It was Mrs. Belle Fotos. The grey of her face matched her hair. She had changed into her purple dress. She was clutching her knitting. The five metal buttons on the bosom of her dress quivered slightly, and then stilled.

Down the stairs came McArthur's assistant, notebook in hand. He slipped on the polished stairs, propped his notebook to seize the rail to prevent himself from piling up on top of Mrs. Fotos. The man's wild-eyed stare met Diamondstone's.

"She musta slipped. Hurt?" asked the policeman.

Diamondstone dropped beside Mrs. Fotos. "No," he said huskily. "Dead. Get Dr. Polk, McArthur. You, cop! Come down here!"

Diamondstone's long fingers raked along the floor near where Mrs. Fotos had fallen. He picked up something, palmed it. The policeman joined Diamondstone. Coming down the steps were Dr. Polk, Greenbush, Wood and Lheureux. Diamondstone seized the law officer by the shoulder and pulled him into the living room. The magician-sleuth's eyes burned with the blue heat of a Bunsen flame.

"Quick," he said, "how did this happen? Who pushed the woman?"

"Pushed— Say, I was standing ten feet behind the old lady. There wasn't any other soul in the hall. I seen her slip. Didn't I slip myself?"

"I saw *you* slip. You dropped your notebook to clutch the stair-rail. Why didn't Mrs. Fotos drop her knitting and do the same thing when she felt herself slipping? Because she didn't *feel* herself slipping. She fell because she was knocked out, and in her critical condition a sharp blow to the head—any serious shock, in fact—meant death."

"Say, listen, if anybody had sapped the old lady I'd have seen it. She *walked* to the top of the stairs—"

Diamondstone left the policeman abruptly and swung back into the hall. Stella Moore had joined the others. She resembled hysteria about to happen, and it was Niki Chartis' embrace that seemed to be holding the redheaded girl together. Dr. Polk got to his feet beside the body and nodded gravely at McArthur.

"Possibly a small fracture. Undoubtedly struck the back of her head on the edge of a step in falling. A sharp blow to the brain-stem such as she received is frequently fatal to younger and sturdier persons. A woman in her condition—" He shook his head. "A most unfortunate accident."

"One, two, three, four, five," counted Diamondstone. "Five buttons on Mrs. Belle Fotos' dress. Metal buttons, round and heavy. Third button from the top is missing. It was missing last night."

"Are you mad?" demanded Wood's futile voice. His narrow face was the color of plaster.

"Going that way rapidly," Diamondstone muttered. Slowly he opened the fingers of his right hand. Nestled in his palm was a round, silvery button—the object he had picked up from the floor beside Mrs. Belle Fotos.

"Button, button, who *had* the button? Who returned it to Mrs. Fotos—so effectively?"

CHAPTER IV

HOMICIDE HOST

S MILING SLIGHTLY, Diamondstone bent over the top of a small drum table which he had monopolized as a stand for his apparatus. In the row of chairs in front of him, was the most unusual audience he had ever performed before. Dr. Polk refused to face the magician squarely, for he said he was skeptical of "tricksters." Morris Greenbush, with his impish grin, promised to be a heckler. Stella Moore was there to titter at Morris Greenbush's witticisms. Lheureux's eyes kept disappearing, for he yawned frequently. Wood, the missing host's secretary, was irritable and nervous.

Niki Chartis, perfectly aware that Diamondstone was playing with dynamite, watched him with wide eyes, and now and again stole a glance at the other spectators. It was three-thirty in the morning. The police had gone and the undertaker's ambulance had called for the bodies of Mrs. Fotos and Consadine.

Diamondstone had never undertaken any magical performance as nerve-wracking. Directly in front of him sat Mr. Mort, whoever he was. And while the others might be fooled, Mr. Mort would not be; he would see through the magic to find evidence of murder that pointed directly at him.

"I wish you'd stop this farce," snapped Wood, after Diamondstone had performed a few preliminary tricks. "You're no amateur magician, and you know it."

Diamondstone smiled. "Thank you."

"I mean," Wood went on, "that you're not just a Mr. Diamondstone. You're *the* Diamondstone. I've read about you. You're a detective, and a damned smart one. You'd have fooled me if you hadn't brought out those tricks. What's it all about? What's the idea of having us sit around here at this hour of the morning and watch you make handkerchiefs and cards vanish? Mrs. Belle Fotos was murdered, wasn't she?"

Diamondstone frowned thoughtfully as he picked up a pharmacist's mortar from the table.

"I wouldn't go so far as to say that," he said slowly. "I do believe we can say that Mrs. Fotos was urged to fall down the steps by an impulse originating outside her own body. But it would be difficult to prove, however." He paused a moment. "Now, for our next little experiment, I require a watch. A gentleman's watch," he added.

Morris Greenbush stared at those about him. "Any gentlemen in the audience?" That brought a silly laugh from Stella Moore.

"Dr. Polk," Diamondstone urged, "will you lend me your watch?"

Dr. Polk frowned. "I suppose I must." He brought a watch out of his pocket and handed it to Diamondstone. The magician-sleuth examined it closely. Niki Chartis had not been mistaken. This watch was a replica of the one Consadine had had—an expensive timepiece of American make.

Diamondstone nodded his thanks. He then dropped the watch into the pharmacist's mortar, picked up a pestle from the table and fell to work on Dr. Polk's watch, apparently.

"Here," Dr. Polk said, as he heard his watch being ground to fragments, "you can't do that to *my* watch!"

Stella Moore tittered. Lheureux stopped yawning. Niki Chartis began to pick her fingers. Morris Greenbush was annoyed. "Sit down, Doc," he said. "I've seen this one. It's a fake."

"Is it?" Diamondstone's eyebrows went up. He tipped up the mortar and poured a handful of broken glass, bent watchcase, wheels, springs and bearings into his palm.

Dr. Polk cursed. "I won't have it. Give me back my watch!"

DIAMONDSTONE EXTENDED the wreckage to him. "If you want it, all right. But I'd rather put it together for you."

"You're damned right you'll put it back together!" Dr. Polk snapped.

Diamondstone then consigned the watch parts to a paper sack, which he blew up. Oh yes, the watch parts were inside the sack. The spectators could hear them rattling. But then Diamondstone popped the sack—an explosion that caused Stella Moore to scream and Niki Chartis to jump out of her chair. But there was no rain of watch parts, nor yet the appearance of Polk's reconstructed timepiece. Diamondstone picked up an apple from the table and handed it to Wood.

"Please cut this apple open," he invited.

Wood took out his knife, fumbled it and the apple, cut his thumb, cursed.

"Here, let me do that," said Greenbush. "What Mr. Diamondstone did was to palm the watch and then stuff it into a slot in the apple. I've seen this before."

And Greenbush took the knife and the apple from Wood, halved the apple, then embarrassedly pulled his long nose.

Diamondstone began to chuckle. "What did you find inside the apple, Mr. Greenbush?"

Greenbush sat down. "Apple seeds."

"But my watch!" protested Dr. Polk.

Diamondstone took a large white handkerchief from his breast pocket held it draped over his left hand.

"My next experiment is an extremely interesting one. I spread my handkerchief over my hand, in this fashion. Then I lift it up and produce Dr. Polk's watch—"

His red-gold brows drew into a puzzled frown. He peeked under his handkerchief.

"Odd. That watch of yours wasn't a Waterbury, was it, Doctor?" He whisked aside the handkerchief to display a large, footed goblet, brimming with water.

Diamondstone put down the glass of water. He went over to Morris Greenbush and began patting Greenbush's pockets. He sighed.

"I thought you might have the watch, Mr. Greenbush." Then he returned to the table, made a pass over the glass of water. There was a *clink*—and Dr. Polk's watch suddenly appeared in the glass of water.

"YOU'LL RUIN that!" Dr. Polk shouted.

Diamondstone was looking at his own wristwatch. "I'm trying to," he admitted. "Ben Consadine had a watch just like this one of yours, Dr. Polk. I am expecting your watch to stop, due to the water getting into its movement. It should require approximately the same time to stop as Consadine's did, when it was submerged in water. What time did Consadine fall into the pool? It must have been close to half-past one this morning, when Mrs. Belle Fotos heard the splash—*one* splash, if you please. A drowning man is not apt to make just one splash, like a rock, unless the man happens to be dead before he hits the water.

"But we know Consadine was *drowned.* If he was dead before he hit the pool, he must have been drowned in his own bathtub, with the special assistance of a murderer. This murderer, sometimes known as Mr. Mort, found it safer to wait until we were all presumably in bed before going to Consadine's room, removing Consadine's body from the tub, and going out the window onto the balcony which circumscribes the entire house. Then Mr. Mort simply pushed Consadine's body over, or should I say through the rusty railing, to let it drop into the pool. Apparently, Consadine had leaned too heavily against the weak railing, and had fallen into the pool.

"And—let's see. Dr. Polk's watch when submerged, stopped in nine minutes and three seconds. Presuming that Consadine's watch stopped in approximately the same time, we know just when Consadine was forcibly submerged in the bathtub.

"To get to the second 'accident', now. Mrs. Fotos lost one of the heavy round buttons off her dress. It was Mr. Mort who found that button and recognized its possibilities as a projectile, when fired by a slingshot. A slingshot can be rather a deadly weapon. It shoots harder and more accurately than most air rifles. Now, a short while ago, just as Mrs. Fotos was about to descend the stairs, Mr. Mort fired the heavy missing button silently and with deadly accuracy at the back of Mrs. Fotos' head—a particularly vulnerable spot, since the nerve center which controls the vital functions is located there.

"Because of Mrs. Fotos' critical condition, the murderer had little chance to fail in his attempt. If he did, no harm done, because the button projectile would have aroused no suspicion. The button might have been torn from Mrs. Fotos' dress in the fall. Fortunately, I noted the absence of the button last night." The magician-sleuth paused a moment to let that sink in.

"Thus, in the killing of Mrs. Fotos, Mr. Mort used a silent, unnoticeable, if not invisible weapon, firing his slingshot from *behind* the policeman who was standing in the hall, then ducking back into the door of his room before the policeman thought to turn around. And, of course, the cop's attention would be focused entirely on the falling Mrs. Fotos."

Diamondstone smiled, bowed. "That concludes my part of the performance. Judge, jury and hangman will attend to the concluding act."

He turned quickly, went into the hall and ran up the steps. He slipped into a small closet in the center of the upstairs hall, where he had noticed an extension telephone resting on a shelf at the back. He picked up the phone.

"Police Headquarters—" Diamondstone began. A crackling sound vibrated in the receiver. Mr. Mort had moved as quick as the magician-sleuth, to cut the line.

Footsteps in the hall. Diamondstone turned quickly. The door of the phone closet, struck on the outside by a lunging form, slammed shut even as Diamondstone threw his weight against it. Again, someone had moved as quick as he. A key turned in the lock, was withdrawn. Diamondstone backed up to buck at the panel, paused to listen to a high-pitched, somehow sinister hiss.

He sniffed, looked upward. In the ceiling, four full feet above his head, was the outlet of an old-fashioned illuminating gas fixture, the origin of the hiss.

Diamondstone dropped to his knees, as a strangled cough escaped his lips.

CHAPTER V

MR. MORT
PACKS UP

FROWNING, **MR. MORT,** his features masked by a triangle of black cloth, stood in the upstairs hall. With him was a man with a cauliflower ear, and another man whose voice Diamondstone had likened to a newly painted park bench. On a little table was a long-barreled, silenced pistol. In front of the table were two sizeable trunks. Beside one trunk lay Niki Chartis, bound and gagged.

"The others lammed out of here before I could sew them up," Mr. Mort was saying. "They'll get the police and crab the whole damned act—the insurance business and the stolen goods business, too."

"If," said the man with the park-bench voice, "you hadn't smashed that puppet, Diamondstone wouldn't have upset the beans."

Mr. Mort sliced the air with his hand. "Nuts! This Diamondstone guy and the girl knew we were up to killing. I knew Diamondstone would come here, looking for murder. I knew he'd know the 'accidents' were something else, even if he didn't have proof. And until I could invent some 'accident' to remove Diamondstone, I had to keep his attention on the wrong track. So I pulled the puppet murder. If we'd stuck to the fence business and left this insurance scheme of yours alone, we'd be in the clear now."

"What you goin' to do wit' de goil?" asked Cauliflower-ear.

"You're going to put a bullet in her," Mr. Mort said. "We ship the dame's and Diamondstone's bodies in these trunks to addresses unknown." He looked at his watch. "Diamondstone has been in there with the gas thirty minutes. Get out the stiff and fit him into the trunk."

Mr. Mort took out a key and opened the phone closet. Diamondstone's big body was stretched at full length on the floor, face up, chest motionless, head toward the rear of the closet.

The murderer got hold of Diamondstone's feet and dragged him into the hall to drop him behind one of the trunks.

"You, Spike," he addressed Cauliflower-ear, "put the slug in the girl. Your gun's right over there. See that you do a better job than you did when you tried to plug Diamondstone."

"Aw, dat guy moved too damned fast," muttered Spike. He detoured around the trunk intended to be Diamondstone's coffin and reached for the gun on the table.

But Diamondstone moved much faster to save Niki Chartis than he had moved to save himself. His limp-looking legs became pistons of power that sent the trunk torpedoing to mow the legs out from under Spike. Then Diamondstone was on his knees, on his feet, a gyrating mountain of power, moving with the elusive speed of an arrow. He seemed but to brush by the table where the pistol lay. Then he whirled across the hall.

The wall stopped him. The gun he had snatched from the table halted the quick draw of the man with the park-bench voice. Diamondstone's lips curved into his suave magician's smile.

"Now all together, my children of the devil," he said. "One compact little huddle. Hands way up. Hold it, Spike; not too close to Mr. Mort. And if, in hell, you trap a man in a lethal chamber, don't forget to plug up the keyhole. I simply knelt, held my nose, glued my lips to the keyhole, then flopped down and played possum when I heard you about to open the door."

"PRETTY DAMNED smart, aren't you?" Mr. Mort said bitterly. Diamondstone chuckled grimly.

"I'm inclined to agree with you, since smartness is a matter of comparison. When I can see how dull-witted you were, I don't show up so bad, after all, do I? When you drowned Consadine in the bathtub, you forgot to remove his watch. The watch stopped at ten minutes past midnight. Watches of that type stop due to water-logging after about nine minutes, as you saw me prove. That meant that Consadine was forced beneath the water in the bathtub at about one minute past midnight.

"Later, when the household was supposedly asleep, you took Consadine out on the balcony, just outside of Lheureux's window. It was easy enough to do, when you consider the balcony runs all around the house. Like the smashing of the puppet, that was to keep me watching Lheureux, rather than you. Then you broke down the iron railing and threw Consadine's body into the pool, to make the drowning appear accidental.

"But the watch showed you up nicely. If Consadine was forcefully submerged in the bathtub at about one minute past midnight, only one person could have accomplished the job. Not Lheureux, because he didn't go upstairs until seven minutes past midnight. But at the time of the murder, Mr. Morris Greenbush was upstairs, presumably looking for Stella Moore's jacket—but actually engaged in one of his thirty-thousand-dollar 'accidental' murders. So ring up the curtain, Greenbush, and let's see you grin!"

Greenbush, alias Mr. Mort, yanked aside the mask. He wasn't grinning now. He was as ugly as a gargoyle.

Diamondstone eyed him contemptuously. "And when I pretended to look for Dr. Polk's watch on your agile person, I discovered something in your pocket that was the unmistakable shape of a slingshot—the simple device you used in shooting that hard button that resulted in Mrs. Belle Fotos' death."

The magician-sleuth's voice was ironic. "And to think that you were making love to Stella Moore! Then, if all had gone well, you'd have killed her like the rest of your star salesmen and saleswomen. Not painfully, of course— You're a sentimental rat." Greenbush snarled in impotent rage, but he was helpless now.

"And what the hell do you think you're going to do about it?" demanded he of the park-bench voice.

Diamondstone didn't answer for a moment. He was listening intently to the scream of a police siren in the distance.

"Evidently," he said, "some of the other guests of Homicide House have contacted Mayfair Beach. I really don't think I have much more to do. There are, as every life insurance agent tells me, *two* universal tragedies—living too long, and dying too soon. I don't think any of you three need to worry about the future at all. You really don't seem to have any. You see, Mr. Greenbush—Mort and Mr. Spike are going to sit on Mr. Park Bench—only he'll have wires attached—"

"And," Niki Chartis told Diamondstone, as he untied her after the Mayfair Beach police had taken charge of Morris Greenbush and his buddies, "I don't see that I have much future, either. You've lost me my job with your detecting and all."

Diamondstone frowned. "One of these days I'm going to relax. And when I do, I want you to be my secretary—so that we can take it easy together."

VI

THREE WISE APES

CHAPTER I

SNAKE AND GUN

UNTIL THAT particularly soggy spring, Diamondstone had been pleasantly unaware of the existence of a firm known as Cashel, Watson, and Tanner. After it had come to his attention, he realized that there was no prettier bit of irony in the English language than that which dubbed Cashel, Watson, and Tanner as a "law firm."

Assuredly, there was very little that was legal about the company except its name, otherwise there would have been no murder. And such were the wages of the sins of the firm that one out of every five persons who had ever had any dealings with it had just cause to murder Messrs. Cashel, Watson, and Tanner.

The firm had been brought to Diamondstone's attention by the following message which had been laid upon his desk in that portion of his magnificent hotel suite he designated as his office:

Dear Sir:
You undoubtedly recall some trouble occurring a few months ago in which this firm was annoyed by the threats of a person named Henry Jorgen, an inventor who, in his peculiar mental condition, imagined that our firm was responsible for certain losses of money and properties which Jorgen incurred.

At that time, police were instrumental in compelling Henry Jorgen to leave the city.

However, on leaving the office last night, I was followed by a man I recognized as Henry Jorgen. It is possible that he has murderous intentions toward me and my partners.

I have heard much of your ability to handle delicate and dangerous situations, from one of our clients, Mrs. Jack Lowery, whom you of course remember. I trust you will find time in the very near future to call on me so that we may discuss some means of disposing of this annoying Jorgen before he becomes dangerous.

Very truly yours,
John Watson,
Cashel, Watson, and Tanner.

There was something very unsavory, Diamondstone decided, about the word "disposing." Was it Messrs. Cashel, Watson, and Tanner's desire that he vanish Jorgen, much as he did a horse in a new magical illusion he was working on or did the word suggest that he simply murder the man?

It was because of this sinister choice of words that Diamondstone paid no immediate heed to the note, and thought nothing more about Cashel, Watson, and Tanner until some weeks later.

HE WAS dining with Niki Chartis that night at the Atrium. Niki was a very lovely hangover from a Florida house party which Diamondstone had crashed when he had discovered that murder was to be the host's chief amusement.

It was very nice with the rain at the windows and the orchestra sweetly keyed to the somnolent sounds of the night itself.

There was nothing about the dinner to suggest Cashel, Watson, and Tanner unless it was the crookedness of the corkscrew the waiter plied in opening bottles.

It seemed, almost, that he was driven to think about Cashel, Watson, and Tanner, by a missing girl named Amy Morton and her dreary-faced guardian. More precisely, he forced himself to be interested in the three lawyers to avoid being interested in the missing Amy.

Amy's guardian, a Mr. Lorin Shotwell, came upon them directly before dessert. He was a small man. His gray hair had given up its unequal struggle with destiny. Above a mouth that was like the pink stitched lips of a rag doll, was a delicate crop of fuzz that might have been blighted by a May frost. He had the merest of noses. His eyes reminded the magician-sleuth of those of a salt fish staring up through brine in a wooden pail. The lenses of the glasses he wore were approximately thick enough to serve efficiently on automobile headlights. He was the proprietor of a small jewelry store on Ohio Street.

Diamondstone reflected that Mr. Shotwell was somewhat less interesting than last night's cold mashed turnips. Some men are dramatic in their sorrow, either in their stagy cheerfulness or in their exuberant grief. Mr. Shotwell was not dramatic. "He weeps inoffensively, like a willow," Diamondstone remarked to Niki afterwards.

Mr. Shotwell borrowed a chair from a neighboring table, hitched it between his legs, and sat down uninvited. He surveyed Diamondstone's

largeness and seemed fa-
vorably impressed. He
introduced himself, and
Diamondstone invited him
to have a bite to eat. Shotwell refused the bite with
a wavering negative and an
apologetic thanks; he
might have said that he ate
nothing but his own heart
and drank only tears, he
was that sad.

**WITHOUT PRE-
AMBLE,** Mr. Shotwell
began: "It's my ward, Amy
Morton. She has been
missing for a long, long
time. She was like a
daughter to me, my
Amy—a sweet, unaffected
girl." Pause for a sniffle.
Then, "I wonder if you
could help me, Mr. Dia-
mondstone?"

He let him have a left to the
jaw and Butch collapsed.

"Uhm," sighed Dia-
mondstone doubtfully, his red-gold eyebrows drawing together above
intensely blue eyes. "Help you what, Mr.—er—Shotwell?"

"Find my Amy," he implored. "I have been to the police. They are no
help at all. They thought for a moment they were on the right track and
my pulse was quickened with the prospect of regaining my Amy. And
then, mind you, they gave me the sickening news that the Amy Morton
they were tracing had died at the age of twelve."

Shotwell inched forward with his chair so that he could rest his
pointed elbows on the table. The coat of his black suit was very shiny
at the elbows.

He must have been in mourning a long time.

"She would be about twenty-four her next birthday," he said, "dark
complexioned and very pretty. I made the police give me back her
picture."

He took out his wallet and fumbled in it.

Diamondstone glanced across the table at a worn snapshot of a little girl of somewhat less than six years of age. And from the picture his eyes traveled to Shotwell's face.

"My dear sir," his voice climbed to the peak of incredulity, "you don't mean that you expected the police to locate your ward from this picture? After all, if the child of that photo is now a woman of twenty-four—"

He let the sentence dangle because to his well ordered mind this was all too fantastic for utterance.

"I know it's hard. Very hard," Shotwell sniffled. "But think of me. She was like a daughter to me—my Amy. If you could find her—"

His grief became insupportable and he sought to bolster it with a pipeful of oddly scented tobacco. Diamondstone, who was very anxious to change the subject, commented upon the pleasant odor of Shotwell's tobacco. Shotwell took the compliment to himself, brightened a bit, and explained the aroma was due to Sarrapia beans added to the tobacco.

"I spent my early years of manhood in South America as a rancher." Lorin Shotwell explained, "and acquired the habit of adding the Sarrapia bean to my pipe mixture."

He removed a black bean, about the size of an unhulled peanut, from his tobacco pouch and gave it to Diamondstone to season tobacco with.

Diamondstone smoked nothing but cigarettes and those only when a routine of magic required it; nevertheless he accepted the bean, put it in his pocket, where it became immediately lost among the number of peanuts he had there for between-meal munching.

"Then you will take the case?" Shotwell almost beamed. "You will find my Amy for me?"

Diamondstone looked across at Niki who nodded her adorable head vigorously. Diamondstone frowned.

"I am extremely busy now, Mr. Shotwell. I have just taken up a new case which occupies all my time."

"What case is that?" inquired Shotwell. "Surely it isn't so important—"

"Ah, but it is," Diamondstone contradicted, elevating his brows. And then the firm of Cashel, Watson, and Tanner popped into his head and became the logical excuse for not starting on Mr. Shotwell's wild goose chase. "I have just agreed to do some work for Messrs. Cashel, Watson, and Tanner."

At the mention of the three attorneys, Mr. Shotwell's chair seemed suddenly to have acquired too hot a bottom. While he roasted at one end, he froze at the other; his face blanched, became rigid. He mumbled something incomprehensible, and faded away from the table. He was seen leaving the Atrium at the same time the waiter approached Diamondstone's table with dessert.

Niki nibbled disinterestedly at her crackers and Roquefort, daubed daintily with her napkin at lips that thinned perceptibly.

"Don't you have anything to do with those Messrs. Shyster, Shyster, and Shyster," she said.

"No?" Diamondstone laughed gently. "Why this sudden flare of protective mother instinct?"

"Purely selfish." Niki wrinkled her delightful nose. "If I'm your secretary, I'll expect some remuneration beside these dinners. After you're finished with Cashel, Watson, and Tanner your pocketbook will resemble a used soap-chip. There was a crack-pot inventor who got himself thoroughly plucked. People who enter the office of Cashel, Watson, and Tanner attach log chains to their watches."

NOW, UNTIL he had been warned about that illegal law firm, Diamondstone had no intention of bothering himself about it. He was extremely wealthy—he didn't know exactly how rich—and the only thing that lent spice to his existence was danger.

At the present time he saw no way of adding this necessary ingredient to his life save through an encounter with Cashel, Watson, and Tanner. So he promptly resolved to make the acquaintance of that unholy trio, in spite of Niki's suggestion that he exert himself to aid the unfortunate Mr. Shotwell.

The following evening, Diamondstone ordered his car from the garage and with Niki beside him drove out Northwestern Avenue to Maplehurst, the wooded, sloping half block that fate and fortune had allotted to John Watson.

"Mostly fortune," he mused aloud as he drove through the drizzle and drip of overhanging maples that edged a ghost-white drive of crushed stone.

Watson's house was not large but it had cost a pretty penny with its Bedford limestone walls and its green copper roof.

Diamondstone got out, his immense shoulders tented by a trench coat, held an umbrella for Niki, helped her from his aluminum-finished car.

Two other automobiles were parked in the drive and both were chauffeur driven.

"There is something magnetic about wealth," he commented philosophically, "which attracts wealth to itself."

When they reached the door, faintly illuminated by a blue globe in a copper lantern, he manipulated the heavy knocker and was ignored. So he took hold of the doorknob, turned it, and stepped across the threshold.

Niki was reluctant to leave even this drizzling dark.

"We really don't know what we are getting into," she said, joining him in the beautifully furnished hall.

"Precisely why I want to get into it," he murmured. "I did try to prevail upon you to keep yourself at home, didn't I?"

She made a face at him, told him it was bad luck to have an umbrella open in the house; which might have explained the events which followed.

From a lighted open door at his right, Diamondstone heard a voice that had the hollow depths of a cistern in it:

"It was a snake, I tell you. I saw it with my own eyes as it slipped over the sill!"

A voice that cracked said, "And he is dead? You're certain of it? Of course you're certain of it. A snake? How fantastic! It's dangerous to be alive in the same room with you, Cashel. I distinctly heard the sound of a gunshot!"

CHAPTER II

MURDER— BUT HOW?

A MAN CAME from the lighted doorway, looking squarely ahead of him. Diamondstone side-stepped politely.

"Well, hello now," he said.

The man from the doorway ran into the magician-sleuth, jolting the hard largeness of the latter with a bumper of fat that bulged at vest bottom and trouser top.

There was a quick intake of breath which indicated that the fat man had found Diamondstone difficult jolting. The fat man's eyes stared directly into Diamondstone's face and were as the eyes of the dead— protruding and staring, yet dully sightless. Quivering, squirming, sensitive fingers rambled up Diamondstone's vest and to his face. Diamondstone slapped them down.

"Here!" he cried. "I have the average good disposition, my friend, but I dislike being fawned upon."

The fat man recoiled.

"Who is it?" his sharp, crackling voice demanded. "Where are you?"

Diamondstone obtained a peanut, shucked it, allowed the hull to fall soundlessly to the thick Chinese floor covering. He tossed the kernels into his mouth and munched while talking.

"I was under the impression that I was in the house of John Watson. Intuitively, I know that I am Diamondstone. However, both impression and intuition may be playing me tricks, and I may be the most dangerous inmate in a madhouse. Why don't you watch where you thrust that tummy of yours?"

Niki Chartis jerked at Diamondstone's sleeve.

"He's blind," she whispered. "It's Mr. Tanner."

The fat man turned around, ran into a small table, knocked off a yellow pottery vase that shattered. He fumbled for the doorway, went through shouting at the top of his lungs: "Cashel, someone is here. Diamondstone, the detective."

And he groped his way to a chair into which he plumped himself, breathless.

Diamondstone stepped ahead of Niki into a book-walled library. Besides the fat man, there was another—a remarkably thin person, sort of a blond Satan with angular brows, an upturned, grinning mustache, and an ace-of-spades face. The steely keenness of the thin man's eyes were fixed upon Diamondstone.

"Mr. Cashel?" Diamondstone inquired mildly of the blond Satan. To which the blond Satan said nothing.

"You'll have to shout," wheezed fat Mr. Tanner. "That hearing aid he wears doesn't amount to much. He's just put it on, and he's stone deaf without it. That's why he didn't hear the revolver shot. Though he might have felt the recoil of the gun!"

This last spitefully accused deaf Mr. Cashel of something that was not to be considered quite the right thing.

"What's this about snakes and revolvers?" Diamondstone shouted.

"There was no revolver shot," said the blond Satan.

His gray eyes shifted to Niki and there was something in their piercing gleam that caused the girl to shrink toward Diamondstone. They were ruthless eyes he fixed upon her; they were thoughtful, too, and capable of transmitting something that was sinister and compelling.

"Tanner is as blind as a bat," Cashel said, "but his ears are acutely tuned to even imaginary noises. Naturally, he did not see the snake." Cashel's was the rain-barrel voice.

Cashel's shoulders shrugged fatalistically. His knitting-needle eyes pointed across the room toward a brown leather chair that was placed next to an open window. Diamondstone looked toward the chair. His red-gold brows soared.

"Oh, hum," he said softly. "Niki, you shouldn't be here."

A man sat in the chair by the window. Nothing could be seen of him except the top of his head, which was bald save for a rim of jet black hairs. His right arm hung over the arm of the chair and it was somehow like the pendulum of a clock that has run down. Rain splashed on the sill and bounced a thin, glittering spray on top of the man's bald head. But he minded neither the cold rain nor the intense blow-torch gaze of Diamondstone's blue eyes.

Diamondstone walked around the short, extended legs of fat Mr. Tanner. He stepped in front of Cashel and decided that it was unwise to have your back to Satan even if Satan was blond. He back-stepped until he was abreast of Cashel, but his eyes did not leave the figure of the man in the chair. Here was quite as dead an individual as Diamondstone had ever encountered.

The corpse was fat, but it was not the mutton-tallow fatness of the blind Mr. Tanner. His jowls were blue with stubble, his black brows overhanging eyes that were partly open, revealing eyeballs of blue-whiteness like a bathroom doorknob.

"Have you phoned the police?" Diamondstone asked softly.

Cashel did not hear. Tanner heard and answered, "There's no phone."

Diamondstone's scowl was frankly puzzled. He ran his long, white, magician's fingers through the waves of his red-gold hair and surveyed the luxurious surroundings from Oriental rugs to impractical arched ceiling.

"Dear me," he said quite loudly, "all this display of richness and no telephone. Was the gentleman medieval minded? But I understand—"

"John Watson could not have used a phone had he had one," said Cashel hollowly.

Diamondstone nodded. "Cashel, Watson, and Tanner. The deaf, the dumb, and the blind. Watson was a mute, I suppose."

And he understood then a very good reason for the firm's existence, apart from swindling clients. It was a sort of three-headed Hydra, each of its heads handicapped by some lack of standard human equipment. Yet the Hydra itself was amazingly efficient.

Diamondstone turned sharply to find Cashel staring at Niki, a thoughtful, altogether impersonal smile on his devilish lips.

"It was exactly eight o'clock when I entered the hall," Tanner was saying. "I was hanging up my raincoat, this being the servants' night off, when I distinctly heard the sound of a revolver shot."

Cashel laughed hollowly. "Yet I was in this room. I saw Watson in the last throes of death. *And I saw a snake crawling over the window sill.*"

CASHEL WAS a barrister, italicizing his words for the benefit of an invisible jury.

"I had not yet put on my hearing aid, but I was certain I would have *felt* the vibrations of a shot had there been one. Does that look like a revolver shot wound to you?"

He stepped briskly to the corpse, pointed dramatically at two small, rosy marks on the throat.

Niki gasped audibly turned her back on the corpse. Diamondstone advanced, bent over John Watson. Fang-like and deep the marks seemed to be. Yet the blood-seeping lips of the two little wounds were rimmed with something that was halfway between gray and tan in color. Diamondstone bent over, sniffed, touched the gray-brown stuff with his finger. It was viscous and formed a thread as he pulled his finger away. He looked at Cashel.

The blond Satan, nostrils dilated, was calmly taking a pinch of snuff from a tiny silver case. Diamondstone conveyed his finger to his nose, sniffed of the tan-gray, viscous something. "Spearmint?" he asked himself incredulously. "Things are fogging up at a remarkable rate. Your snake must have been addicted to chewing gum."

Diamondstone and Niki finally left after the police arrived. Diamondstone had sent Niki out to phone for the officers. He took her home and then started out again.

Deep blue globes of light cast purplish shadows across the rain-curtained entrance of the police building on South Alabama Street. Diamondstone, alone, stepped through the drizzling curtain into dry shelter. His orange-tan shoes said *sodge-sodge* along the corridor as he approached the office of Chief of Police Markly.

Outside the office was Mr. Samuel Koyusha, who, in spite of a Japanese moon of a face, was proclaiming to a Headquarters detective:

"I am a highly respecting American citizen and dealing in Oriental goods in my shop on Illinois Street, thank you," he said.

"Thank *you*," said the detective, who was an admirer of the mustached Marx brother.

"And this night," went on the small, yellow man, "I locking up my shop only to behold that some despicable individual has desecrated my establishment by throwing something at my sign and breaking."

"It could be the Chinese bombers coming over here to retaliate," said the Headquarters man. "Will you run along now? Chief Markly is occupied elsewhere with a murder."

"This is not to be laughing," said Koyusha indignantly. "On sidewalk in front of my door are broken bits of my sign which are plaster images of three wise monkeys. So please, your eminence, I are requesting reciprocation for taxes paid and are you catching and holding the culprit."

"Hello!" said the detective, over Koyusha's head to Diamondstone. "Hear you and your lady turned up a corpse."

"And a couple of bad pennies as well," Diamondstone said.

He waited for the detective to open the door of the office. Then he went inside where Detective-sergeant Prout rested weary feet on Chief Markly's desk top. Yet in spite of the eminent position which Prout had allotted to his feet, it was his sizable mouth which dominated immediate attention to whoever looked upon him. That mouth grinned in such a manner as to express a genuine liking for Diamondstone as well as to produce a surprising display of molars.

Diamondstone dropped into the chair indicated by the sergeant.

"Oh, hum, what a night!" he sighed. "Those three shysters. Imagine! One of them insists that Watson was bitten by a snake. The other swears that he was shot with a revolver. The confusion is understandable when you consider that Cashel couldn't have heard the shot had it been three inches from his ear, and Tanner couldn't have seen the snake with a microscope if it had been as big as a boa constrictor. Poor Markly! Cashel and Tanner are such accomplished liars that Markly can't get anything straight. Furthermore, he has completely overlooked the truly significant detail of the whole set-up."

PROUT LAUGHED, not happily, for he suffered from indigestion.

"I could shake the hand of the man who murdered John Watson. Cashel, Watson, and Tanner settled up my Aunt Mary's estate. When they got through there wasn't enough left for you to have yourself a good time in front of a chewing-gum machine."

Diamondstone nodded. "This overwhelming desire to congratulate a murderer—is that the reason you're warming that chair?"

"I am," said Prout, "supposed to be searching for a man named Jorgen— a nit-wit inventor who got skinned by those three lawyers and once threatened to kill them. I forget what this Jorgen looked like so I am having a detective look up his picture for me. What's this significant point Markly has missed?"

"The chewing-gum around the wound in Watson's neck," Diamondstone told him. "What's it for? To keep the murderer kissable—I don't think!"

Prout took his feet off the desk and looked interested.

"You tell me."

Diamondstone thoughtfully massaged the back of his neck. "Chewing-gum is a very sticky substance."

"Any heel knows that," Prout panned dryly. "So what?"

"So it could have been used to hold some sort of poison, that is not sticky, to a metallic instrument which was used to pierce Watson's throat."

"Lots of people chew gum," Prout declared wisely.

CHAPTER III

THREE WISE MONKEYS

THE DOOR of the office opened and short, plump Mr. Koyusha entered, bowing and smiling.

"Patience," he said, "are accomplishing miracles. You are undoubtedly Chief Markly."

"I am like hell," shouted Prout. "I said I wasn't going to see you—"

"I prostrate myself before your eminence," said Koyusha, not doing anything of the sort. "But if you are in authority I beg that you lay hands on culprit who throw brick at my sign and breaking off wise monkey."

Diamondstone frowned, looked at Prout. The sergeant saw no significance in what Koyusha said, rose wrathfully to his feet to lay hands on Mr. Koyusha.

Koyusha was a little adept at laying hands on, too, for he seized Prout by the fullness of his shirt, sliced the air with the flat of his hand which connected with a point below Prout's Adam's apple.

Prout was stunned to the point of staggering. Furthermore, he had considerable trouble getting his next breath. Fists clenched, he would have attempted annihilation upon Mr. Koyusha had not Diamondstone stepped between the East and West.

Diamondstone regarded Koyusha with new respect.

"No possible reason for mopping up the floor with our police department, my dear sir," he said. "No reason at all, really."

"So sorrowful," murmured Koyusha. "I believe I misinterpret."

"Prout," Diamondstone soothed, "was simply going to flick a bit of lint from your collar."

"Get out of my way," snarled Prout, "and I'll flick a bit of Japan off the map."

Diamondstone raised hands in a placating gesture.

"Did I understand you to say, Mr. Koyusha, that your sign was of plaster and represented the Three Wise Monkeys?"

"Assuredly," was the reply.

"And would you mind telling me more of the nature of this accident?"

"Number one monkey was knocking down and breaking up," said Koyusha.

Diamondstone went back to his chair and sat down. Habit forced him to shuck a peanut, but he did not put it in his mouth.

"Well, what, of it?" asked Prout, massaging his throat.

"The admirable Koyusha has hit on something inadvertently," Diamondstone said softly, "It hardly seems a coincidence. Three wise apes. Cashel, Watson, and Tanner. The number one monkey hangs on to his mouth—he speaks no evil. Speak-No-Evil is destroyed. So is Watson. The only reason Watson spoke no evil is because he couldn't speak at all. Speak-No-Evil, See-No-Evil, Hear-No-Evil. Watson, Tanner, Cashel. Three wise apes. It is hardly coincidence."

Nor was it coincidence that Diamondstone entered the Emerald Cafe in Illinois Street shortly after Mr. Cashel, the following evening. Mr. Cashel had been the object of considerable attention from Niki, Absalom—the magician-sleuth's colored servant—and Diamondstone himself.

They had worked in shifts and had managed to keep the blond Satan pretty well within sight during the past twenty hours. Of the law firm, Cashel was by far the most dangerous.

However evil might be the thoughts in Mr. Tanner's brain, his lack of eyesight prevented him from being anything like a worthy opponent for Diamondstone.

Cashel had not entered the Emerald alone. With him was a square-shouldered man wearing a hounds-tooth checked topcoat. Though

Diamondstone had not seen the man's face, he felt certain it was not a lovely thing to look upon.

It was remarkable how Diamondstone could accomplish virtual self-effacement when he wanted to, for he managed to enter the cafe and take the dining stall adjoining the one occupied by Cashel and his companion without Cashel being any the wiser.

HE WAS chuckling inwardly over his fine position for eavesdropping, while ordering food he did not intend to eat, when it occurred to him Cashel and his companion would probably not say anything of any possible interest. Mr. Cashel was deaf. Diamondstone had forgot that for a moment, and now, as no whispered words came from the next stall, he realized that if the man in the checked topcoat had any secret to confide to Cashel he would have had to shout it.

"Which," Diamondstone murmured, "would prevent it from being a secret any more."

Yet he felt absolutely certain that a man of Cashel's wealth had not selected the Emerald's cuisine from choice. The blond Satan and his companion were hatching some sort of a plot.

During a diminuendo in dish clattering, Diamondstone detected the unmistakable scratching of a pencil in the next booth. That would be the checker-coated man's method of speaking with Cashel; and how Diamondstone was to find out what was written taxed his ingenuity to the utmost. Outside of pulling his gun and demanding to see what had been written by Cashel's friend there was no other way.

Then it was that he heard Cashel say, "You'll call him from here. It's best to use a public phone. I'll write down exactly what you're to say,."

There was more pencil scratching, during which Diamondstone's blue eyes scouted the table in front of him, alighted upon a square pat of butter in a little paper dish. The butter was intended for his waffles which were cooking, but he had resolved to put it to quite another purpose.

Butter in hand, he arose and walked with quiet swiftness to the only telephone booth in the cafe. He went inside and closed the door.

A screwdriver which was a part of his pocket knife aided him in removing the perforated metal disk of the telephone dial. That done, he gave the under side of the disk an even coat of butter, or perhaps margarine, and returned the disk to its proper place. Some butter had got on the upper surface of the disk, and this he wiped off cleanly with his handkerchief, especially the inner edge of the finger holes in the dial.

As he left the phone booth, he got a very good look at Cashel's companion, for the man in the checked topcoat was heading for the phone.

Instinctively, Diamondstone christened the man "Butch," for it appeared that he had got his dished-in face from stopping too many knuckles. The fact that his tow-colored hair was clipped close to his billiard ball skull detracted nothing from the man's right to the name Diamondstone had given him.

Diamondstone went over to the lunch counter at one side of the room and became tremendously interested in jets of steam from the waffle irons until Butch came from the phone booth. Then he wandered toward the booth to step inside as soon as Butch had returned to Cashel.

He took from his pocket a tiny flashlight from which he slanted a beam across the phone dial. Butch's pudgy fingers had carried enough butter up from the under surface of the dial to clearly mark exactly which holes he had used. His number had been on the Lincoln exchange, as indicated by the letters "LI." For numbers, he had dialed a six, a four, an eight, and a zero, which could have been arranged in all sorts of combinations. Diamondstone carefully noted the numbers on a piece of paper and left the booth.

Returning to his table he found that his waffles had arrived and Cashel and company had vanished. He took his check up in a hurry, paid the cashier, and strode out of the Emerald. Search the street as far as his eye could reach, he failed to see anything that was like Butch's flagrant topcoat.

Diamondstone's immense shoulders helped him heave a ponderous sigh.

"I may quite as well go back and eat my waffles and top off with a bicarbonate," he murmured as he went back into the cafe.

But it was the telephone book he devoured rather than waffles. It was something more of a task than he had anticipated to find all the possible combinations of six, four, eight and zero on the Lincoln exchange. It was not until he had gone nearly to the end of the book that he found something which caused a figurative pricking up of his ears. The telephone number of Shotwell's jewelry shop was Lincoln 8640. At once he decided to pay the woebegone little jeweler a visit.

He had left his car a block south of the Emerald. As soon as he had regained it, he drove two blocks down Illinois Street and slowed in front of a small show window labeled oriental art shop. Leaning far to the right in his seat, Diamondstone saw something that caused him to jam on the brakes and his heart to beat faster.

The shop was undoubtedly the one owned by the little, yellow Mr. Koyusha, for dangling above the door on an iron bracket was a single plaster monkey brightly painted with brown, gold, and red. And the iron bracket was quite large enough for three such monkeys.

Diamondstone sprang out, got to the sidewalk. Beneath the monkey sign, and distributed unequally over some twenty square feet of concrete, were the painted plaster remains of the second wise monkey—See-No-Evil.

"And," Diamondstone mused, "Mr. Cashel is still alive."

CHAPTER IV

MADMAN'S LAUGHTER

S UCH IS the physical law of reflection of light that Diamondstone was aware of a presence behind him without turning around, for he had seen the man in Koyusha's window. The man had alighted from a car and was coming toward Diamondstone vainly counterfeiting nonchalance. No one, who could be appropriately christened Butch, could ever succeed in being nonchalant.

Exactly why Butch was following him was not apparent at the time, but Diamondstone concluded that in this game it was perfectly fair for Cashel to have put a hound at Diamondstone's heels in retaliation for the shadowing that Diamondstone had given Cashel that day. So he decided to humor Butch to the extent of leading him on a little.

Diamondstone, instead of returning to his car, walked briskly on up the street, turned into the first dark and dismal alley he came to and proceeded, without looking around, to an even darker doorway that was a service entrance for some of the shops in the district.

The doorway was closed by an iron grating eight feet back from the alley, but that made little difference to Diamondstone since he bounced from the doorway almost as soon as he entered it, thereby coming face to face with Butch. Diamondstone had got his flashlight into his hand and its white beam needled the surprised and squinting eyes of Mr. Cashel's comrade in crime.

"Well, Butch," Diamondstone said softly, "I heard a noise behind me, and it occurred to me it was that horribly loud topcoat you are wearing."

Butch blinked.

"How'd you get *that* stuff?" he said out of the side of his mouth.

Whereupon Diamondstone let him have a left to the jaw and informed Butch that he got that stuff from eating spinach.

Butch was a heavy man and he had been in fights before, but then he had never seen anything of Diamondstone's proportions that could move with anything like speed, except a crack streamlined train.

THE BLOW Diamondstone handed him started somewhere down near the magician's knees. It had some distance to travel before it encountered Butch's jaw and its capacity for acceleration seemed unlimited. Butch simply crossed his eyes slightly and collapsed.

Diamondstone bent low over the fallen Butch and quickly weeded out the contents of the man's pockets—a sap, an automatic of cannon proportions, a small wad of bills, watch, a handkerchief, a package of breath perfume, cigarettes, a pencil, a piece of white cardboard. It was the cardboard that he had hoped to find; for on it, in writing too refined to belong to Butch was the following:

> We have your ward. Place one hundred thousand dollars in a steel box and tie same to last pile of Old Pier near where Bellefountain runs into the river. Do this before midnight tomorrow and your ward will be handed over to you.

And that was, in all probability, what Cashel had ordered Butch to say over the phone to Mr. Shotwell. Where Shotwell was to obtain that much money was the mystery that staggered Diamondstone for the moment. Somehow, he could not associate Shotwell with wealth.

Also, in the threat message Butch had phoned, a couple of important elements were conspicuously absent. It was amateurish—this ransom message—decidedly not the usual sort of thing you would expect from kidnapers. Yet Diamondstone was averse to considering Cashel in the light of an amateur criminal.

He got out of the alley quickly, regained his car, turned at the next corner into Ohio Street, and picked out the modest neon sign of Lorin Shotwell's store.

Though it was by now nearly nine o'clock, Shotwell's store was apparently still open. It was not an elaborate store, and its old-fashioned counters were modestly stocked. A man wearing a leather jacket and blue corduroy pants was lounging across the counter, talking to Mr. Shotwell about a watch.

"That ain't a gold case," said the customer. "Not at that price."

Mr. Shotwell looked sad that his word was doubted.

"That is genuine fourteen carat gold-filled, with a seven jewel movement," he said, as though he had said it before. "At the price, you can't beat it."

"Still don't look like gold," the man insisted. He looked up at Shotwell's face. "Lemme see your glasses a minute. They're gold, sure."

Shotwell sighed deeply, removed his glasses, and handed them carefully to the man.

"Please be careful. Those are very special lenses. I could not have them duplicated in less than a week."

The customer picked up the glasses and held their gold bows against the case of the watch he was examining. Then he laid the glasses down on the counter and reached inside his coat for his wallet.

"I'll take the watch. I guess it's okay."

Shotwell, smiling faintly, squinting blindly, reached out for his glasses.

"You'll never regret buying it, I'm sure."

Then Diamondstone, who was standing in the door, witnessed one of the most unusual and unmotivated crimes that had ever occurred. The customer's elbow brushed along the top of the counter, struck Shotwell's glasses, knocked them to the floor in front of the counter.

"Did something drop?" inquired the customer, at the same time stooping to look at the floor and deliberately crunching the lenses of Mr. Shotwell's glasses to bits beneath his heel.

There followed a tempestuous minute when Shotwell demanded that his customer pay him for the broken glasses. The man in corduroy declared he would do nothing of the sort; that Shotwell's glasses should not have been lying on the counter. And it all ended with the customer leaving the store without buying the watch and without paying for the broken glasses.

As the man went out, Diamondstone gave him an intense glance. The man had a sullen face, thick lips, and very little forehead. Then Diamondstone approached the unfortunate Shotwell.

"Mr. Shotwell," he began. The jeweler squinted and tried to get his salt-fish eyes to focus on Diamondstone's face. "Mr. Shotwell, I may be able to help you," Diamondstone offered kindly.

Shotwell leaned across the counter, small mouth open.

"Is it—" he stammered, "is it Mr. Diamondstone? That clumsy yokel has broken my glasses—"

"Diamondstone," the magician-sleuth acknowledged. "I think I know the villains who have snatched your ward. I am going to try to find her for you—"

Shotwell's face became pasty.

"No—no," he sputtered, after he had rediscovered his tongue. "Don't think of it. Really—thanks, of course. My ward, my Amy. I know where she is. She isn't missing. She simply went on a vacation. She's returning soon."

He bustled from around his counter and shooed Diamondstone toward the door.

"Time to close the shop. Thank you very much. Don't trouble yourself. A very good night to you, sir."

Diamondstone backed through the door and had it shut in his face. Then he turned around and started for his car. "Sometimes," he muttered, "I wonder if a great number of persons, whose acquaintance I have recently made, aren't altogether insane."

He spotted Mr. Shotwell's recent customer seated at the seat of a car that was far too elaborate for a man in corduroy breeches. Beside him, his satanic face illuminated by pale green lights from the instrument board, was Mr. Cashel. The car was parked on the opposite side of the street and the driver had just turned over the motor.

Diamondstone sprinted from the curb and rapped on the window of the car just as it had begun to roll. The car stopped and the sullen-faced driver lowered the window to say, "Well?"

"Mr. Cashel!" Diamondstone shouted.

Mr. Cashel turned and blinked the surprise from his gray eyes.

"Mr. Diamondstone!" he said, hollowly.

"Mr. Cashel, you will find one of your minions sleeping on the hard bricks of the alley up yonder," Diamondstone said in silky tones. "I am surprised at you! The thoughtful employer is buying Beauty-Sleep mattresses for his servants' rest periods, these days. And by the way, have you inquired after the health of Mr. See-No-Evil Tanner within the past few hours?"

Mr. Cashel thumped his driver on the arm.

"Start," he snapped.

DIAMONDSTONE HAD but a split second to get his foot off the running board before the big car accelerated down the street.

Diamondstone had regained his car and started the motor but was prevented from leaving the curb because of the warning wail of a siren in the next block. A police car rocketed across the intersection, passed Diamondstone, squealed to a stop beyond, went into reverse, and came back abreast of Diamondstone's car.

Sergeant Prout leaned from the window of the police car.

"Hey!" he said.

"Why are you burning up the taxpayers' gasoline in this fashion?" Diamondstone inquired mildly.

"I've got a tip," Prout announced. "Got Watson's killer located about eight blocks up the street."

"Watson's killer? Then Tanner's, too, because Tanner is either dead or rapidly approaching that deplorable state. Another monkey has been knocked off Koyusha's sign—the blind monkey."

Prout whistled.

"You don't expect to catch a clever killer in that yowling chariot, do you?" Diamondstone asked. "Better get in with me."

Prout popped out of the police car, told the driver to go back to the police station. He got in beside Diamondstone.

"This killer isn't clever," he said. "He's Jorgen and he's crazy. Nobody but a crazy man would see the connection between those monkeys and Cashel, Watson, and Tanner."

"You are not very complimentary," Diamondstone said, as he slid over the lever of the automatic transmission. "Know what killed Watson yet?"

"Cyanide," Prout said. "It was stuck on to something sharp with chewing-gum, like you said. Cyanide works fast once it gets into the blood stream."

Diamondstone drove on in silence to stop in front of a grocery store that was dark except for an electric sign which advertised somebody's milk.

He and Prout got out, and Diamondstone saw the sergeant hunch his shoulder as he always did to feel the reassuring weight of his revolver in its clip. At one side of the grocery store was a stairway leading up to a cheap flat above.

Prout went ahead into the stairway which, three steps up, swallowed the light which came off the street. Half-way to the top, he slipped, fell back against Diamondstone, then went into a crouch.

"Holy hell!" he whispered.

Diamondstone had his pencil flashlight out before Prout could think which pocket his was in. He beamed it over Prout's shoulder and Prout said hoarsely, "A stiff!"

CHAPTER V

SECOND MURDER

WHITE LIGHT found the fat, mutton-tallow face, the round head that was wedged into one corner of the steps. The body had been doubled up considerably to get it in such a small compass.

"It's See-No-Evil," Diamondstone said.

"Yeah. Tanner. I guess this is the right place, huh?"

Prout cautiously stepped over the body, while Diamondstone lingered behind and determined that which the sergeant missed entirely, for which he was not to blame.

Rigor had set in, but the doubled up arm of the corpse, when Diamondstone moved it, hinged limply. Diamondstone knew that rigor, once broken by force, does not return.

Tanner had not died on the steps in that peculiar position. He had been killed elsewhere and deliberately planted on Jorgen's steps some time after death.

Diamondstone ran up behind Prout, who had come to a stop near the top of the flight. Beyond a doorway, up there in the darkness, somebody, laughed. It was not the sanest laugh imaginable.

"The crack-pot," Prout whispered. Then he stepped through the doorway into a maelstrom of motion. There was a *thuck,* an "Ooom" from Prout. Prout dropped at Diamondstone's feet, sapped.

Diamondstone sprang over the sergeant, went into a crouch with the intention of pulling his baby hammerless revolver from the clip that was strapped to his right ankle.

He didn't draw the gun because there wasn't a chance. There was a sudden light, the mad, gleaming eyes of Henry Jorgen looking over the sights of an automatic. Diamondstone straightened.

"Hello," he said.

Jorgen was a big man, worried and wasted down to the bone. He was gray-haired. His lips drew back from set teeth.

"Laugh," he said huskily.

"Ha," said Diamondstone, "ha."

His hand went to the pocket of his tan coat and came out almost at once as Jorgen shook his head warningly.

His intense, blue gaze traveled over the room. It contained an iron bed, a table, a couple of chairs placed at opposite sides of the table. Jorgen motioned Diamondstone into one of the chairs and sat down in the other.

"Wasn't it funny?" said Jorgen, laughing. "Tanner on the stairs curled up like a fat anchovy in a bottle."

"No end funny," Diamondstone said. "Tanner was an anchovy. Did you kill him?"

"Seven times in my sleep." Jorgen nodded. "I killed Watson, too. And Cashel. Only the third time I killed Cashel I pulled out his devil's mustache a hair at a time. He howled like anything."

"And did you knock down a monkey each time you committed murder?" Diamondstone asked.

"Monkey?" said Jorgen. "No. You're crazy, aren't you?"

"Definitely balmy. But I hate Cashel, Watson, and Tanner almost as much as you do. Let's club together and roast them like wieners on a stick."

"Like anchovies," said Jorgen. "Only I don't trust you."

The white, supple fingers of Diamondstone flicked in toward his palm. A dollar-sized palming coin appeared magically and apparently from thin air. Then another and another clinked from fingertips to the table.

"I hate rich people," Jorgen said. "I am going to kill you. I think it's the right thing to do."

"Oh," Diamondstone said, "I'm not that rich."

He experimented with catching the rays of the light globe above on the surface of the shiny coin, turning the reflected rays against the opposite wall.

"I am going to kill you." The madman laughed. "You're Cashel, Watson, and Tanner."

Diamondstone twitched the coin in his fingers, brought a tiny ray of blinding light to Jorgen's eyes. Jorgen winced, shot with his eyes closed.

And then Diamondstone wasn't where the bullet could have found him. He was more than halfway under the table, upsetting it, lifting it.

The table became both shield and battering-ram. It drove into Jorgen as the latter tried to stand up. It sent Jorgen crashing back against the wall. Plaster dropped. Jorgen's arms were pinned to the wall. He emptied the gun, but only at the floor.

Sergeant Prout staggered to his feet behind Diamondstone.

He yelled, "I'm coming!" and came.

"What for?" asked Diamondstone mildly, keeping the madman against the wall. "Jorgen is as helpless as an—er, anchovy."

"I guess it's finished," Prout said disappointedly.

"I was never so sure of anything," said Diamondstone, "as that it isn't finished."

ALL THE next day and late into the night, Diamondstone and his assistant, Absalom, worked in the shop which Diamondstone had recently acquired for the birthplace of many magical tricks his inventive brain was continually producing. This was not a new trick. It was, in fact, merely the remodeling of an old stage trick of his by means of which he had escaped from a gigantic milk can.

The changes they made consisted chiefly of supplying the can with a new air duct in the form of a hose which they cleverly camouflaged with hemp fibers until it looked like a rope. At ten o'clock that night they had stored this can in a group of willows down near the Old Pier where Shotwell was to place his hundred thousand dollars in ransom money.

At eleven o'clock, Diamondstone went downtown to his hotel for the sole purpose of having a few words with Niki. He had not seen as much of that lady as he would have liked that day. Her suite was directly above his, but he took the precaution of calling her on the phone before going out of the lobby. But Niki didn't answer.

"Miss Chartis went out about an hour ago," the captain of the bell-hops told Diamondstone. "She went out with a man."

Diamondstone frowned.

"What sort of a man?"

The bellhop was unable to describe the man because he hadn't been on duty at the time. He had simply heard, from one of the boys he had relieved, that Miss Chartis had gone out with someone besides Diamondstone.

Worried, Diamondstone went outside and made inquiries of the hack driver who was posted there. Yes, the driver remembered taking Miss Chartis and a man from the hotel. Miss Chartis had looked extremely nervous and the man had kept closer to her than was necessary.

"He was sure a queer egg," said the driver. "I thought he told me to drive to College and Sixty-ninth Streets. I said 'Sixty-ninth, sir,' and he came right back with, 'Yes, it's a very pleasant night.' Now, you can see for yourself, Mr. Diamondstone, that it's been drizzling rain most of the night, and—"

"You took them where?" Diamondstone cut in.

"Why, to College and Fifty-ninth. He claimed to have said Fifty-ninth and not Sixty-ninth. There was a car waiting for them there, and Miss Chartis and the man got into it. I don't know what happened after that."

"I'm afraid to think," Diamondstone muttered. "The reason you and your fare got your numbers mixed was because he was deaf, don't you think? Did he have a face like the ace of spades only light complexioned?"

"He did," said the cabby. "Know him?"

"All too well, I'm afraid." And Diamondstone strode off to his own car.

Cashel had Niki. Well, it was only a matter of an hour or so before Diamondstone would have Cashel. He tried to consider the matter coldly. It was such a bewildering mess of villainy that it defied reason. Did Cashel imagine that he could get by with wholesale kidnaping? Had Cashel killed his partners in order that he might not have to divide the spoils of his crimes?

Then Diamondstone recalled the action of that sullen-faced, low-browed individual in Shotwell's store; recalled that deliberate breaking of Shotwell's glasses. And things became remarkably clear to him. Cashel did not have the missing Amy Morton, and possibly never had had her.

He was pretending to have kidnaped her, would collect the money, and hand over Niki Chartis to Shotwell, who, without his glasses, would be none the wiser. He would see Niki's loveliness simply as a brunette blur, and Shotwell had described the missing Amy as a brunette about Niki's age.

But if Cashel didn't have Amy, who the devil did? And the answer to that question came to Diamondstone when he was not in the best position to do anything about it.

IN THE midnight darkness, Diamondstone and Absalom waited. There was a whisper of wind in the willows that arched from the river bank, and out over the water was the sputtering splash of rain drops. Diamondstone peeked around crumbling blocks of concrete that had once formed one end of the pier. He saw a rowboat fighting the swift current. In the boat was a lone occupant—Lorin Shotwell.

They watched the jeweler tie a sizable metal box to a pile standing sixty feet out from the shore, turn his boat around and row away.

As soon as he was out of sight, Diamondstone and his servant went to the shadowy shore where a rowboat containing Diamondstone's especially constructed milk can was waiting.

They immediately put off for the pile, where they removed the box which Shotwell had tied there and fastened the milk can in its place. The can rested on the prow of the boat, its air-conducting rope tied to the pile. Diamondstone removed his coat and prepared to get into the can.

"Boss," Absalom whispered, "dis box got nothin' but a bunch of old newspapers in it."

"Eh?" Diamondstone turned around, nearly knocking the milk can off the boat. "What's that?"

"Newspapers, boss, cut up like money. Little jewelry guy mus' be tryin' to fox 'em."

Diamondstone frowned. "Then why grant Cashel's demands at all, unless, of course, Shotwell was simply putting on an act to decoy Cashel out here on the river while Shotwell made some sort of an attack on Cashel's stronghold. Well, we'll see soon enough."

He calmly got into the giant can, snapping an end of his suspender doing so. Then he told Absalom to put the lid on tight because he had no desire to have water slopping over the mouth of the can.

What he did not know until the can had been shoved off the boat was that a portion of his broken suspender elastic was visible between the lip of the can and the lid.

Curled up in his cramped quarters, Diamondstone was robbed of some of the pleasure of anticipating the surprise he intended to hand Cashel by the uncertainty of all this. What was little Mr. Shotwell up to? What would Shotwell do if he discovered the lady Cashel had kidnaped was Niki Chartis instead of his beloved Amy?

Diamondstone got his tiny revolver into his right hand. His left snaked down to his trousers pocket for a peanut. His fingers got hold of a nut, attempted to crack it. But the nut refused to crack. In fact, it was not a nut at all.

It was a Sarrapia bean.

Diamondstone felt himself going cold all over. Paradoxically he found light in this total darkness. And what it illuminated in his mind was not a pleasant thing....

CHAPTER VI

DEATH WEAPON

LEANING OVER the white prow of a motor launch that had bumped the last pile of the Old Pier, Cashel's hollow voice said, "Give me a hand with this can, Groover."

The man whom Diamondstone had christened Butch joined his chief. He grasped the milk can. "It's large enough to be a locomotive boiler," he said. "If there's a hundred grand in there, it must be in pennies."

The can, however, was lighter than they had anticipated, and they managed to get the ropes unfastened and get it aboard. The man called Groover turned a flashlight on the can, uttered an oath that Cashel could not have heard.

"Somebody's suspenders sticking out from under that lid! It's a damned trap."

Cashel could see if he could not hear.

"One of Diamondstone's tricks," he snapped.

Groover pulled his automatic.

"Let me drill it," he said. "Knock the guy off before we let him out of there. Dump him in the drink."

Again Cashel did not hear. He put his hand on the lid of the can.

"Cover him as soon as I open he ordered, "even Diamondstone can't move very fast cramped up like that."

Then he pulled the lid off and Groover jammed his flashlight and gun into the opening.

"For gosh sake, the damn thing's empty!" Groover gasped. "There ain't no bottom in it!"

"Oh, there was a bottom," said a soft spoken voice. "A very nicely fitted bottom."

Groover pivoted, saw Diamondstone half out of the water at the stern of the boat, a small gun gleaming in his right hand. The terrier bark of Diamondstone's gun was drowned by the thunderous bellow of Groover's gun, but it is not so much the noise a gun makes as how accurately it is aimed. Groover did an ungraceful half-turn into the river. Water geysered over the deck of the little craft.

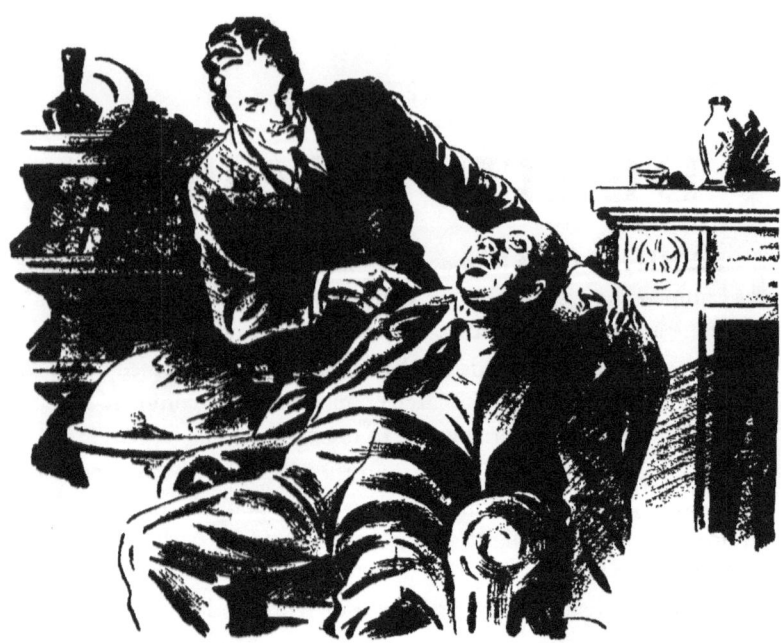

Cashel pointed to the two small marks on the throat.

CASHEL THOUGHT he knew where Groover's gun fell and scrambled for it, but Diamondstone had floundered over the stern and was crouching there.

"Ah-ah. None of that, Cashel," he shouted. "I'm not killing you until you tell me what you've done with Miss Chartis."

Cashel, who had seen one man dive into the water, had no great desire to try it himself. He was more in the mood to bargain.

"I'm not fooling," Diamondstone said sternly. "Shotwell didn't hand out any ransom money tonight. He used newspapers. That means he thinks he knows where his ward is and is going after her this moment."

"He could have donated the money, nevertheless," Cashel said calmly. "He's the richest man in this town."

"I see," said Diamondstone loudly. "I see the game now. Shotwell doesn't want his ward alive. That much was indicated in the phone message you had Butch—I mean Groover—give him. In that message the usual phrase, 'You will never see your ward alive again', was omitted. Am I right in the conjecture that Shotwell's hidden wealth is the result of his swindling his ward out of rightful riches?"

"You are," Cashel agreed. He scraped a match on his thumb and lighted a cigarette. "Amy Morton was a pauper child placed in Shotwell's

custody years ago. Shotwell deserted the kid, not knowing she had an uncle who had struck it rich in the African diamond fields.

"When the uncle died, his fortune was left to Amy Morton, in the trust of her legally appointed guardian, Lorin Shotwell. Shotwell didn't know where the kid was and didn't care. He had the money. My late lamented partners and I dug all that up."

"And tried to extort money from Shotwell by saying you had found the missing Amy," Diamondstone continued. "Shotwell tried to find the missing ward on his own hook. Then you told him you had her in your custody and would hand her over to him to do with as he pleased upon payment of a hundred thousand dollars.

"A very pretty swindle! If Shotwell didn't pay you, you threatened to tell Amy she was the rightful heir to millions and legally support her claim."

"The big joke is that Amy Morton is dead." Cashel chuckled. "She died at the age of twelve. There isn't any Amy Morton. But there is a Niki Chartis, and if Shotwell knows where she is and thinks she is Amy Morton, what the hell are you going to do?"

Diamondstone sprang at Cashel, flattened him on the deck with a blow of his fist. He jammed his little gun into the center of Cashel's forehead.

"I'm going to blow your brains out of your ears, if you don't tell me where Niki is. You kidnaped her after your hirelings had kept me shadowed so they would know when I wasn't around the hotel.

"You were going to pass her off as Amy Morton. Shotwell wouldn't have known the difference, even though he had seen Niki, because you destroyed his glasses. You know damned well he'll kill her, just as he killed Watson and Tanner. And for the same reason to keep his appropriation of the Morton fortune under cover."

"Shotwell killed Tanner and Watson?" Cashel gasped. "I thought—"

"You thought Jorgen did. That's what everybody was supposed to think. That's why Shotwell knocked off one of Koyusha's wise monkeys every time he made a kill. You were to be next and then Hear-No-Evil would have been knocked down. He wanted the killing to appear the work of a madman. And then to clinch the frame, he planted Tanner's body at Jorgen's door."

"Well?" said Cashel. He was as cool as his gray eyes.

"Well, I'm going to kill you slowly. You'll have plenty of time to talk before you die. You are going to tell me where you've got Niki."

"You should have tried to buy one of my men into telling you," Cashel said. "That's probably what Shotwell did. No, I won't tell you, because you won't kill me as long as I don't tell."

Diamondstone's eyes blazed. He jabbed a thumb into Cashel's left eye.

"I'll take you apart! I'll—"

"Not necessary," said Cashel softly. "All I want is your guarantee that you'll say nothing about my part in the affair to the police. It will be your word of honor against mine."

"Bargain!" said Diamondstone. "I'll give you twenty-four hours to get out of town. More, if you like—"

"That's quite enough," said Cashel. "Your Niki is in my penthouse on top of the Gaymode Apartment on Meridian Street."

"Then nose the boat to the south shore and dig it into the mud."

THAT NIGHT Diamondstone's silver car made a record for itself that would have flattered its advertisers. Its low-slung, front drive chassis hugged the pavement tightly. It rocketed along through the night while Diamondstone in water-soaked clothes, sent it slewing around turns with one hand at the wheel and the other on his gun. For blond, satanic Mr. Cashel was beside him.

"You and Tanner were both right the night Watson was killed," Diamondstone shouted above the roar of the motor. "The murder weapon looked like a snake. But to blind Tanner it sounded like a revolver. There's only one such weapon. It would take a man who lived in South America long enough to get in the habit of seasoning his tobacco with Sarrapia beans, to know how to use the weapon. I never guessed the weapon until I came across that bean in my pocket, and—"

"Here!" Cashel said. He jerked his head toward a tall apartment building in front of him.

Diamondstone braked, craning his neck in an effort to see the penthouse on the roof. There were lights in the penthouse. And Niki was there, perhaps—

Diamondstone sprang from the car and urged the lawyer to take the lead. They went into the elaborate lobby of the exclusive apartment building.

An indicator told Diamondstone that the elevator was halfway down the building, descending. He grabbed Cashel's arm, and together they ran up a flight of steps to catch the elevator at the second floor. Diamondstone ordered the operator to take it to the roof.

The elevator crawled. Cashel grinned. Diamondstone cursed quietly and methodically. And then the elevator came to the top where they had to climb a short flight of stairs to the roof. They were halfway across the penthouse terrace when Diamondstone stumbled over a body beneath his feet.

Not Niki. Pray God it was not Niki— He jerked out his light and beamed it downward to strike across the face of the low-browed individual who had broken Shotwell's glasses on Cashel's order.

"If Niki's like that, I kill you, Cashel!" Diamondstone said tensely, in a voice he scarcely recognized.

For the snake that made a sound like a revolver had bit into Cashel's servant's throat.

Diamondstone nearly tore off the penthouse door getting it open. He dashed into a small hall, stopped, listened. In the next room, he could hear Niki's clear, young voice, tremulous with fear:

"I'm not your Amy. Really I'm not. I couldn't be. Mr. Cashel kidnaped me, but I'm not your Amy. I don't care what anybody told you. Don't, *please*—"

In a brass urn standing in the hall, was an umbrella with a crooked handle. Diamondstone seized it. He was up against a new weapon. Sleight-of-hand would avail him nothing. Even a well-placed gunshot might not drop the killer before his weapon could inflict its tiny, deadly wound.

Diamondstone sprang into the room. Lorin Shotwell stood in the middle of the floor; Niki shrank into one corner. Coiled at Shotwell's feet was the snake—a snake about fifteen feet long; a leather-lashed, South American bull whip. At the end of the whip were tiny barbs of gleaming steel, each coated with a thin layer of chewing-gum which held cyanide to the barbs. Cyanide used in gold refining, would have been easy enough for Jeweler Shotwell to get hold of for his purpose. And it took only a scratch from those barbs—

"Don't bother to use that whip thing," Diamondstone said. "Terrible waste of energy, really."

Shotwell swung around, gripping the butt of his whip. The leather snake came to life, uncoiled, cracked out. It was a brown bolt of lightning; it was as deadly as lightning. It hissed like a snake; it was deadlier than a snake. It cracked like a revolver; it was more accurate, in Shotwell's hands, than a revolver.

Diamondstone was holding the umbrella by its tip. As the lash swung out, he waved the umbrella in a swift moving arc. It required perfect timing. It required that he watch the lash, when instinct insisted that he close his eyes and cover his face with his hands. The umbrella handle slashed across the path of the whip. The leather snake, weighted by the poison barbs at its tip, coiled three times around the umbrella handle.

Diamondstone was surprised to find himself alive and in motion. He gave the umbrella a jerk, got his hands on the middle of the lash, hauled Shotwell within range of a lightning left jab to the jaw. It was highly probable that wizened Mr. Shotwell did not know the exact moment he struck the floor.

"Oh, darling—" Niki sobbed, as she rushed into Diamondstone's arms.

Diamondstone and Niki watched Cashel pack, and Diamondstone was not sullen about it. He had given his word that Cashel would have twenty-four hours. Now he was keeping his word. Cashel went about it all calmly, a cigarette dangling from his lips. He went to the door, bags in hand.

"I'll be seeing you," Diamondstone shouted.

A wry smile spread across Cashel's thin lips.

"No need to shout. When you jumped on me out there in the boat, something snapped in my head. I can hear perfectly now. Next time we meet, I shall be a more dangerous opponent. I am sure we shall meet."

"My dearest hope," said Diamondstone politely, as the last of the three wise apes went through the door.

AFTER THAT, there was the business of tying up Shotwell with his own murder weapon. Then Sergeant Prout had to be called. Diamondstone sat on Cashel's best table and used Cashel's phone to do the calling. His, blue eyes glinted happily as he looked into Niki's upturned face.

"What was it you called me a moment ago, Niki? Was it darling?"

"Well, I can't call you Diamondstone, can I?" Niki flushed. "If you'd tell me your first name, I wouldn't have to call you darling."

"I am very much afraid," he said, "that I have no first name. Or perhaps I've forgotten it. And I certainly shan't try to remember."

ABOUT
THE AUTHOR

G .T. FLEMING-ROBERTS is tall, slim, a quiet sort of person who is usually seen with a pipe in his mouth, one of the hundreds in his collection. Born in Indianapolis in 1910, he grew up with no literary ambitions except to please his English instructors, which he found easy because of his love of words. He graduated from Purdue University back in the depression years with a B.S. degree and a dilapidated typewriter. While waiting on action for a teacher's license, he wrote four short detective stories, which he promptly mailed magazine editors, which they promptly rejected. Mr. Roberts then acquired an agent who pointed out the flaws and how they could be avoided in the future. Fleming-Roberts took the agent's advice to heart and rewrote one of the stories, which sold, his first, to *Ten Detective Aces* for 25 dollars. That did it! He forgot about the teaching profession and decided to earn a livelihood by writing. Since then he has sold every story he has ever written.

Unlike so many fiction writers who must look to another source for a regular income, Mr. Roberts is one of the select few whose craft pays real dividends. Since 1932, with the exception of a brief trick in the Air Corps during the last war, he has depended entirely upon his detective-mystery writing.

Mr. Roberts' chief literary critic and adviser is his pretty wife, Agatha, whom he married in 1940. They reside in picturesque Brown County (the Greenwich Village territory of Indiana), in a rustic home of square-hewn logs called the "Witch House." Perched high on a hill, which gives them a perfect view in all directions, it is sinister in name only. The Roberts' decided to call it that be ause of its quaint resemblance to the candy and gingerbread cottage in the tale, *Hansel and Gretel*.